Praise for

A Roux of Revenge

"A good read from beginning to end. The mystery kept me glued to the pages and the writing style had an easy flow that made it hard to put down . . . I can't wait to see what happens next in this delightfully charming series."
—*Dru's Book Musings*

"This book is rich in stories about relationships . . . I highly recommend this series to anyone who loves culinary cozies!"
—*Melissa's Mochas, Mysteries & Meows*

"The third Soup Lover's Mystery builds nicely as clues and key characters fall into place."
—*RT Book Reviews*

"A great series based on one of my favorite things: soup. Connie Archer gives readers a likable heroine and a great mystery in *A Roux of Revenge* that keep them guessing all the way to the end."
—*Debbie's Book Bag*

A Broth of Betrayal

"Murder in the past, murder in the present, and an assortment of interesting characters in a small town, rife with secrets mixed together to serve up a soup du jour of mystery that cozy lovers are sure to enjoy."
—*MyShelf.com*

"An action-packed page-turner with memorable characters I look forward to revisiting again and again!"
—*Melissa's Mochas, Mysteries & Meows*

O9-ABF-808

continued . . .

little
stain
outside
pages
12-2-2016

"This book is full of wonderful mysteries, a skeleton discovered, a missing person, and a murder. The pages flew by. Archer has created such lively characters. Lucky is a strong protagonist who doesn't mind finding herself 'in the soup' as she tries to save her friend or catch a killer."

—*Escape with Dollycas into a Good Book*

A Spoonful of Murder

"Snow in Vermont, soup, and murder. What could be more cozy? . . . A charming new amateur-sleuth series."

—Julie Hyzy, *New York Times* bestselling author of the White House Chef Mysteries

"An engaging amateur sleuth due to the troubled heroine and the delightful Vermont location."

—*Genre Go Round Reviews*

"Plenty of small-town New England charm."

—*The Mystery Reader*

"A 'souper' idea for a cozy mystery series! . . . [Archer] has set a great foundation for this series. We have met the star and recurring characters and they have been left with plenty of room to grow. The setting is ideal."

—*Escape with Dollycas into a Good Book*

"The way cozies should be written. A small town with lovable characters and a plot that leaves you satisfied at the end."

—*Girl Lost in a Book*

Ladle to the Grave

Connie Archer

BERKLEY PRIME CRIME, NEW YORK

THE BERKLEY PUBLISHING GROUP
Published by the Penguin Group
Penguin Group (USA) LLC
375 Hudson Street, New York, New York 10014

USA • Canada • UK • Ireland • Australia • New Zealand • India • South Africa • China

penguin.com

A Penguin Random House Company

LADLE TO THE GRAVE

A Berkley Prime Crime Book / published by arrangement with the author

Berkley Prime Crime Books are published by The Berkley Publishing Group.
BERKLEY® PRIME CRIME and the PRIME CRIME logo are trademarks of
Penguin Group (USA) LLC.

For information, address: The Berkley Publishing Group,
a division of Penguin Group (USA) LLC,
375 Hudson Street, New York, New York 10014.

ISBN: 978-0-425-27311-1

PUBLISHING HISTORY
Berkley Prime Crime mass-market edition / March 2015

PRINTED IN THE UNITED STATES OF AMERICA

10 9 8 7 6 5 4 3 2 1

Cover illustration by Cathy Gendron.
Cover design by Diana Kolsky.
Interior text design by Kristin del Rosario.

For the girls—
You know who you are.

Acknowledgments

Many thanks to Paige Wheeler of Creative Media Agency, Inc., for her hard work, good advice and expertise, to my terrific editor, Faith Black, whose insights have made each book all the better, to Valle Hansen, thank you for catching all my errors, and to Danielle Dill for her enthusiasm and support of the Soup Lover's Mysteries. Huge thanks go to everyone at Berkley Prime Crime who contributed their talent and energy in bringing this series to life.

Special thanks as well to the writers' group—Cheryl Brughelli, Don Fedosiuk, Paula Freedman, R.B. Lodge and Marguerite Summers—for their criticism and encouragement. And a very special thank-you to Elise Varey who can take credit for inventing a last name for Meg! Meg thanks you and she is thrilled to know she'll be playing a much larger role from now on.

Last, but certainly not least, thanks to my family and my wonderful husband for their tolerance in living with a woman who is constantly thinking about ways to kill people.

CONNIE ARCHER
CONNIEARCHERMYSTERIES.COM
FACEBOOK.COM/CONNIEARCHERMYSTERIES
TWITTER: @SNOWFLAKEVT

Chapter 1

THE WOMEN MOVED slowly, shuffling into the clearing in the woods, careful not to trip on the long white robes they had been instructed to wear. A few stole surreptitious glances at one or another of their group as they formed a loose semicircle before the slab of stone in the clearing. A chill wind blew through the trees, and the sound of beating wings came from above.

Cordelia Rank took her place at the designated altar. Behind her, a brazier flamed on the ancient rock. She surveyed the gathering critically. "Sisters, please! You *can* do better. Form a *semicircle*!" she ordered, indicating her wishes with a sweep of her arm. Each woman glanced to her left and right and, stepping carefully over the pine needles and damp earth, shifted position to form a more uniform shape.

Cecily Winters took a deep breath, wondering, not for the first time, whether joining the Snowflake Coven was such a good idea. Her sister, Marjorie, certainly hadn't been happy about it. It had sounded just so wonderful when she had first heard of the plan. Beltane Eve, April 30, a night to celebrate the coming of spring and the first buds of May with a bonfire, feasting, candlelight and song. Their small iron container would have to do. A bonfire in the woods at midnight could be dangerous. Cecily shuddered involuntarily. The crackling flames formed eerie shadows in the night, flickering against the tree trunks. *If only Cordelia hadn't appointed herself high priestess*, she thought, *insufferable woman, it might have been fun.*

At a nod from Cordelia, one of the group, holding a candle cupped in her hand, moved within the inner circumference of their small circle and lit the candles clutched in the hands of the other women. When all the candles were lit, Cordelia nodded.

"Now we begin," she announced. She turned back to the stone altar and, raising her arms, spoke in ringing tones. "Mother Earth, we have gathered together here, in this wood, to honor you, to celebrate the light of coming spring. Beltane is a time for love and the union of souls, the union of minds and the union of bodies."

Cecily looked up quickly. This was the first she had heard of the union of bodies. She glanced around the circle to see whether anyone else had noticed the phrase.

"We have been called to replenish the earth," Cordelia continued. "Our fire and our candles will light the sacred union of fertility, as our pagan ancestors have done for centuries. We will assist in bringing the sun's light to earth, so that the earth may awaken from its long winter sleep. Our bodies, our minds and our spirits will alight with joy. We are ready to cast away all the doubts and fears of the winter. Our dream will be of hope and harmony."

Cecily's nose was itching. The band of flowers in the headdress she wore was slipping down over her forehead. She needed to scratch, but holding the candle and her too-long robe together, she had no free hand. She moved her shoulder up and turned her head, rubbing her nose on her arm. Cordelia glared at her from the stone altar. Cecily dropped her arm but before she could stifle it, she erupted with a thunderous sneeze.

Cordelia sighed her disappointment. Addressing the

women, she said, "We now dedicate our herbs to the glory of Mother Earth. Each of us shall drink of our May wine." She turned to the woman on her left. "You, Sister, shall be the first to drink of our draught tonight." Cordelia filled a shallow bowl from a cauldron that sat next to the fire. "With these herbs of sweet woodruff, strawberry and honey, you shall partake."

One woman stepped forward and doused her candle on the stone altar. She grasped the bowl in both hands. Cordelia paused, about to speak, but before she could utter a word, the woman drank the brew in its entirety. Cordelia stared at her, then filled the bowl again as a second woman stepped forward.

A strangled sound came from the lips of the first woman to drink. She gasped, clutching her throat. Her eyes grew large in panic as she tried to speak. Her chest heaved with the effort to breathe. She dropped to the ground as her legs crumpled beneath her. The others watched helplessly as the woman lay before them, retching and gasping for air.

"Agnes!" Emily cried out.

"What's wrong?" Cecily asked.

Someone replied in alarm. "She can't breathe. Help her!"

"Let me through. I know CPR." Emily Rathbone pushed the women aside. They stepped back and stared as Agnes continued to gasp. Emily struggled to lift Agnes's head and open her jaw while Agnes writhed violently.

"Help me hold her," Emily shouted. Two of the women knelt. One held Agnes's arms and the other, her legs. Emily tilted Agnes's head and checked her throat. "There's nothing there. Nothing's interfering with her breathing. Maybe it's an allergic reaction." She deftly rolled Agnes to her side. Agnes's head fell forward, her movements still violent. She retched again and whispered, "Help me." Then her body went limp.

Complete stillness filled the clearing. No one spoke. Someone finally whispered, "Is she breathing?"

Emily felt for a pulse while the women watched in silence. She looked up at their concerned faces. "Agnes is gone."

Chapter 2

LUCKY JAMIESON PUSHED the button on the CD player behind the counter, and a quiet guitar instrumental filled the restaurant. She heard a tap on the glass of the front door. Elizabeth Dove stood outside and waved. Lucky hurried over to let her in.

"I guess I'm too early," Elizabeth said.

"Not at all. Come on in. Just getting ready to open." Elizabeth followed Lucky to the counter. "What can I get you?"

"Just a cup of coffee. I've already had breakfast." Lucky was always happy to see Elizabeth, especially when they had a few moments to chat. Elizabeth had been a dear friend of her family. Since Lucky's parents' sudden death in a car accident, Elizabeth had been a surrogate mother to her—renting her an apartment and giving her a car to drive. Returning home to Snowflake and the By the Spoonful Soup Shop would have been so much harder without Elizabeth's love and support. Retired now from teaching, Elizabeth had been elected Mayor of Snowflake, Vermont, and consequently had little time to herself.

"Hello, Sage." Elizabeth called out to Sage, the Spoonful's chef, already hard at work in the kitchen. Sage peeked through the hatch and smiled a greeting.

Lucky set a place mat, napkin and silverware on the counter for Elizabeth and poured a mug of coffee. "A little cream?"

"Yes, thank you, dear." Elizabeth stirred the cream into her mug. "Where's your grandfather?"

"Jack's gone to Lincoln Falls to pick up some supplies. He'll be back in an hour or so."

"Oh."

Lucky looked at her quizzically. "Is something wrong?"

"Well, I'm the bearer of some bad news, I'm afraid. You know that women's group that Cordelia Rank formed?"

"Not really. I heard there were some meetings at the library—something like that."

"Well, apparently Cordelia organized a May Day celebration in the woods last night. I gather it morphed into something that . . . Well, some people have dubbed it a coven, with Cordelia officiating. But last night . . . one of the women died suddenly."

"Oh no! Who?"

"A woman named Agnes Warner. I didn't really know her. She lived outside of town with her husband."

Lucky thought for a moment. "I think I know who she is but I haven't seen her in years. My parents might have known her." She leaned over the counter on her elbows. "That's terrible. How did it happen?"

"Well . . . that's what I wanted to talk to you about. Nate Edgerton called me early this morning to let me know. The women brewed some wine with herbs that Jack had picked for them and they're suspecting—mind you, just suspecting—that Agnes might have . . . Well, I guess they're thinking she had a bad reaction to the herbs."

"What are you saying? That Jack's herbs had something to do with this?"

"No, not necessarily. I didn't mean to alarm you. I just

wanted to give you a heads-up about this. She could have had a reaction to medication, or a stroke or heart attack . . . anything . . ." Elizabeth continued. "But Nate will probably want to talk to Jack at some point."

Lucky sighed. "Well, I can't imagine that anything Jack gave them caused any harm, but I appreciate your telling me."

Lucky heard a knock at the front door. "Oh, I forgot to unlock." She hurried to the entrance, flipped over the OPEN sign and opened the door. A slight woman dressed in a long brown skirt and sweater entered. Her dark hair was streaked with gray and pulled into a bun at the nape of her neck. She wore thick eyeglasses and carried a small bundle of flyers.

Elizabeth swiveled on her stool. "Hello, Greta!" she called out.

Greta smiled nervously and approached the counter.

Elizabeth turned back. "Lucky, have you met Greta?"

Lucky shook her head.

"Greta Dorn . . . Lucky Jamieson." Elizabeth turned to Lucky. "You and she are neighbors in your building now."

"Oh, how nice." Lucky's apartment was just around the corner on Maple Street in a four-unit building that Elizabeth owned.

Lucky smiled. "Nice to meet you, Greta. Welcome to the building." Lucky offered her hand across the counter. She realized upon looking closer that the woman was much younger than she had first appeared, perhaps late thirties or early forties. "Can I get you something? Coffee?"

Greta accepted the handshake, shifting the bundle of flyers to her other arm. "Oh, no. Thank you. I just stopped in to see if I could leave some of our flyers for the library drive with you."

"Of course. I'll put one in the window and we can offer them to people when they pay at the cash register. Are you volunteering at the library?"

"Uh, yes, just helping out with whatever I can."

"That's great. You'll have to stop back whenever you have a minute."

Greta nodded. "Thank you." She hesitated as if unsure where to go. "I'll be on my way now." She turned and hurried out to the sidewalk.

Lucky turned to Elizabeth. "She's a nervous little thing."

Elizabeth nodded. "She is. Greta's a widow and rather lonely, I think—at loose ends. She was living with a relative for several years in a neighboring town but decided to move closer in. I think she'll be a good neighbor."

"She's volunteering at the library, she said?" Lucky asked.

Elizabeth looked up quickly. "Oh. You mean she might have been with those women last night?"

Lucky nodded.

"Hmm. I have no idea but I'm sure we'll be finding out all about it." Elizabeth took a last sip of her coffee. "Oh, before I forget. The cleaning company for the building has misplaced some keys. It's very worrying. You haven't seen anything like that around, have you?"

"No, but I'll keep my eyes open."

"Thanks, dear. It's just not safe. If they don't turn up, I'll really have to have all the locks changed." Elizabeth dropped her napkin on the place mat. "And now I must be going. I'll see you later." Elizabeth blew her a kiss and headed for the door.

Lucky cleared away the coffee mug and finished laying place mats and napkins along the counter. This was her favorite time of day at the Spoonful. Soup was bubbling on the stove, breads warming in the oven, gentle music playing, the pleasant clatter of Sage working in the kitchen and a few moments of peace and quiet before the busy day began.

"Hey, Lucky," Sage called from the kitchen.

Lucky turned and peeked through the hatch. "Sophie says she'll stop by this afternoon. She wants to show you something."

Lucky smiled at him. Sage looked so relaxed and happy. He was about to become a newlywed. He and Sophie, her best friend from childhood, had decided to hold their wedding later in the month. Sophie's favorite flower was lilac, and since Jack's large garden was completely bordered by well-established lilac bushes soon to be in bloom this month, they had asked to hold their private ceremony there.

"What's the surprise?" she asked. "Do you know?"

He smiled mysteriously. "I know, but I'm sworn to secrecy. You'll just have to wait."

Chapter 3

A COUPLE OF hours later, the busiest part of the morning rush was over. Only a few customers remained. Lucky sighed as she cleared off the counter, wishing she could be outdoors. Sunlight was streaming through the yellow gingham curtains at the windows and reflecting off the wide pine floorboards. Several vases of forsythias, long branches covered with small, bright yellow flowers, filled the large front window. The first of May promised to be a perfect spring day but certainly not a quiet one.

"Heathens! That's what they are," Flo Sullivan announced loudly to the entire restaurant, her halo of orange frizz wiggling violently.

Lucky sighed. Flo had been holding court for the past hour. Not surprisingly, the news of Agnes Warner's death had spread throughout the village of Snowflake. Lucky wondered whether others held the same opinion of Cordelia's group.

Flo spun on her stool at the counter and surveyed the room. "This may be a terrible thing to say, but those women, messing around with occult forces, what did they expect? They got no better than they deserved."

Barry Sanders and Hank Northcross, at their usual corner table, looked up and then away, studiously avoiding becoming embroiled in Flo's harangue.

"I was raised in the Church," Flo announced. Lucky remained silent and continued to clear dishes away. "And the Pope himself says he's very upset about this rise in idolatry. It's just not normal. And why someone like Cordelia Rank would dream up something like this, I just can't imagine."

Lucky, from the corner of her eye, saw the swinging door from the corridor open a crack. Lucky's grandfather Jack peeked through the opening an instant before Flo swiveled back to the counter. Taking in the scene, he quickly ducked back before Flo spotted him. Lucky caught the movement and stifled a laugh. Flo had nursed an interest in Jack for a long time—to no avail—and Jack had become expert at avoiding Flo's flirtations. Lucky could imagine him now, listening on the other side of the door and gnashing his teeth until the coast was clear.

Flo leaned across the counter. In a conspiratorial tone, she said, "I haven't seen your grandfather yet, Lucky. Where is he hiding?"

Lucky cleared her throat and struggled to keep a straight face. "Well . . . uh . . . I think he was planning to pick up some supplies in Lincoln Falls this morning. He won't be back for a while."

"Ah. Well. In that case, I'll be on my way."

As Flo stood, a large shape blocked the sunlight at the front door. The bell jingled and Horace Winthorpe entered, followed by his dog, Cicero.

Flo sensed a fresh audience. "What do you think, Horace?" she hollered across the room.

"Eh?" Horace approached the counter, taking a stool one seat away from Flo. "Did I miss something?" he inquired.

"Well, surely you've heard, haven't you? About Agnes Warner and that disgusting devil worship going on in the woods last night?"

Horace's eyebrows rose. "Oh, yes, of course. Everyone at the market was talking about it. I'm sure the whole town's heard by now. But it's hardly devil worship, you know."

"Hmph." Flo sniffed. "I don't know what else to call it."

"From what I've heard"—he smiled and nodded as Lucky poured a mug of coffee and placed it before him—"they were merely celebrating the rites of spring. Beltane. The first of May. Nothing sinister at all about that. In fact . . ." Lucky could see that Horace was warming to his subject. A retired history professor, Horace was erudite on many subjects. "Many European and Scandinavian cultures to this day celebrate that date. Of course, everyone now conveniently chooses to overlook its pagan roots."

Flo sniffed again. "Is that so?" She stared critically at Horace.

"Why, yes. In some countries, it's known as *Walpurgisnacht*—Walpurgis Night—particularly in cold northern countries, like Latvia or Sweden or Finland, but others as well. It was, and still is, an important festival because it represented the driving out of winter and the inception of warm weather."

"And just who was this Walpurga man?" Flo replied suspiciously.

"*She*," Horace replied, "was a missionary of the sixth century. Saint Walpurga. The fact that the festival is named after a woman rather betrays its pagan roots, don't you think?"

"I don't know about that. I've never heard of a Saint Walpurga, but it still just doesn't seem right to me, holding that kind of thing in the woods!"

Horace shrugged. "I'm rather sorry I wasn't invited. I would have enjoyed it—to see how Cordelia and the other women interpreted the festivities. Of course, I'm sure it didn't involve bonfires and orgies, but interesting nonetheless."

"I should hope not." Flo sniffed and hopped off her stool. "Well, Horace, I'm sure you know a lot more about all that than me, but I still don't approve of those shenanigans." She turned back to Lucky and smiled. "You'll let Jack know I stopped by, dear, won't you?"

Lucky nodded. "I sure will. He'll be sorry he missed you." Lucky cringed inwardly, hoping Jack hadn't overheard this last remark.

Flo leaned forward and whispered, "I know how busy the lovebirds must be by now"—she nodded her head in the direction of the kitchen—"but maybe you could give them a little nudge?"

Lucky stared blankly at Flo. "Lovebirds?"

"Yes," she said. "I know they're busy, but they need to get a move on. I check my mailbox every day but I haven't seen my invitation yet."

Lucky's eyes widened. "Ah . . ." was all she could think to reply. "I . . . uh . . . I'll pass that on." Flo was expecting an invitation to Sophie's wedding? Lucky shook her head. Whatever had given her that idea? Or was it a ploy to get closer to Jack?

"You'll take care of that, won't you?" Flo remarked as she headed for the front door and slammed it behind her.

A few moments later, Jack poked his head through the swinging door. He glared at Lucky. "I'll be *sorry*?"

Lucky had all she could do not to burst out laughing at Jack's distress. He shook his head, muttering to himself, and joined Horace at the counter. Jack held a paper napkin in his hand. Cicero made almost human sounds as he anticipated a treat. Jack unfolded the napkin and held out a generous hunk of chicken. Cicero wolfed it down instantly. Horace had inherited Cicero after the dog's original owner had died under terrible circumstances. Cicero had come by his name because of his efforts to talk, albeit in a language humans couldn't possibly understand. Nonetheless, Cicero gave it his best effort and managed to get most of his desires fulfilled, particularly his love for restaurant treats.

"Horace!" Barry Sanders called out from his corner table.

Horace turned on his stool. Hank raised his coffee mug to Horace in greeting. "Why didn't ya chatter on some more about whatever pagan thing she was going on about. I thought she'd never leave!"

"Oh, I apologize if I extended the torture." Horace smiled shyly. "I just thought she needed a dose of reality, not to get so worked up about a spring festival. That's all."

Barry smiled back. "S'all right, Horace. Just pullin' your leg."

The bell over the door jingled once again. Nate Edgerton, Snowflake's Chief of Police, stood in the doorway and surveyed the restaurant. Lucky's heart skipped a beat, remembering her conversation with Elizabeth. Nate spotted Jack at the counter and walked over to him.

"Jack, how are you?" He remained standing.

"Good, Nate. Have a seat."

"Uh." Nate cleared his throat. "Could we have a quick word . . . in private?"

Jack, surprised, looked at Nate. "Why, sure. What's going on?"

Lucky noticed the dark circles under Nate's eyes. He had probably been up all night dealing with the death in the woods. "You can use the office if you like, Nate," she said.

Nate nodded and pushed through the swinging door to the corridor. Jack rose and followed him. A shudder of anxiety ran up Lucky's spine.

"Horace, I'll be back in a minute." She wiped her hands on a dish towel and headed down the corridor, entering the restaurant's tiny office. She caught the last of Nate's remark.

". . . we think she might have been poisoned."

Chapter 4

LUCKY SAW THE stunned look on Jack's face. She glanced at Nate, a question on the tip of her tongue.

"Poisoned?" Jack asked.

"Well, we don't know for sure. It's possible she had some sort of allergic reaction to whatever was in that drink they brewed," Nate replied.

"What are you saying, Nate?" Lucky grasped Jack's hand, a sinking feeling in the pit of her stomach.

"Apparently, these ladies brewed their own wine. 'May wine' they called it. According to Cordelia Rank." Nate sighed heavily. Lucky was sure Nate hadn't had an easy time dealing with the prickly Cordelia. The woman was undoubtedly making his job more difficult than it already was.

"According to Cordelia, they mulled it with herbs that Jack had given them. That's why I need to know exactly what was in that mix." He turned back to Jack. "Do you remember what you gave them?"

Jack's jaw dropped open. "Nate, I . . ." He shook his head. "Just what I grow in my back garden and some herbs I gathered near the woods. They asked me for woodruff and strawberry leaves and I made up a basket for them."

"That's all? Woodruff and strawberries?"

"That's it. Both harmless. I had Sage double-check the recipe for me. Woodruff's only harmful if you take it in huge amounts; then it might make somebody sick, but definitely not kill them. It's just used for flavoring. And the strawberries that I grow, I eat myself. Nothing wrong with them."

"What about the leaves of the plant? Are they edible?"

"Pretty sure they are. Of course, I don't eat the leaves myself, but some people brew teas from them. I don't think they'd harm anyone, certainly not cause anybody to die." Jack rubbed his forehead distractedly. "You don't think . . ." Jack trailed off.

"Is it possible you maybe made a mistake?" Nate questioned gently, but Jack had no response. "Maybe you thought you picked woodruff, but you picked something else?"

Jack shook his head. "I was real careful, Nate. I'm sure I was." Lucky saw a fleeting moment of doubt cross Jack's face.

She felt the need to step into the exchange. "I'm sure he's right, Nate. Jack is very careful in his garden, and he certainly knows his plants. I doubt he'd make a mistake like that. Besides, could a poisonous plant cause someone to die so quickly?"

"Generally, no. Although I imagine some toxins could cause a fast reaction." Nate turned to Jack. "You wouldn't mind if I stopped by, maybe tomorrow or the next day, and had a look? And maybe you could show me where you found the woodruff?"

"No. Of course not. Happy to."

Nate nodded. "Like I said, it's possible Agnes had an allergic reaction to something. It's also possible she had a heart attack or a stroke. We just don't know at this point. I've got a call in to a plant specialist—and if there's anything left over, I'll have them check any leaves that weren't used up. The morgue can examine her stomach contents and what we have of the wine and any substances in the containers or the bowls. Whatever caused her death acted pretty quick. I suppose it's a good thing nobody else was hurt."

Jack nodded but remained silent, his forehead furrowed in worry.

"What about Cordelia? Perhaps she added something she shouldn't have. Have you questioned her carefully?"

"Yes, I have. I'm certain she didn't get creative with her recipe. Her husband confirmed her story." Nate stood. "I'll be on my way, then." He stopped at the door. "Jack, I'm sure you're right. Whatever killed this lady coulda been anything. Who knows? I just had to ask. I don't want you worrying yourself about it."

Lucky turned in her chair. "Has Elias had a chance to examine her yet?" Elias Scott, the love of Lucky's life, was the only doctor in Snowflake and also served as the town's coroner. "Did he have anything to say?"

Nate scratched his head. "He couldn't be definite, but he was leaning toward some form of poisoning or allergic reaction, given the vomiting. But he didn't want to hazard an opinion until the pathologist completes an autopsy."

"I see." Lucky glanced at her grandfather. Jack still hadn't said a word. "Thanks, Nate."

"See you later." Nate shut the door behind him.

Jack was staring at the floor.

"I'm sure it's nothing, Jack. I'm sure it had nothing to do with the herbs you gave them."

His face was pale. "What if I made a mistake?"

"Jack, you've been doing this for years. You didn't. I'm sure you didn't." She squeezed his hand in encouragement.

"My eyesight isn't so good these days."

"That may be, but I doubt you'd have anything poisonous growing in your backyard. And whatever you gathered near the woods was fine too."

"Lots of everyday plants and flowers are poisonous, you know, very dangerous." He took a deep breath. Jack still didn't seem convinced. "You better get back out front, my girl. You'll have more customers by now. It's just gone four bells."

"I will, but I plan to talk to Cordelia myself as soon as possible." She squeezed his hand one last time. Even in times of stress, Jack still told time by the bells. It was second nature for him. And she was one of the very few people who could interpret his references. Most of Jack's life had been spent in the Navy and, for him, the walls were still the bulkhead and the floors, the deck. His health had improved a great deal over the past year when his symptoms had been diagnosed as a vitamin deficiency. But from his days in the Pacific in World War II, he suffered from a post-traumatic stress disorder generally set off by stress or, particularly, the sight of blood. The last thing she wanted was for any suspicions to linger about him or for him to worry he had played a part in anyone's death.

Lucky returned to the counter. Janie and Meg, the Spoonful's two young waitresses, were busy. Meg had covered the counter in Lucky's absence, and Janie was taking orders from a few new arrivals. Horace had already gone on his way, and Barry and Hank were settling in for a game of chess at their table. She quelled an unsettled feeling in her chest. Jack couldn't possibly have made a fatal mistake. She was sure of it.

Chapter 5

Lucky pushed her way through the untrimmed bushes that threatened to block the drive. Sophie had rushed on ahead.

"Come on, slowpoke. Hurry up!" Sophie called gaily from the top of the hill.

A small twig struck Lucky's face. She brushed it away, huffing the rest of the way to the clearing at the top of the dirt drive where Sophie's childhood home stood.

When Lucky caught up with her, Sophie spun in a circle, her arms held straight out. "Here it is! Remember?"

Lucky laughed. "Of course I do. How could I forget? I always loved to come to your house."

"Well, it's pretty basic but it was home when we were all kids."

Lucky was an only child and had always envied Sophie's noisy family. Sophie was the baby of the brood, her three siblings years older, but all of them were welcoming and kind to Lucky when her mother would allow her to visit.

Sophie grabbed her hand and led her up the wooden stairway to the front porch and through the open doorway.

"My grandfather built this. Isn't it incredible?" She pointed to the huge stone fireplace in the front room, a fireplace that was large enough to grace a mansion.

"It sure is. We used to roast marshmallows in that when we were little kids."

"And sleep in front of it in our sleeping bags too. He built it all by himself with river rock. It's gorgeous and just as solid as the day he made it." She spun on her heel and held her arms out. "This is what I wanted to show you." Sophie's expression grew serious. "Sage and I have decided we're going to live right here. We'll have our very own home right on the property."

"Here?"

"Well, mostly. Structurally, what's here is pretty sound. We can replace some of the wood that's not so good. We'll extend the porch and knock out a few walls inside. Sage is having a friend draw up some plans. New roof too. There are three tiny bedrooms. We want to open up the inside and add a kitchen and another bedroom toward the rear of the property. It'll be a proper house. It'll take a while 'cause we plan to do the work ourselves, but we can do it. It shouldn't be that hard," Sophie said hopefully.

"What about your brother?" Sophie's father had abandoned the family years before. After that, her mother became sick and died after a long illness. Her older sister had taken the lead in raising Sophie, and then she in turn left home after Sophie graduated from high school. That sister died only a few years later. One brother had been killed in a car accident. Her remaining brother, Rick, at least twelve years Sophie's senior, was the last of her siblings.

"I've written to Rick—e-mailed him, I should say. He's over in New York State right now, or at least he was the last I heard. Sage and I have both been saving our money and I've asked Rick if we could buy him out. I know he doesn't want to come back to Snowflake, so I don't see why he'd care. We'd give him a fair price. It's just him and me now— we're the last of the family. I'm sure he has no interest in living here again, so hopefully, nothing will go wrong."

Sophie watched her friend's face carefully. "What do you think, Lucky? Do you think it's a crazy idea?"

"No. Not at all. I think it's a fantastic idea."

"Rick hates this place. Even more so after my mother died. But I don't feel that way at all. Maybe I'm trying to re-create something I didn't have as a kid—security, a feeling of safety. Maybe that's why I'm so attached to this place. I look at this fireplace and I see everything that's possible."

"It'll take a lot of work . . . and money."

"I know, but we can stay where we are and work on the house in our spare time. It'll take a year or two to get it livable, but it's possible. I just can't stand the thought of letting my grandfather's chimney and fireplace go to waste. And I can just picture Sage and me cuddling up in front of a roaring fire in the winter."

Lucky gazed silently at the five-foot-tall hearth surrounded by a wall of rounded gray rock. "What about your dad? Have you or Rick ever had any contact with him?"

Sophie shook her head. "Never. I can't speak for Rick, but I've never heard from him." She shrugged. "And nobody in the family would even mention his name after he left. I finally gave up asking. It was like I was the only one who cared. It's funny you should ask, though. I've found myself thinking about him a lot lately. Or at least what I can remember about him. Maybe because my life is going through such a big change now. I was so young at the time, but I always felt like the heart went out of this place when he left. Do you think I'm crazy to take this on?"

"Not at all. I'd probably feel just the same if I were in your shoes."

Sophie hesitated a moment. "There's something else too."

"What?"

Sophie took a deep breath. "I got a letter from a lawyer for the Resort. They're interested in buying this property and the acreage we have on the other side of the hill. They want to extend a ski run, and the parcels on the other side of the hill are right in their way. I haven't contacted them yet, but they want to meet with me."

"Really? Would you want to sell to the Resort?"

Sophie shrugged. "It's interesting, kind of, to know you own something your employer wants, isn't it? But there's no way I'll sell the land that the house is on. If I did, the Resort would just mow everything down. Truth is, they don't need this portion; it's the parcels on the other side they need to expand that run." During the winter months, Sophie worked as a ski instructor for the Snowflake Resort. Summer was on its way and she would have some part-time employment at the Resort giving swimming lessons, but during the warmer months she was much more able to set her own schedule.

"Would that interfere with your view?"

"Not really. Those parcels are hidden behind us. I doubt we'd even be able to see a run over there. And we'd still have plenty of land around the house for privacy."

"If you sold that land, it would solve your money situation, wouldn't it? You'd have the cash to remodel the house."

"True." Sophie picked up a stick from the hearth and poked at the ashes. "I'm just scared their lawyers have been in contact with Rick. They must have researched the title to know about me. They've probably contacted him by now too." Sophie grimaced. "I'm just hoping they don't want to buy the whole property. If that's the case, they'd be able to offer Rick more than Sage and I ever could."

"Sounds like you're getting ahead of yourself. Why don't you wait till you hear from your brother?"

"It's been a few weeks since I e-mailed him. I'm really starting to worry that he hasn't gotten back to me."

"Have you heard much from him over the years?"

Sophie shrugged. "Rarely. Now and then. He's a funny guy—kind of a lone wolf. Of all of them, he and I have probably been the least close. So I can't really say I know my brother at all. He was gone before I hit junior high."

Lucky checked her watch. "Hey, I better get back to the Spoonful."

Sophie laughed. "How many bells is it?" she asked, referring to Jack's method of telling time.

"Just gone six bells." Lucky smiled.

Sophie looked down at the soot on her hands. "Give me a minute. I'll rinse off my hands in the creek. No running water in here now." She left by the back door and Lucky watched her from the window as she scurried down the slope to the creek that ran below the house.

Lucky shut the front door behind her and walked down the wooden steps at the front of the house. She perched on a large rock at the top of the drive to wait for Sophie's return. She was thrilled that Sophie and Sage were getting married and had a chance at their very own home. She leaned back and breathed in the warm spring air. Wildflowers were blooming over the hillside. The setting was inexpressibly peaceful. She felt her shoulders relax and closed her eyes, letting the sun warm her face.

Sophie's screams cut through the air.

Chapter 6

LUCKY CLAMBERED OFF the rock and raced toward the sound, scrambling down the rise. She tripped and almost slid the rest of the way. Sophie stood at the bank of the creek, staring at a dark green bundle wedged between two rocks floating in the water.

"Sophie?" Lucky approached.

Sophie turned to her without speaking and pointed at the dark mass in the creek.

The dark green bundle was a man's jacket floating and inflated like a balloon. Lucky recognized the shape of a white hand under the water. Denim jeans covered a pair of legs that protruded from the jacket. A dead man was bobbing in the water.

She touched Sophie's shoulder. "Are you okay?"

Sophie gulped and nodded. "I just didn't realize what I was looking at." They stood in silence staring at the corpse for several moments.

"Is he really dead?" Sophie asked.

Lucky nodded. "Looks that way." Burbling water gushed

over the rocks. The body had been snagged by an overhanging tree branch entangled in the coat.

"We need to check, don't we?" Sophie said. "What if he's just unconscious?"

"I really think we're too late." Lucky turned away and grabbed a long, sturdy branch that lay on the ground. "But I think we should have a look at him."

Sophie nodded. "Go ahead."

Carefully maneuvering the long branch, Lucky snagged the edge of a pocket and pushed gently. The body rolled over slowly. The man's face was a mask of bloody flesh.

"Oh, dear God," Sophie groaned. "I think I'm going to be sick."

"Okay. You'll be okay." Lucky dropped the branch. "Let's leave him and call Nate. We shouldn't touch anything."

"How did he get here?"

"He must have washed down from the top of the hill. Maybe he got banged up on the rocks or . . ."

"What?"

"Animals? Maybe." Lucky leaned in closer for a better look.

"Come on. I can't look at it." Sophie grabbed Lucky's hand and started to drag her back up the hill.

Lucky could barely pull her gaze away. She turned and let Sophie lead her back to the house. "We have to call Nate right away."

NATE EDGERTON ARRIVED on the scene fifteen minutes later, looking as if he still hadn't slept from the night before. Bradley Moffitt, his deputy, also appearing very pale, rode with him.

Lucky walked toward the cruiser as Nate climbed out. Sophie remained seated on the steps, her hands covering her face.

"Where is he?" Nate asked.

"Take that path right there." Lucky pointed to an opening between the trees. "He's in the creek down below."

Nate nodded and gestured to Bradley to follow.

Lucky joined Sophie on the steps of the battered front porch as Nate and his deputy disappeared from sight. Lucky pulled out her cell phone to call the Spoonful to let them know she'd be delayed. She only hoped she'd be able to get cell service from their location. She breathed a sigh of relief when Sage answered the phone after a few rings. She quickly filled him in about what was happening and told him not to worry. She promised they'd tell him everything when they returned.

A few minutes later Lucky heard the crashing of branches. Nate Edgerton reappeared on the path between the trees. His shoes and pant legs were soaked to his knees. His complexion was gray, and dark circles outlined his eyes. He sat down heavily at the edge of the stairs and pulled out a notebook. "What brought you two up here?"

Sophie spoke first. "I wanted to show Lucky my mom's property. It's been a long time since she's been here. Sage and I are hoping to buy out my brother's interest and redo the house." Sophie's hands shook. "I thought it'd be a fun surprise to tell Lucky about it."

Nate whistled. "That'll take a lot of doing."

"I know. But we want it to be a real home again. And I don't want my grandfather's chimney and fireplace to go to waste."

Nate nodded. "I can understand that. It's a beauty, all right. All river rock, all perfectly joined too." He made a few scribbles in his notebook. "I wish you lots of luck. Don't let this thing today get in your way. I'm sure we'll find out who this man is and I'm sure there's a reasonable explanation how he ended up in your backyard. What made you go down there, anyway?" He nodded in the direction of the creek.

"My hands were all sooty from the fireplace. And there's no running water now, so I just wanted to wash up." She looked down at her half-clean hands and rubbed them self-consciously on her jeans.

"Elias is on his way," Nate said to Lucky. "I don't know

what he can tell us. Given the way this guy looks, it's hard to say what killed him."

"Do you think he could have fallen and hit his head and washed down this far?"

"Possible." He looked at both women carefully. "Anything about him either of you recognized?"

Sophie shook her head violently. "Nate, there wasn't anything to recognize. I've never seen anything like that."

"I'll bet you haven't. Sorry you had to discover him, but if you two hadn't come along, well . . . who knows when he would have been found. Coulda been there for months, maybe years. At least we got him when there might still be some identifying marks."

They all turned as a car approached up the dirt drive. Lucky recognized Elias's silver sedan. He climbed out and walked toward them, reaching down to place a protective arm around Lucky's shoulders. "Are you all right?"

Lucky just nodded.

"Sophie? How are you doing?" he asked.

"I'll be okay, Elias. Just a bad shock."

Nate gestured toward the path that ran down to the creek. "You'll find Bradley down there."

Elias nodded. "I'll be back up as soon as I can."

When Elias was out of sight, Lucky asked, "What do *you* think happened to him, Nate?"

"Don't know. He could have slipped and fallen in farther upstream. Maybe knocked unconscious and drowned. But . . ." He trailed off. "I don't know. That damage to his face . . ." Nate shook his head in disbelief. "Doesn't seem like the rocks could've done that."

"Is there any identification on him?"

"Nothing I could find. No ID, no wallet, which is pretty strange. We pulled him out of the water for now. Looks like he's maybe been in there a few days. Once Elias has a look, I'll have Bradley wait for the coroner's van to get over here from Lincoln Falls." He ran a hand through his thick gray hair. "I don't know what's going on anymore. Two deaths in less than twelve hours." He stood slowly, holding a hand against his lower back. "Why don't you two go back to town? We've got this covered."

Lucky agreed. She was still unnerved by their discovery. "Tell Elias I'll catch up with him later?"

Nate nodded and watched as they climbed into Sophie's car and reversed onto the road. Sophie was silent on the drive back to town.

Lucky glanced over. "You're very quiet all of a sudden. You sure you're okay?"

Sophie's jaw was clenched. "This feels like a bad omen, Lucky."

"Don't even say that. It's horrible, but it's probably an accident. It has nothing to do with you—or with Sage."

Sophie shivered. "I only hope you're right."

Chapter 7

SAGE STEPPED OUT to the corridor as soon as he heard the back door slam. "What happened?" He looked as if he had been worrying since he had received the phone call. "Isn't Sophie with you?"

"She's fine, but she wanted to go straight home."

"Tell me everything."

"Sophie walked down to the creek to wash her hands and she found a man—dead, floating in the water."

"A dead man? Who?"

"Nobody knows. And Nate said he couldn't find any identification at all."

"Look, will you be okay if I take off a little early? I just want to make sure Sophie's all right."

"Sure, you go ahead. Janie and Meg are here. I'll man the kitchen and they can take care of the front. You go home."

"Thanks, Lucky. I just don't want to leave you in the lurch."

"You're not. Go ahead. Where's Jack, by the way?"

"Uh . . . he left about an hour ago. Didn't say where he was going."

"Really? That's odd. Was he okay?"

"Just very quiet. Like something was on his mind."

"Ah. I'll bet I know what it is." She sighed. "I'll catch up with him later. Too much stuff is happening all of a sudden. Uh, Sage, can you wait just a minute? I need to make a phone call before you go."

"Sure, I'll wait."

Lucky hurried into the office and looked up Cordelia Rank's home number. Norman Rank, Cordelia's husband, was their landlord, the owner of the space the Spoonful occupied. Their number was on her Rolodex. It was Norman who answered.

"I was hoping to talk to Cordelia. Is she available?"

"No, I'm sorry, Lucky. She's resting right now. She's very upset about . . . well, I'm sure you know."

"Yes, Jack's concerned too. I'll talk to her later. Please let her know I called, though."

"I will."

Lucky sighed. Norman, for all his idiosyncrasies, was a breeze to deal with. Cordelia was another story altogether. Lucky returned to the kitchen and said good-bye to Sage. She looked around. Three large slow-cooking pots stood full. She lifted the lids and stirred each with a wooden spoon, making sure nothing was drying out. Each pot bubbled with Sage's specials of the day: an Asian tofu soup with ginger and green onion, a beet and apricot soup, and a potato kale that was Lucky's favorite. All the sandwich ingredients were in containers in the refrigerator, and the rolls and breads were already sliced and covered in preparation for the next rush at supper time.

Janie had chosen one of Jack's CDs to play. This one was an upbeat big band sound that kept a steady rhythm going. *Good choice*, Lucky thought. The restaurant was full. The music would keep everyone on their toes.

THE NEXT HOURS passed quickly. Lucky filled thirty orders of soup and twenty of sandwiches, made five pots of coffee and ten cups of tea. She had a new respect for Sage's organization. Her back was aching, and this wasn't even a particularly busy day.

As the last customers were leaving, she realized Jack had never returned. She wiped her hands on a dish towel and dialed his home number from the kitchen phone. It rang fifteen times—no answer. She shook her head in frustration. Jack refused to get an answering machine. He always said if anybody really wanted to talk to him, they could just ring his doorbell. After all, he would say, how did everyone manage before there were answering machines?

She was definitely worried. If he were home, he'd answer his phone. And if he hadn't been at the restaurant all afternoon, where had he gone? It wasn't like Jack to leave them like this and not make sure everything was secure for the night.

Lucky was the last to leave. She hauled the last trash bag out to the Dumpster and climbed into her car. When she turned the key in the ignition, the engine coughed and died. She tried again to no avail. In frustration, she banged the steering wheel. "Not now. This is all I need." In her daily routine, she had no real need of a car. Her apartment building was on Maple Street, just around the corner. She could easily walk back and forth every day. In fact, most of the places she visited in town were within walking distance. But over the next two weeks she'd be busy helping Sophie with her wedding plans. She'd need transportation if she had to drive to Lincoln Falls to pick up flowers or supplies or anything else. She sighed and rested her head against the steering wheel.

Jack sat motionless at the kitchen table. Outside it had grown dark and only a small bulb over the kitchen sink offered relief from the night. His eyes were closed, hands held over his face, as he replayed in his mind the steps he had taken that day in the woods. He was sure he could find that same place again, the spot where he had found the woodruff. It was along a path that led past the meadow toward the small pond, a shady, water-fed spot, a perfect place for woodruff to grow. He saw himself walking, searching, then kneeling and trimming the plant. Had he made a mistake? Had there been something else growing there that he hadn't seen? His eyesight wasn't what it once was, he knew, but surely he would have spotted anything strange, something that didn't belong? Other things could be growing near, that was true, but he would have recognized them. Had he been careful enough? Had he sorted through the plants on his kitchen counter? Yes, he had. He was sure it was only woodruff he had picked. He took a deep breath to calm himself. Could he trust his own memory? It sometimes failed him; there were times he could recognize a face and knew the name, but couldn't bring it all the way into his mind. Had something like that happened? Had he been careless? Had someone died because of him?

Lucky tried to start the car again. Again the engine coughed and refused to turn over. She groaned. It was too late to call Guy Bessette at the Auto Shop. She'd call tomorrow, and tonight she could walk the few blocks to Jack's house on Birch Street. She climbed out of the car and hurried down the alleyway to Broadway. It had worried her all evening that Jack hadn't returned to the Spoonful. She knew he'd be concerned about Nate's questions, but she was positive that whatever had happened to Agnes Warner in the woods the night before had nothing to do with the plants he had provided.

The first evening of May promised delicious warm days. Fragrant lilacs would bloom soon, but the evenings were still chilly. She wrapped her sweater tighter around her and turned the corner on Birch Street. She climbed the steps to Jack's house and peeked through the window in the front door. A light was burning at the back of the house. Jack was still awake. She knocked on the front door and waited. No answer. She retraced her steps and walked down the driveway. Jack's car was there, parked in front of the garage. She continued along the side of his house and stood on tiptoe to peer through the kitchen window. Jack sat at the table, his head in his hands. She tapped on the glass.

"Jack. It's me."

He looked up, an anxious expression on his face.

"Can you let me in?"

Jack rose slowly and walked to the back door. He unlocked it and held it open for her.

"Lucky, my girl. Did you walk over? You shouldn't have bothered." His complexion was drained, as if he had aged in the few hours since that morning.

"I was worried about you. You didn't come back."

"I just couldn't face anybody—especially if they're all thinking I caused . . . you know."

"You're taking too much on." Lucky sighed. "I don't think you made a mistake. I'm sure whatever plants you gave them were fine. Besides, I've never heard of anyone having an allergic reaction to woodruff. It's used all the time as a flavoring ingredient."

"I just can't get it out of my head—that maybe I did something wrong. Wasn't careful enough."

"Oh, Jack. You've got to stop thinking like that. For all we know, the poor woman had a stroke. Please. Don't let this gnaw away at you. Let's find out the facts before we jump to any conclusions." She reached across the scarred wooden table and squeezed his hand.

He took a deep breath. "You're right. I know you're right. I'm a worrywart. I know I am."

"We'll find out exactly what happened to her in a few days. Until then, stop blaming yourself for things you had no control over, okay?" Lucky realized she had to add to Jack's worries. She'd rather he heard from her than from someone else. "I haven't had a chance to tell you what happened this afternoon."

Jack's eyebrows rose as she filled him in on the discovery of the body in the creek.

"You shoulda called me."

"Well, I called the Spoonful and spoke to Sage, but you might have already gone home. Besides, there was no need for you to be worrying about me. We were fine. Nate and Bradley got there right away. And then Elias. We talked to Nate for a bit and then we drove back." She looked at him carefully. "Anyway, you need to get some rest. What have you been doing all afternoon? Sitting here worrying?"

"Nah," Jack denied. "Look, can you come and have a peek at the herb garden? I went out there earlier to check, but I couldn't see anything wrong."

"Okay. If it makes you feel better."

Jack grabbed a flashlight from the kitchen counter. Lucky wondered how many trips he had made to the backyard this afternoon to check on his plants.

They trudged silently across the lawn. The yard was shaded by a maple tree and tall lilac bushes along both sides of the wooden fence. Jack's small vegetable and herb garden was laid out in short, neat rows behind low hedges at the rear of his property where the plants would get the best sunlight. He shone his flashlight on a section planted with tomatoes, carrots, potatoes and Swiss chard. There were plants of sage, mint, parsley, thyme and oregano. The next row was basil and strawberry plants and a large borage plant for the bees. "I've checked for any weeds that might have come up, but I just weeded a few days ago and didn't see anything."

"That's 'cause there's nothing to see. This garden is immaculate. Nothing's growing here that shouldn't be. If that woman was poisoned, it's more likely they decided to experiment with their wine and added something she was allergic to. Now will you stop worrying?"

"I guess you're right. I'm making a mountain out of a molehill."

She tucked her arm through his and led him gently back into the house. "I'll say good night. Will you promise me you'll go straight to bed? Sleep in tomorrow if you like. No need to be at the restaurant early."

Jack smiled for the first time since the morning. "Oh, I don't sleep very much anymore, my girl. I'll be there bright and early."

"Well, all right, then. If not, I'll tell Flo you're feeling bad and might need some help." She chuckled.

Jack stopped in his tracks and stared at her. "You wouldn't do that to your defenseless old grandfather, now, would you?"

"Wanna bet?" She laughed and blew him a kiss as he shut the door behind her. Lucky tested the knob to make sure it was locked. The light in the kitchen was extinguished, plunging the driveway into darkness. She headed for the street and continued on through the still night, not meeting another soul. When she reached her apartment building, she climbed the stairs and locked the door behind her, so grateful to fall into bed after a long, strange day.

Chapter 8

SOPHIE SAT AT the counter sipping a mug of coffee. It was a few minutes before opening time. Jack had arrived early as promised and now sat at a front table reading his newspaper.

"Sure you don't want something to eat?" Lucky asked.

Sophie shook her head. "Nah. I just walked over with Sage. I have a few errands to run today. I'll come back later to help you out if you need me." Lucky was grateful for Sophie's loose spring and summer schedule. She was always willing to lend a hand if things got busy. Lucky had offered to pay her for her time, but Sophie adamantly refused payment, saying she enjoyed being able to hang out with everyone at the restaurant.

Lucky glanced toward a stack of CDs at the counter. "What should we play this morning?"

"Hmm." Sophie picked through the CDs. "How about this one?" She pushed the plastic container toward Lucky. "I used to love to listen to this in high school." Sophie had chosen a collection of classic rock songs.

"That's great. It'll wake everybody up. And I can really use the help. I'm waiting for Guy Bessette to come by."

"Something wrong?"

"Hopefully nothing expensive. My car just wouldn't start last night."

"If Guy has to tow yours in, just take mine. I can always use Sage's."

"Are you sure?"

"Yes, no problem." Sophie reached down and hauled her purse onto her lap. "Here," she said, passing the keys across the counter to Lucky. "It's parked in the back next to yours."

"Thanks, Sophie. I do have to drive out to Horace's later. He has some boxes of my mother's in the attic and I know one of them is full of sewing supplies. Oh, and there's something I should mention to you." Lucky cringed, fearful of Sophie's reaction.

"What's that?"

"Did you invite Flo Sullivan to your wedding?"

"Huh?" Sophie looked blank. "Are you kidding me?"

"She told me to give you a nudge because she hadn't received her invitation. I thought it was odd because you said you wanted your ceremony to be very private."

"What did you say to her?"

"I was speechless. I didn't know what to say. I told her I'd remind you."

Sophie groaned and rolled her eyes. "I can't believe this. Why in heaven's name would Flo get the idea she was invited to a private wedding? I have nothing against her—I mean, she's a weird character—but we're not close friends or anything."

Lucky shrugged. "Who knows? Maybe she figures it's such a small town everyone is invited?"

"Don't even say that." Sophie looked panic-stricken. "What do I do?" she squeaked.

"Don't worry about it for now. Flo will probably forget all about it in a day or two. But please remember, we have to do some final fittings for your dress. We're getting close." Lucky was referring to Sophie's wedding dress, which she had volunteered to sew.

Sophie groaned. "Oh, right." She glanced up. "I don't

mean to sound ungrateful. I can't thank you enough for doing all that work—it's just that I feel so awkward in a dress. I don't think I even own another one. Where would I wear them?"

Lucky laughed. "Well, I'm not much better when it comes to that stuff, but this is your absolutely special day. I want everything to be perfect for you. You're beautiful and you should look amazing on your wedding day."

"It's ironic, isn't it?"

"What?"

"You have no interest in fashion, yet you're such a perfectionist with dressmaking."

"True, but my mother always said sewing has more to do with patience than skill. And I do think your dress will be stunning." Lucky had chosen a pattern with an empire waist, a sweetheart bodice and elbow-length sleeves. The skirt was cut on the bias and would flow gently to the floor. The material was an eggshell white with a matte finish and would set off Sophie's coloring and dark curly hair. Sophie had nixed the idea of lace or anything fussy.

"I just have to hem the dress, but if I can't find the notions I need, I'll have to make piping from the leftover material for a lacing at the back. That'll take me at least another night."

"Thanks, Lucky. Not just for the dress but for everything else." Sophie was referring to Lucky's efforts over a year ago in freeing Sage from a possible jail sentence. "If it hadn't been for you . . ." Sophie trailed off.

Lucky poured a little more coffee into Sophie's mug. She blushed in response to Sophie's praise. "It was nothin'."

Sophie balled up a paper napkin and threw it at her head. "Don't even say that. All this . . ." She waved her arm in the air, indicating the restaurant, Jack's health, Sage and herself. "None of this would be here if it weren't for you."

Lucky looked up when she heard a knock on the front door. Nate was on the threshold. "I'll get it, Jack," she called out. She unlocked the front door and opened it for Nate. She reached up to flip the sign over to read OPEN.

Nate grasped her hand before she could turn the sign. He looked her straight in the eyes. "Hold off, Lucky."

Lucky's eyes widened.

"You'll need to wait a bit." He glanced around the restaurant, realizing that only she, Jack, Sage and Sophie were there. Sage peered through the hatch from the kitchen. Nate nodded to him, indicating Sage should join them in the front.

Sophie had turned on her stool, gazing curiously. When she saw Nate beckon Sage to the front of the restaurant, she frowned.

Nate approached Sophie and took her hand. "Let's sit over here," he said, leading Sophie to Jack's table. Sage and Lucky joined them as Jack, aware that something was wrong, folded up his newspaper and put it to the side. Nate turned his chair toward Sophie and took both her hands in his. "The man you discovered yesterday . . ."

Sophie gulped and nodded.

"We think he could be your brother."

Chapter 9

SOPHIE'S FACE WAS blank, uncomprehending.

"What?" She shook her head as though she were unable to hear Nate's words.

Nate glanced around, taking in all of them. "We didn't find any identification on the body—nothing. But there was a small pen in one of the inside pockets of the jacket. It had the logo of the Snowflake Resort on it. You know, one of those pens they leave in the rooms for guests to use."

Sophie continued to stare at Nate. Sage moved closer to her and placed a protective arm around her shoulders.

Nate continued. "We checked with the Resort. They don't have a lot of bookings right now so it wasn't too hard to figure it out. Everyone's accounted for except one room hasn't been slept in for at least a couple of days." He watched Sophie's face carefully. "It was reserved under the name of Richard Colgan. Sophie, we think it could be him. Your brother."

Sophie seemed to sink in upon herself. "Rick? Rick was here?" She spoke in a barely audible whisper. "How can you be sure it was Rick?"

Nate heaved a sigh. "We can run a DNA test, with your

permission. That would clinch it. Other than that, did he have any identifying marks? Birthmarks? Tattoos? Anything like that you might remember?"

Sophie shrugged, still unable to take in all that Nate was saying. "I . . . I really don't know my brother all that well. He's been gone since I was . . . what, eleven, I think. And I've only seen him once in all these years. He came back when we buried Mom. If he had any birthmarks or anything, I never saw them."

"And there was nothing about that body you found that made you think it might be your brother?"

Sophie shook her head.

"What's he been doing all this time?" Nate asked.

Sophie shrugged. "I don't really know. I don't even have an address for him. Just an e-mail. He wrote once and said he was working for a private investigator. Doing some process service work in New York—somewhere near Utica, I think. I had the impression he was thinking of getting his own license."

"Hmm. Interesting," Nate said. "Then, if that's the case, it should be easy to trace him if he's licensed with New York State."

Lucky and Jack had remained silent, watching their exchange.

Nate hesitated. "We can't be absolutely sure at this point, Sophie, but it's definitely pointing in that direction. I'll check out what I can with New York. If it turns out there's no one who can identify him, I'd like to set up an appointment for a DNA collection in Lincoln Falls. It'll just take a minute. A swab is all they'll need."

Sophie sniffed and nodded silently.

"I'm sorry, Sophie. Sorry I had to come to you with this." Nate stood and walked to the door. "I'll be in touch." Nate exited without looking back.

Sage followed Nate and locked the door behind him, making sure the CLOSED sign was still turned toward the outside of the glass. He returned to the table and sat, taking Sophie's hand in his. All three were quiet, watching Sophie carefully.

She looked around the table at them. "I don't know what to say. I'm not really *feeling* anything right now."

"That's understandable," Lucky replied. "I guess he was a stranger to you . . . really."

"He was. But still . . . my only flesh and blood in the world. I feel like I should feel something."

Jack reached across and touched her shoulder. "If it really is your brother they found up there, you'll come to grips with it. You'll sort out your feelings."

Sage leaned closer. "Look, if you're upset or want to postpone the wedding, we can. We'd all understand."

"No!" Sophie's response was vehement. "No. I can't sort it out, but I don't want to be putting our lives on hold. I didn't even know my brother and he's been gone for a long, long time. If that was him, I'm real sorry, but putting off the wedding won't help a bit. It's a terrible accident but there's nothing I can do about it."

Silence fell over the table. No one wanted to suggest there might be more to this death than an accident.

Chapter 10

"MAYBE I SHOULD take you home?" Sage offered.

Sophie shook her head. "No. No, I'm fine." She leaned over to give him a kiss on the cheek. "You have work to do and Lucky needs to open. I'll be okay. I have to get a few things done and I'll come back later. I refuse to be upset. Especially since we don't know for sure who that man in the creek was. No one could possibly identify him from his face anyway."

Sage seemed to accept Sophie's decision. "All right. As long as you promise to call me if you're not feeling well."

"I promise." Sophie stood. "By the way"—she turned to Sage—"I need to use your car. Lucky's going to borrow mine till she can have hers looked at."

"What's wrong with it?" Sage asked Lucky.

"Just wouldn't start last night. Guy's coming by soon to see what he can do. I can wait until he gives me an opinion, if borrowing Sophie's car is inconvenient."

"No. It's fine. Go right ahead. Let me know if you need any help with that."

"Thanks, Sage."

Sophie slung her purse over her shoulder. "Thanks,

Lucky . . . Jack. I appreciate your concern with all this. I really do. But I don't want you worrying about me. I'll be fine."

Lucky smiled her encouragement and waved as Sophie headed through the swinging door to the corridor. A minute or so later, they watched as she pulled out of the alleyway in Sage's car and turned onto Broadway.

Jack sighed. "Keep an eye on her, you two. This could hit her real hard if it turns out Nate's right."

Sage rose and, turning over the sign at the door, headed back to the kitchen. He hadn't said a word. Lucky knew he'd worry about Sophie all day. She just hoped there would be no need for their concern. She craned her neck to look out the window. "Time to open up. I see Hank and Barry coming down the street."

The two men entered the restaurant and called out their greetings. Jack leaned over and whispered to Lucky, "Do you think we should say something to them? About Sophie?"

Lucky shook her head. "No. Not yet. Not until we absolutely know for certain."

"Hey, Jack," Hank called out. He sat at the corner table, his pince-nez glasses on his nose. Hank had always reminded her of a friendly scarecrow. He was tall and thin and his glasses gave him the look of a bookish professor. Barry was his foil, short and stocky with a protruding belly that threatened to break through the buttons on his plaid shirt.

"Coffee?" she asked the men as she returned to the counter.

"Thanks, Lucky," Barry replied.

Lucky carried two mugs filled with coffee on a tray to their corner table. "Here you go."

Barry leaned closer and whispered, "Lucky, we were just wondering"—he glanced toward the kitchen hatch, as if concerned that Sage might overhear—"what kind of presents do you think we could get the newlyweds?"

"Oh, I'm sure they don't expect anyone to buy them presents." She wondered whether Barry and Hank were under the impression they were invited guests too. Neither of them had exactly said that, but she wondered if the question of presents was an indication they planned to attend the ceremony.

Hank spoke up. "That's not right. We come in every day and eat delicious food thanks to Sage. We'd just like to show our appreciation. It's the least we can do."

Lucky nodded. "Well, that's very thoughtful of you both. I'll try to find out if there's anything they could use. How's that?"

"Great," Barry responded. "Just let us know."

The bell over the door rang as Lucky returned to the counter. Marjorie Winters entered alone. Generally she and her sister arrived together every morning and ordered in duplicate. Whenever one was alone, it usually indicated a rift between the two. Marjorie slid onto a stool. She was neatly dressed, and her blonde hair was perfectly in place.

"The usual, Marjorie?" Lucky asked.

"Yes, dear. Thank you."

"Cecily's not coming?"

Marjorie pursed her lips. Too late, Lucky realized she had put her foot in her mouth.

"No," Marjorie replied curtly. "She's at home reflecting on the error of her ways."

Lucky poured Marjorie's tea and brought her a cup. "Ah. I see," she replied neutrally.

"It's just so embarrassing that my sister would become involved with that mad crew. Celebrating spring rites! For heaven's sake. Running around in the woods with robes and flowers in their hair worshipping the earth goddess. Did you ever hear of anything so daft?"

Lucky wasn't sure how to respond. "Well, I think a few people in town might share that opinion."

Marjorie sighed heavily. "And to have witnessed Agnes Warner dying like that."

Lucky cringed, hoping Jack hadn't overheard that last remark. She glanced quickly across the room where Jack sat reading the morning paper. If he had heard, he gave no indication.

"I really hope this teaches them all a lesson. And for

Cordelia Rank to have organized it . . . She's always on about how important she is to the town. Has she taken leave of her senses?" Marjorie's voice had risen. She glanced over her shoulder, suddenly realizing everyone's attention was on her. Fortunately, only the Spoonful's crew and two of their regulars were in attendance.

"Sorry, dear. I don't mean to go on at you about this. But it's just appalling. I don't think Cecily even wants to show her face in town at this point. She's home, under the covers, pretending to be sick—like a six-year-old!"

Lucky reached for Marjorie's order. It was ready and waiting on the hatch. She delivered it to the counter. "How many people were there in the woods the other night? Do you know?"

Marjorie sniffed. "I gather there were seven, including my sister and Cordelia, the *high priestess*—of all things to call herself!" Marjorie was clearly fuming about the gathering and her sister's involvement.

"I had heard something about a women's group at the library or a study group of goddess-based religions. But I had no idea they planned a . . . What would you call it? A gathering, I guess?"

"Some sort of ceremony." Marjorie shook her head. "Practically turned into a sacrifice. According to Cecily, their interest was piqued by the travelers who were here last fall and all that talk about the Stones outside of town being sacred to them. Pagan nonsense." Marjorie was referring to the Neolithic stone structure that stood on a hill above Snowflake. Marjorie took a bite of her croissant. "One woman lives up in Lincoln Heights—a newcomer—and another one lives out of town." Lincoln Heights was the name given to a newer development in town, filled mostly with executives of the Snowflake Resort and their families.

"Frustrated, aging hippie women, if you ask me. And Emily Rathbone, our librarian, attended as well. Thought she had more sense!"

"She has a helper now, doesn't she? A volunteer. She came by to leave flyers for the library."

"Oh yes, that nervous little thing. What's her name? Greta?"

"I believe so. Is she part of the group?"

"Cecily never mentioned her. I don't know. Maybe the woman has too much sense to be involved with all that crazy nonsense." Marjorie finished the last bite of her croissant and wiped her lips with a napkin. "Well, dear, I'll be on my way to open the shop. Hopefully my darling sister will see fit to get over her shock and come to work."

Lucky nodded. "See you tomorrow, Marjorie. I do hope she's feeling better. It must have been a terrible shock."

"Hmph! I'll give her a shock if she doesn't develop a bit more sense." Marjorie slipped off her stool. "Oh, before I forget. What type of outfit do you think would be appropriate for the big day?"

Lucky hesitated. "The big day?"

Marjorie's eyes widened. "The wedding, of course! This is so exciting. Snowflake hasn't had a wedding in years."

"Uh . . ." Lucky couldn't think of a quick response. Was she to tell anyone who asked that Sophie and Sage's wedding was a private affair? She had no idea what to say.

"I think something soft and feminine would be right. Nothing too formal. Don't you agree, dear?"

Lucky nodded her head a few times. "Perfect. That sounds perfect." She'd have to have another word with Sophie. It seemed that everyone in town knew about Sophie's wedding and everyone assumed they were invited.

Marjorie reached the door as Horace was about to enter. He held the door for her.

"Thank you, Horace," she said, reaching down to pat Cicero's head. Cicero wagged his tail happily. Marjorie turned and strode purposefully down the sidewalk to her shop.

Horace said hello to Jack as he came through the door, and raised a hand in greeting to Hank and Barry. He took a stool at the counter. "Is Marjorie all right?" he asked Lucky.

Lucky poured a mug of coffee for Horace. "She's just a little upset about her sister's involvement with the group that

Cordelia Rank organized." Lucky heard the phone ringing in the kitchen. It stopped after two rings. Sage must have answered.

"Hey, Lucky," Sage called out. "It's Guy Bessette . . . about your car."

"Oh!" She turned back to Horace. "Give me a second, Horace. I need to talk to Guy."

"Car trouble?" he asked.

"'Fraid so." Lucky wiped her hands and pushed through the swinging door to the kitchen. She grabbed the phone. "Hello, Guy."

"Hi, Lucky. Some good news and bad news, I'm afraid."

Lucky groaned inwardly. "Okay," she replied hesitantly.

"Your starter's gone, but that can be replaced. The bad news is the timing belt is bad and it's gonna take me a while to find one. It's an older car, not so easy to find parts."

"What's the good news?"

"Your battery's in good shape. No need to replace that."

"How long will this take, Guy?"

"With luck, maybe six, seven days."

"Why so long?" she squeaked.

"Like I said, I have to hunt up a new belt. Not something I keep around. But I'll keep you posted. You have something you can use for now?" he asked.

"I'm okay. Sophie's loaned me her car. Thanks, Guy, for calling."

"I'll get it done as soon as I can." He rang off.

Lucky returned to the counter.

"Uh-oh. Bad news?" Horace asked.

"Well, not horrible. It's just going to take some time for Guy to find the parts he needs."

"Ah." Horace nodded in commiseration.

"More coffee?" Lucky asked.

"Yes, thank you." Horace offered his cup as Lucky refilled it. "What were you saying before . . . about Cordelia? That Cordelia had organized the gathering in the woods? I thought Emily Rathbone was the driving force behind that thing. Sadly, this might not do her library drive any good.

People are always happy to donate books, but this may have created a mini-scandal in town, and now with Agnes Warner dying like that . . ." Horace trailed off. "People do get very worked up about these things. Although it's a movement that has many adherents in the world right now."

"You mean paganism?"

Horace furrowed his brow. "No, not paganism, per se, but reclaiming women's role in religion, as in early Christianity. I think the women's movement has had a lot to say about male-dominated religions." Horace chuckled. "Pastor Wilson is beside himself right now. 'Apoplectic' might be a better word. I saw him on my way over this morning and he really wanted to bend my ear about it. I wonder if he secretly thinks Agnes's death was God's punishment on wayward souls, although I'm sure he would never come right out and say that."

"I should hope not," Lucky answered. A small plate appeared on the hatch with Horace's muffin, butter and jam.

"So tell me." Horace leaned forward. "How are the wedding preparations coming?"

"Oh, I'm so glad you reminded me. Would it be all right if I stopped by to take those last few boxes of my mother's that are in the attic?" When Lucky had inherited her parents' home, she realized she couldn't possibly afford to pay the mortgage on their house. Horace had arrived in town and was looking for a place to rent long-term to work on his book about the Revolutionary War years in Vermont. He fell in love with the house, and Lucky was relieved she wouldn't be forced to sell it at what would have been a loss.

"Of course. Anytime. Those boxes are no bother to me, if that's what you're worried about."

"It's not that. I'm looking for buttons and things to finish Sophie's wedding gown and I'm pretty sure one of those boxes has tons of my mother's sewing supplies."

"Ah, yes, for Sophie's wedding. I wanted to talk to you about that. What do you think they'd like as a wedding present?"

Lucky smiled. "You're planning to come, then?" *Wait till Sophie hears this*, she thought.

"Oh, I wouldn't miss it for the world! I understand there hasn't been a wedding in Snowflake for a long time. And this is the perfect month to hold it."

Lucky sighed. There was no escaping this. "Well, everything's organized. We've hired a harpist to play for the ceremony. Sage wants to do the food himself. It'll be buffet style but they plan on wine and champagne. Sophie's dress is almost ready. Jack has a gazebo in his garden that we'll decorate with tulle and flowers. And I guess that's it. Hopefully, everything will go very smoothly, no glitches."

Lucky looked up as the bell at the door jingled. Elias stepped in and joined Horace at the counter. Lucky dropped a slice of bread into the toaster and poured a cup of coffee for him. Elias smiled at Lucky.

"So, Elias, any news?" Horace asked.

Elias raised his eyebrows. Lucky could tell Elias wasn't quite sure which body Horace was referring to. News of both discoveries had spread throughout town, but Lucky was sure no one else had been taken into Nate's confidence about the possible identity of the dead man.

Elias shook his head. "Too soon to tell. Autopsy results on both should, with luck, come back in a few days. Nate's asked them to expedite, if possible. That's all I can say for now."

Horace nodded. "I understand." He was aware that Elias undoubtedly knew more than he could speak about. He looked down at Cicero. "Ready for your walk?" he asked the dog. Cicero made a yearning sound in his throat and wagged his tail happily.

"Oh, wait," Lucky said. She leaned into the kitchen hatch and asked Sage for a hunk of chicken meat. He passed it through and she handed it to Horace for his dog. Cicero inhaled the meat quickly and continued to wag his tail. Horace picked up the leash and headed for the door, waving good-bye to Hank and Barry.

The bread popped out of the toaster and Lucky quickly buttered it. She carried the plate to the counter and brought a pot of jam for Elias. He reached across the counter and grasped her hand. She blushed, grateful that no other customers were seated there. "Dinner tomorrow night?" he asked.

"Sure. Love to. You cooking?"

"Of course. I was thinking a small pork roast with a plum wine sauce and mashed potatoes."

"Mmm. Sounds heavenly. Yes, ply me with food." Lucky, who served food all day, had no desire to cook when her day was done. For Elias, cooking was a relaxing enterprise that broke his routine of seeing patients. He was still alone at the Snowflake Clinic since his last hire had left town under suspicious circumstances, a woman who had sent Lucky into paroxysms of jealousy. Before that, his medical partner had left town after a scandal involving his wife. It meant that Elias's schedule was still extremely hectic, as was hers, so the time they spent together was extra precious.

"With anything I can," he said, smiling seductively.

Lucky blushed furiously. Their romance had been back on track for the past several months. Not simply on track, but growing deeper every day. She rubbed her cheeks hoping the flush would disappear before anyone noticed.

Chapter 11

SOPHIE WAS BALANCED on a small stool while Lucky knelt on the carpet on her living room floor. She held a pin between her teeth and placed the pincushion within reaching distance.

"Hold still," she ordered through gritted teeth.

Sophie sighed. "It's perfect, Lucky. There's no need to fuss over the hem this way."

Lucky removed the pin from her mouth and stuck it in the pincushion. "I know you think it's perfect, but it's not. This material slides around and you want it to show only the very front of your shoes as you walk. Trust me. It's worth it to take the time."

"If you say so. I love you, and I love that you're going to all this work for me, but we just want this to be a small, informal ceremony—with lilacs all around us."

"Uh . . . about that . . ."

Sophie looked down at her with a suspicious eye. "What?"

"I told you about Flo Sullivan."

"Yeees," Sophie replied cautiously.

"Well, Marjorie asked me what type of dress would be

appropriate and Horace wanted to know what you'd like for a wedding present. Uh . . . and so did Hank and Barry."

"I can't believe this!" Sophie tried to turn around. The stool wobbled and she quickly returned to her pose. "We just wanted you and Elias and Jack and Sage's brother Remy and maybe my two work friends. Isn't it possible to do anything in this town and not have everybody get involved?" Her voice was rising.

Lucky grimaced. "Sophie, I really didn't know what to say to any of them."

Sophie groaned. "We're doing it this way so it's inexpensive. I can't afford to rent a hall and hire caterers for tons of people."

"I know. I understand. What do you want me to tell them?"

"It's not your problem, Lucky. You shouldn't have to tell them anything." Sophie sighed. "Let me talk to Sage and see what he thinks. If a few more people want to come, and Jack doesn't mind, maybe he can prepare a little extra food." She looked down, doing her best not to move her legs. "Are we done yet?" she asked impatiently.

"Almost. Just one more touch." Lucky stood and marked a spot slightly below Sophie's waist. "I want to take it in just a bit right here."

Sophie groaned.

"Hush. This will make the line from the waist flow better." She made a mark with tailor's chalk and then checked the other side of the dress. "There," she said, finally satisfied with her work.

"*Now* are we done?"

"Just a sec," Lucky replied, quickly checking the hem once again. "Stop fidgeting!"

Sophie stood still.

"And stand up straight, please."

"Yes, ma'am."

Lucky moved two of the pins down a sixteenth of an inch on either side of the dress. She breathed a sigh of relief as she placed the last pin. "Okay, now we're done."

"Thank heavens!" Sophie slumped. "Get me out of this beautiful creation of yours, please, before I scream."

"I'm sorry it's taking so long. I'm really not an expert dressmaker, but I do want you to look gorgeous and perfect."

Sophie raised her arms as Lucky lifted the long dress over her head. She hung it carefully on a padded hanger and hooked the hanger over the door. "I need to find some ribbon or make some piping to lace up the back. That will be the finishing touch, Cinderella."

Sophie laughed. "Right. Actually, I should probably wear one of my ski outfits and Sage could wear his white jacket. That would really be appropriate."

"Nah. It's fun to make a big deal over a wedding. It's something you hopefully only do once in your life." Lucky frowned. "By the way, what would you like for a wedding present? You still haven't told me."

"We don't want you to buy us anything. I told you that. You're making my dress and Jack's volunteered his garden. That's so much already."

"Yes, but I do want to get you and Sage something that's sentimental, that you'll remember as a wedding present from me," Lucky replied. "Isn't there something you'd love to have?"

"Well . . ." Sophie thought for a moment.

Lucky was sure something definite had occurred to her friend. "Tell me."

"No."

"No? What do you mean, no?"

"I don't think it's something you could get."

"Sophie! What?"

"I absolutely adore the blue pottery you have. I know it was your mother's and knowing you, you'd give us the shirt off your back. And if you tried to give us that, I'd never, ever accept it."

"Oh," Lucky replied. "I'm not sure exactly where my mother found those dishes. I think they were made by a local potter."

"They're so beautiful. If you ever remember where she found them, could you let me know? I wouldn't get the exact same kind, but I just think they're so charming and quaint. I'd love to find that artist."

"You've got it. Maybe I can figure it out."

"But I *don't* want you to buy us anything, okay?" Sophie was adamant.

"Okay. I hear you. But I will try to find out who made them." Lucky squeezed her eyes shut.

"What's wrong?"

"Oh, nothing. I'm just trying to remember what's stored at Horace's house. I brought bunches of material over here to the apartment when I moved in, but there's more boxes in the attic. I plan on picking them up and going through them. I'm pretty sure at least one of those boxes has lots of notions. I hope so, anyway. It'll save me a trip to Lincoln Falls." Lucky placed the pincushion on the coffee table. "Come sit down and have a glass of wine with me before Sage comes by."

Sage had insisted on walking over to meet Sophie. He had been anxious about Sophie's emotional state since Nate's news that morning.

"How are you feeling about everything?" Lucky asked as she poured two glasses of a white wine that Sage had recommended.

Sophie rested her arm on a sofa cushion. "You mean the . . . the man we found?" Sophie sighed. "I feel bad that I really don't feel anything—at least not yet. Maybe you all think I'm in a state of denial but I don't think I am. First of all, we don't know that the . . . body in the creek really is Rick. And there's no way to identify him by his face." Sophie shuddered involuntarily.

"What about dental records?"

Sophie shrugged. "You know how poor we were. I don't ever remember even seeing a dentist when we were kids. I guess we were lucky; we had real strong teeth. I have no idea if Rick saw anyone when he was younger, and who knows what dentists he might have seen since he moved away. Nate's contacted authorities in New York, but until we hear back, we just won't know." Sophie swirled the wine around in her glass. "To tell you the truth, I've been thinking more about my dad than anything else these days."

Lucky raised her eyebrows, surprised. This was the second time her friend had brought up the subject of her father. Over the years, Lucky could never remember Sophie speaking so openly about him. Lucky had never met the man. He had abandoned the family years before she and Sophie met at school. It was the unspoken event in Sophie's household. Sophie's mother, older sister and brothers were always friendly and welcoming to her when she would visit as a young girl, but no one had ever spoken about the man who had deserted them.

"Do you think that's strange?"

"No. Not at all. Getting married is a big transition. It's pretty normal that you'd think a lot about your parents or childhood, I guess."

"I've been hoping for weeks now that my brother would get in touch. And now"—she shook her head as if to drive away the thought—"we don't even know if he's still alive. What if Nate's right, Lucky? What if that was my brother's body in the creek? Oh." Sophie groaned. "I can't even wrap my head around it all. Wouldn't I have known instinctively if that man was my own flesh and blood?"

Lucky reached across and grasped Sophie's hand. "I wish I had an answer for you, but I simply don't know. And it'll take a little time to find out for sure anyway. It's just something you have no control over."

"You know it wasn't just the property that I wanted to talk to Rick about."

"No?"

"Remember I said he was working for a private investigator at one time. I don't know if he still is, but I thought . . ." Sophie trailed off.

"What?"

"I wanted to talk to him about trying to locate my father . . . our father."

Lucky nodded. "I'm sure he would do that for you; wouldn't he?"

Sophie shook her head. "I don't know. He was always pretty weird and angry on the subject. Now? I have no idea what his reaction would be. What am I saying? I don't even know my brother at all. I've seen him once in the last twelve years and that was only for a few hours. I have no idea what he'd say."

"Don't get ahead of yourself. First we need to find out who that man is that we found in the creek. Nate mentioned a DNA swab, didn't he? When are you planning to do that?"

"Tomorrow. Actually, Nate arranged for a tech to come to the police station here. I'm supposed to meet them tomorrow morning."

"That's good," Lucky replied.

"I was wondering . . . do you think you could take a break and come with me? I know it's silly, but it kind of freaks me out."

"Sure, I don't mind. If you want me there," Lucky answered.

"They won't have results right away. Nate says it'll still take a few days to confirm. That's why I don't want to even consider postponing our wedding because of this. It could all be for nothing. That man could be a total stranger. And if it is Rick, why would he come back to Snowflake and not contact me?"

"Does he know you work at the Resort?"

"Yes, I told him—a few years ago. It was just an e-mail but I think he'd remember." Sophie took a sip of her wine. "By the way, you were supposed to let me know how much you've spent on all the material and stuff."

Lucky shook her head. "No way. Don't even ask. I'm paying for it."

"But you're doing all the work," Sophie yelped.

"Yes, and I'm paying for it too, so I don't want to hear any more about it, okay?"

Sophie opened her mouth to argue but the doorbell interrupted her. Lucky placed her wineglass on the coffee table but before she could rise, Sophie jumped up. "There's Sage now. We'll discuss this later." She narrowed her eyes in a mock threat.

"No, we won't. I'm gonna win," Lucky replied, smiling.

Sophie walked to the front door of Lucky's second-floor apartment and opened it. She was leaning over the banister to watch Sage as he climbed the stairs.

Lucky grabbed the dress from the door and rushed it down the hall to her bedroom. It was a silly superstition that the bridegroom should never see the wedding dress before the ceremony but she wasn't going to take any chances. She didn't want to risk anything going wrong on Sophie's big day.

Sage stood in the hallway, a puzzled look on his face. "Something wrong?"

Lucky smiled as she walked back down the hallway toward him. "You know it's bad luck to see the bride's dress before the wedding."

"I thought it was bad luck to see the bride."

"Both! Glass of wine before you go, Sage?"

Sophie threw her arms around Sage's neck and kissed his cheek. "My knight in shining armor." She laughed.

"Your worn-out knight. But here to escort you home, miss." Sage turned to Lucky. "Thanks, but no, Lucky. No wine for me. I'd rather just head home." He followed Sophie into the living room as she pulled on her sweater. "By the way, who's your nosy neighbor downstairs?"

"Huh?"

"When I came in, I saw the door in the rear apartment open a crack." He laughed. "Every building has one, I guess."

"Oh, that must have been Greta. She's in the first-floor apartment in the rear, just under me. She seems nice, but a little skittish. Why do you ask? Did she say something to you?"

Sage shook his head. "No, she just peeked out and stared at me for a second. Neighborhood watch, I guess. I said hello, but she scurried back in."

"Maybe she was expecting someone. Or maybe she's just checking on who's in the building."

"I guess it's a good thing to have someone keeping an eye out. By the way, you should make sure that front door lock catches. It wasn't closed all the way tonight."

"Ah. Good. I'll check it at night. There's a man in the

front apartment downstairs who's a little careless. It's just the three of us right now. The second-floor front is vacant and Elizabeth is looking to rent it. If you know anyone you'd recommend, can you put them in touch with Elizabeth?"

"Sure, we will," Sophie answered. She grabbed her purse and headed out the door with Sage.

Lucky locked the door behind them and kicked off her shoes in the hallway. She returned to the living room and picked up the wineglasses. She had no sooner lifted the glasses from the table than one of the legs gave way and the table tipped to the floor. Lucky groaned. She had glued the thick maple leg back into the slot underneath, but obviously the glue hadn't held. She carried the wineglasses back to the kitchen and dug the wood glue out of the drawer.

So annoying, she thought. *Why won't this leg stay in place?* She turned the table over and squirted glue into the wood slot, maneuvering the table leg back into place. As she got to her feet, she heard a shout from the street below. She rushed out of the apartment and peeked out to the street from the hallway window. Sophie was standing at the bottom of the outside stairway. Sage was crossing the street, heading back toward Sophie.

Lucky opened the window and leaned out. "What's going on?" she called down to them.

Sage shook his head and shrugged. Sophie turned and looked up at the window.

"Hang on." Lucky slammed the window shut and ran down the stairs. She pulled open the front door. "Was that you I heard?" she asked Sage.

He nodded. "There was a guy lurking on the other side of the street. Something about him . . . He was definitely watching us. I told Sophie to wait and I turned back to walk over to him. As soon as I did, he took off."

"Strange."

"I saw him too," Sophie said.

"Did you get a good look at him?" Lucky asked.

"Nah," Sage replied. "And he's gone now. Go back inside, Lucky. Make sure that front door's locked, okay?"

"I will." She waved good night and climbed the stairs to her building, glancing around at the street. She usually never worried about her personal safety. Snowflake was such a quiet village where everyone knew one another. Everyday crime was almost unheard of here. Granted, there had been murders in the past, but there had been reasons for those. She shuddered as she climbed the stairs, remembering that two people had died under suspicious circumstances within the past two days.

Chapter 12

NATE PULLED THE cruiser to the side of the road and turned to Jack. "Is this where you were?" They had driven about half a mile from town along the Old Colonial Road.

"This is it." Jack nodded. "There's a path down to the pond from here. Near the water is a good place to find certain plants."

A newer-model sedan pulled up behind them. A botanist from the University, Professor Lois Hightower, had followed Nate's cruiser in her own car. She climbed out and waited for the two men. Jack nodded to her and started down the path. Nate and the Professor followed him.

The day had grown quite warm, and the first sweet fragrances of summer filled the air. Bees swarmed over flowering bushes and insects flitted in the air. The woods felt as if everything had come alive. When they reached the pond, Jack turned and followed a well-worn path to a shady area. "Here we are," he said, pointing to a hearty clump of sweet woodruff. "I picked those leaves right here, Professor."

"Please, call me Lois." She smiled and knelt down. "Well, this is definitely our sweet woodruff, *Galium odoratum*. I'm sure you know, Jack, that it's an herbaceous perennial." She picked a small leaf and held it to her nose. "If this was all you picked, then I can't see how this could have caused a problem for anyone." She stood and surveyed the area, then walked in a circle around the tree, studying the ground and nearby vegetation.

"You see anything interesting?" Nate asked.

Professor Hightower looked up and smiled. She was a tall blonde with a ruddy complexion that betrayed the time she spent outdoors. "I'm just checking the area. There are lots of everyday plants that are terribly poisonous, even some houseplants. People die or become sick every year because they pick the wrong kind of leaf or the wrong type of berry, particularly children who like to put anything they find in their mouths. Sometimes it's all parts of the plant that are poisonous and sometimes just the leaves or seeds. Even everyday foods can cause harm—uncooked potatoes, things like that."

Nate nodded in agreement.

The Professor continued. "Elderberries contain high levels of cyanide, just like apple seeds. Jimson weed is a member of the nightshade family. Foxglove can cause convulsions and heart problems. Hydrangeas, even tulip bulbs; the list goes on and on. Be careful what you eat or touch, and let the experts do the food harvesting." She turned and moved closer to the water. "I'll just have a look around."

Jack turned to Nate. "Well, even this woodruff, if you ate enough of it, could cause some people to be sick, even though it's not poisonous. That's why I picked it now before the plant starts to bloom, and I didn't give the ladies too much of it."

Professor Hightower turned back. "He's right. Good thing you picked the young leaves. It's considered safe to use as a flavoring in alcoholic drinks, but there have been instances where ingesting it in large amounts has brought on paralysis and even coma and death." The Professor moved to the other side of the patch of woodruff and knelt down. She was suddenly quiet.

Nate approached closer. "Anything wrong?"

She pointed to a cluster of plants with thick stems colored

with purple blotches. "Yes. Something rather bad, actually. This is water hemlock, also known as false parsley or cow-bane. A very dangerous plant."

Nate looked at Jack. "Do you recognize this, Jack?" The men approached the spot where the Professor knelt.

"Sure, I do. I know better than to pick something like that. Nate . . . you don't think I'd ever . . ."

"I'm sure you didn't, Jack," Nate reassured him.

The Professor smiled. "You seem pretty knowledgeable, Mr. Jamieson. I'm sure you were very careful." She turned to look at the patch of plants and shook her head. "Water hemlock grows all over North America, usually near ponds but in meadows too. It's such a dangerous plant because people mistake it for coriander or parsnips. Kids have made blow darts out of the stems and died just from that. The roots taste sweet and have even been known to kill large cattle. Horribly dangerous plant."

"I know I'd never mistake hemlock. I was warned about that when I was a kid. I didn't really notice it that day, to tell you the truth. But I'm sure I was real careful when I picked the woodruff leaves."

Professor Hightower pulled a pair of pruning shears from her jacket and snipped off a section of the hemlock plant. She pulled a tissue from another pocket and dropped the clipping into a plastic bag, careful not to touch the sample.

"I'm sure you were, Jack." Nate patted the older man's shoulder. "Don't worry about that now. We just wanted to see where you found the woodruff. Come on—I'll drive you back to town."

Jack nodded. He wiped perspiration from his brow. He could feel his heart beating rapidly. Had he made a terrible mistake?

Chapter 13

THE OFF BROADWAY Ladies' Clothing Shop carried women's clothing almost exclusively, but often Marjorie and Cecily kept the odd bolt of fabric, buttons and various accessories in stock. Lucky had finished the final touches on Sophie's wedding dress but she wanted to embellish it further—some pearl beading, she thought, perhaps along the top of the bodice and the neckline. She wasn't sure, but she felt she'd recognize the exact thing that would make the dress come to life. She hadn't consulted Sophie in this matter, since Sophie would more than likely have nixed the idea, but she could picture the finished dress in her mind and how lovely it could look. She was sure Sophie would be happy with her efforts.

She pushed through the front door. Marjorie was behind the counter and Cecily stood at the other side of an L-shaped glass display case. She was arranging blouses on hangers. Cecily smiled and waved.

"Hello, Lucky," Marjorie called out. "What can we do for you?"

"I was just wondering if you had any netting or beading on hand, or anything like that?" Lucky asked.

"Hmm," Marjorie replied. "We have a few things—in the back storeroom. Cecily can show you." She smiled broadly. "Is this for Sophie's wedding dress?"

"Yes. It's almost finished. I'd like to add some embellishment and I need to find something that would work for a veil."

"Oh, we might have just the thing," Cecily replied.

Lucky heard the door to the street open behind her. She turned to see Greta carrying a tote bag full of books. She wore the same brown dress and sweater she had worn the first day Lucky had seen her at the Spoonful.

"Greta, hi," Cecily said. Greta nodded shyly in return. "You're here for the books?"

"Yes," she replied.

"Hang on just a second, Lucky." Cecily hurried into the storeroom and returned with a stack of five hardbound and three paperback books. "Can you manage these in your tote bag?" she asked.

"Oh, yes. Just put them all in here." Greta held the heavy cloth satchel open while Cecily slid the books into it.

"Lucky, have you met Greta yet?" Marjorie asked. "She's doing a lot of volunteer work for the library."

"Yes. We met at the Spoonful." Lucky smiled. "And we share the same apartment building. Nice to see you again."

"Hello again." Greta nodded and attempted a wan smile.

Lucky wished there were some way she could put the woman at her ease. She always appeared so nervous. "By the way, Greta, I have a lot of books that moved back to Snowflake with me. I'll go through them and donate them if you think you can use them for the library."

"That would be wonderful. Our drive has been very successful so far. We appreciate anything you'd like to give." She turned back to the sisters. "Thank you so much for these, Cecily . . . Marjorie." She ducked quickly out the front door.

"Well, that was quick," Marjorie remarked. "She skittered away so fast you'd think she was afraid of us."

"I know," Cecily said. "I've seen her at the library. She's afraid of her own shadow, poor thing." She shivered. "She makes *me* nervous." She smiled quickly, dismissing the feeling. "Come on back, Lucky," she added, indicating Lucky should follow her into the rear of the store.

"We do have some things—a small supply we keep just in case. No point getting rid of it; it's all useful for something." Cecily opened the door to the small storeroom in the rear of the shop. A long table took up most of one wall. On the other side was a sewing machine with a rack of spools of thread hanging on the wall above. Next to that, a bureau with deep drawers. On the far wall were shelves and several bolts of fabric carefully protected in plastic.

"Is the dress white?" Cecily asked.

"More of an eggshell color, if you know what I mean. Very simple and flowing. It'll look beautiful on her with her dark hair. I need some soft netting material for a veil and maybe some beading for the dress."

"Oh, how romantic," Cecily breathed. "I can't wait to see her on her wedding day!"

Lucky realized she'd reached a point at which she'd need to keep a list for Sophie and Sage.

Cecily pulled down one of the bolts and laid it on the long table. She carefully slid the plastic covering away from the fabric. "This is lovely stuff. Hard to find, you know."

Lucky picked up an end of the soft material. There was no stiffness to it. When she lifted the cloth, it hung easily. "This is perfect. Right color . . . gorgeous."

"What are you using for the headdress?"

"Haven't quite decided yet. I was thinking of going over to the big fabric store in Lincoln Falls to see what they have."

"Hang on, dear. We might have something." Cecily hurried to the bureau and opened the top drawer. Inside were hat and shoe accessories in plastic cases, bags of buttons, hem binding and zippers. Cecily rummaged some more and retrieved a large plastic bag of small pearls, already prepared with tiny holes for sewing. "How's this?" She held the bag up to show Lucky the contents.

"Oh," Lucky breathed. "These are perfect, Cecily. Thank you!"

"And," Cecily announced triumphantly. "Look at this!" She turned back with a circlet of clustered pearls in her hand. "We did a June bride display a few years ago. These are the things that didn't sell, but they're in perfect shape. You could use this to secure Sophie's veil."

Lucky took it from Cecily's hand. "It seems a little big," she remarked.

"Not really. You see, it fits over the forehead, like this," she said, slipping it on. "I like the look, actually: a little medieval and romantic."

"I see what you mean. It's different but lovely, and I can attach the veil to it with little stitches. I think she'll like this. Can you cut me three yards of the netting?"

"Sure thing," Cecily said, flipping the bolt over a few times on the table and lining the material up with the yard-stick attached to the front edge. "Do you really need three yards for her veil?" she asked.

"Just in case. Two would be enough, but an extra in case I make a mistake or anything."

"Okay," Cecily replied.

Lucky hesitated to broach the subject, especially since Cecily and her sister seemed to be on good terms today, but curiosity got the better of her. She sat on a stool next to the table and leaned her chin on her hand as Cecily lined up the netting. "How are you holding up, Cecily?"

Cecily glanced at her sharply. "You mean since . . ." She trailed off.

"Since your meeting."

Cecily smiled. "That's a nice way to put it—our meeting." She shook her head. "My sister was so upset with me that I was involved with them—but it just sounded like so much fun!" she exclaimed. "I didn't see anything wrong with it. I still don't. And if Cordelia Rank wanted to run herself ragged organizing it, I thought, well, why not?"

"I didn't hear what happened until the next day. Elizabeth told me first and then Flo Sullivan showed up first thing in the morning at the Spoonful and went on and on about it. It must have been horrible."

"Oh, it was." She sighed. "Believe me, it was. But I still don't think there was anything wrong with that wine. I'm sure when they figure things out, they'll realize poor Agnes had some condition or something."

"Cecily, Nate questioned Jack about the herbs he provided. And Jack has been really disturbed about it, thinking he might have made a mistake."

"Oh, I doubt that. He certainly knows what he's doing. He's been gardening for a long time."

"I understand you picked up the basket from him?"

"Yes. I did." Cecily had finished neatly cutting the edge of the material and folded it into a large square.

"And you took it straight to Cordelia's house?"

"That's right." Cecily turned to look at her. "Lucky, you're not thinking that it sat around in the open somewhere and someone could have tampered with it?"

"It did cross my mind."

Cecily shook her head. "Nothing like that happened, believe me. I put the basket in my car and drove it straight to Cordelia's. She was making the May wine and, knowing her, I'm sure no one else was allowed in the kitchen."

"Did Cordelia ask you to bring anything else?"

"No. Nothing."

Lucky nodded. "Good to know. I'm sure you're right. It couldn't have anything to do with Jack's herbs, but I guess we'll have to wait till the results of the autopsy come in."

"Will one bag of these pearls be enough, do you think?"

Lucky was jolted out of her reverie. "Uh, yes. Yes, I'm sure that'll be plenty."

Cecily folded each item into tissue paper and then placed the netting, pearls and circlet into a plastic bag. "There you go, dear. You can pay Marjorie at the counter."

"Thanks again, Cecily. I'm sorry to bring it all up. I didn't mean to pry. It's just that Jack has been worried about this since he heard about it. I am curious, though . . ." Lucky hesitated. "There's something else, if you don't mind my asking?"

"Of course not. What is it?"

"Who else was there in the woods?"

"Well, besides myself, there was Cordelia, Emily Rathbone from the library, Agnes Warner, of course, and Greta. Let's see, that's five. One woman who lives up in Lincoln Heights—I forget her name—and another woman who came over from Lincoln Falls. I didn't know those two before, actually. Cordelia wanted to have a group of thirteen, but she couldn't talk anyone else into it. She finally decided to settle on the seven of us." Cecily shook her head. "I can't imagine anyone deliberately wanting to hurt Agnes. She was such a harmless woman. She was so quiet. Struck me as a somewhat oppressed creature, if you know what I mean. I'd rather think that Cordelia—our high priestess—would be a much more likely murder victim." Cecily chuckled.

"Oppressed? That's an odd word to use."

"Yes. Well. You see, Agnes's husband always dropped her off and picked her up. She was always so concerned that we'd finish late and he'd be kept waiting. I didn't care too much for him. He was polite enough but I always felt he was one of those men who rules the household with an iron hand."

Lucky heard footsteps in the corridor. Cecily looked alarmed. "Shh! I don't want Marjorie to hear me talking about this."

Lucky nodded in acknowledgment.

The footsteps came closer. "Here you go, Lucky," Cecily said in a slightly louder voice. "Marjorie will ring you up. And I just can't wait to see the bride on her wedding day!"

Lucky made a mental note to add one more person to the guest list.

Chapter 14

LUCKY WALKED SLOWLY up the brick path to Elias's restored Victorian on Hampstead Street. He had purchased the house several years before and renovated it himself. She had always admired this house, but had to admit it had been in need of some tender loving care before Elias bought it. The three-story Victorian was topped with a peaked roof over a half-moon-shaped window. A round window of stained glass shed light on an interior staircase. The house had been repainted its original white but now the shutters were a soft lavender color that matched the lilacs just beginning to bloom along the side of the property. She breathed deeply. Even though the buds were still forming, the scent was intoxicating. She loved to come to Elias's beautiful house at any time, but particularly when he was in the mood to cook.

She peeked through the etched glass windows at the double front door. Dinner aromas assailed her nose. Suddenly she was ravenously hungry. She rang the bell and saw Elias's shadow in the doorway to the kitchen. He hurried down the hall and opened the front door a moment later.

With a dish towel draped over his arm, he bowed. "Enter, madame—uh, excuse me, mademoiselle. Dinner is served . . . almost."

Lucky laughed and reached up to his face where a small leaf of parsley clung to his cheek. "I think some of our dinner is clinging to you."

Elias grinned and wiped his cheek. She crossed the threshold and he enveloped her in a hug. "Missed you," he said.

"Missed you too," she replied.

He kissed her quickly. "Hurry. I don't want anything to burn."

She dropped her small purse on the hallway table and followed him into the kitchen. The table was set and two candles were lit in holders in the center. Elias pulled out a chair for her as she sat.

"Tonight we are serving a pork roast with figs and a plum wine sauce, mashed potatoes and asparagus." Without asking, he poured white wine into two glasses and handed one to her. "A toast—to more relaxed evenings like this."

"I'll second that," Lucky said as they clinked their glasses together. She took a sip. The wine was delicious, a slight woodsy taste and not too dry. "This is wonderful. What is it?" she asked, reaching for the bottle.

"A German wine that I really like."

Lucky knew Elias was getting a small section of his basement organized to create space for his collection. He had remodeled the entire house, pretty much on his own, except for some expertise from electricians and plumbers, and the wine storage in the basement was his last touch. It wasn't exactly a wine cellar—more of a wine closet—but Elias was excited about finishing it and adding to his collection.

"I wish I knew more about wine," she replied.

"Somehow this seemed like the right one to serve tonight, given that it's springtime and all."

Lucky looked up at him quickly. "Oh! Are you saying this is May wine?" she asked.

He grimaced. "Don't remind me. No shop talk tonight."

He turned back to the stove and slid a roasting pan out of the oven. He transferred the roast to a large plate and then delivered it to the table with bowls of mashed potatoes and asparagus.

"Hungry?" he asked.

"Starving. I only nibbled at the Spoonful today. I wanted a big appetite for what you're cooking."

"Eat up, my lovely." He sat across the table and draped a linen napkin onto his lap.

There had been many nights over the past year or so that Lucky's appetite had abandoned her. When she and Elias first began to see each other, it was soon after the sudden death of her parents. She knew Elias enjoyed cooking, but on those occasions, she felt guilty that she hadn't been able to enjoy his meals. Now that life had become more settled, their dinners were wonderful events she always looked forward to. She took another sip of wine.

"This really is a nice wine. There's something to it, a slight under taste."

"See, you're learning. I hate to say this, but it actually is what is called a May wine."

She raised her eyebrows. "You mean like the drink that Cordelia brewed in her cauldron?"

"Not quite. This one won't make you sick."

Lucky frowned. "Elias, you don't think Jack gave them the wrong herbs, do you?"

He could see the worried expression on her face and was suddenly serious. "I don't know what he donated from his garden. Nate never told me."

"He said they asked him for sweet woodruff and strawberries."

"Nothing wrong with that. Woodruff could possibly make someone sick, but they'd have to eat a huge amount of it. And I think, added to alcohol, it's harmless. That's what you taste in the wine tonight. It's a flavoring used in certain white wines. It couldn't cause anyone's death. Unless . . ." He trailed off.

"Unless what?"

"Well, I was going to say unless they had an extreme allergic reaction. I suppose that's possible, but I would think it highly unlikely. I've never heard of anyone having that type of thing with woodruff, but I'm not an allergist or a poison expert."

"What do you think that woman died of, then?" she asked.

He stared off into the distance. "I can't say for sure. And in any case, only the pathologist who's going to do the autopsy could hazard an opinion. Just on a cursory examination, I'm inclined to think it could be some form of reaction because of the symptoms that the women observed and the vomiting and sudden gasping for air. But . . . those observations are thirdhand . . . Those symptoms could be indicative of a lot of things."

Lucky listened carefully. "Jack's very worked up about it. He's really worried that he gave them something bad or poisonous."

"Ah. Well, Jack worries too much. If those plants came from his garden, I'm sure they were fine." He looked across the table. "Where did he get the woodruff?"

"He said he picked it near the edge of the woods. I'm not sure where."

"I know it grows all over the place." He smiled. "I thought we weren't going to talk shop. More potatoes?"

"No, thanks. I'm fine. They're delicious." Lucky realized she was so hungry she was wolfing down her food. "How would they go about identifying the stomach contents to see what she could have ingested?"

Elias groaned in mock displeasure. "You just can't help yourself, can you? Do we have to talk about this now?"

"Sure. I have a strong stomach."

"All right. You were warned, though. I have a general idea how it's done but my knowledge might not be up-to-date. The lab would use some sort of solvent to isolate elements of the sample. Then they'd probably use a gas chromatography method. Different compounds move differently through an inert gas and can be identified that way. They also move at different speeds and it's recorded and printed on a graph. Often that's enough. If it isn't, mass spectroscopy is another way to go, either in addition to or in conjunction with. They'd be able to pinpoint exactly what the chemical makeup is. Of course, if they have an idea before they start, I suppose they could look at the sample with that in mind. That might speed up the process."

"Okay, you've lost me, but I won't ask for further explanation."

Elias smiled across the table. "Speaking of stomach contents, you have a very healthy appetite tonight."

She laughed, her mouth full of potatoes. "Umm, sorry." She swallowed quickly. "My compliments to the chef."

"As long as we're talking shop, how's Sophie doing? I talked to Nate and he told me what he suspected. That the body you discovered in the creek could be Sophie's brother."

Lucky sighed. "She seems fine, but I'm worried about her. It's as if . . ."

"What?"

"As if she doesn't believe that could possibly have been her brother in the creek. As if she doesn't *want* to believe it."

"That's understandable. Maybe she's just having a very practical reaction. She's not going to get upset, or wonder if she *is* upset, until the body is identified. Why do you think that's weird?"

"I don't know. If it were me, I guess, I'd be worried. I guess I'd feel something. I just worry that Sophie's not really taking it in."

"You told me she didn't know her brother very well. Plus, she hadn't seen him for years, really didn't have any kind of relationship with him. Seems to me it's understandable she might not have a big reaction."

Lucky nodded. "It all sounds perfectly reasonable when you lay it out that way. I hope that man we found *wasn't* Rick Colgan and I hope you're right. She's getting married in a little over two weeks. I don't want anything to spoil that for her. I don't want her to fall apart at a time she should be happiest." Lucky laid down her fork. "And speaking of the man we found in the creek."

"Yeees?" Elias drew out the question.

Lucky smiled across the table at him. "You know I'm curious! Can you talk about it?"

Elias sighed. "Here we go again . . ."

"I just want to know what you think, Elias."

"About what?"

Exasperated, Lucky knew he was baiting her. "How he died, for heaven's sake!"

"Oh, that." Elias popped an asparagus spear into his mouth. "Well, since Nate really doesn't know who he is, maybe I'm not breaking any oaths here. But please don't repeat this anywhere."

"I won't."

"What I think is this—if he fell into the creek farther up where the water is moving very quickly, and even if he landed on his face, which is unlikely—"

"Why?" Lucky interrupted. "Why is it unlikely?"

"Because if he were conscious, his first instinct would be to hold out his hands, break his fall and protect his head, his face. But to continue before I was so rudely interrupted . . ." He smiled impishly at her. "I just don't think that even if he was knocked unconscious, that amount of damage could have been done to his face. He had a severe blow to the back of his head, but it didn't look—and this is just cursory; the autopsy will have the final result—it didn't look like the type of injury you'd get from hitting your head on a rock. Hard to say, but it seemed like he suffered a blow to his head from a small object, something like the head of a hammer. And I don't believe he would have sustained such damage to his face. I think that was done deliberately to make identification extremely difficult."

"What you're saying is . . . he was murdered."

Chapter 15

LUCKY SHIFTED HER weight on the hard oak bench in the waiting room of the police station. Sophie, still as a mannequin, sat next to her, silent the entire time they waited to see Nate. She knew Nate was hoping, as was she, that the body in the creek was not that of Rick Colgan. Lucky only hoped the technician from Lincoln Falls was ready to meet with Sophie and wouldn't take a great deal of time.

They had been waiting for several minutes and Lucky was growing impatient. Someone was with Nate in his office, and Bradley was insistent that Nate not be disturbed. Now Bradley sat at the front counter, shuffling paperwork from place to place, doing his best to appear busy and important.

Sophie stood. "Bradley." She approached the counter. "Any idea how much longer Nate will be?"

"Sorry, Sophie, not really. But I don't think it'll be too much longer."

"Who's in there with him?"

Bradley hesitated but finally offered the information. "He's with Leonard Warner and the boy."

Sophie looked blankly at Bradley for a moment and then recognition dawned on her face. "Oh!"

"Yes. Oh," Bradley replied.

"Agnes's husband and son?"

"Husband and grandson."

"Got it," she replied. "Okay, you're right. Those poor people. We can wait." She returned to the long oak bench and sat heavily, then turned to Lucky. "I can't help it. I just feel like this is such a waste of time. All I want to do is get ready for the wedding and go over my to-do list. Does that sound horrible?"

Lucky shook her head. "No. It doesn't, Sophie." She grasped her friend's hand. "It must seem totally unreal to you."

"'Unreal' isn't the word. I can't believe it," she said. "I won't believe it until Nate has some definite proof." She fell silent for a moment, then turned back to her friend. "Lucky, what if it really is? Really Rick, I mean?"

For the first time, Lucky heard a frisson of panic in Sophie's voice. "If it is, we'll deal with it. We'll all help you deal with it."

"The thought scares me at some level, but I don't feel . . . I mean, I don't think I'd feel any grief." Sophie leaned back against the bench. "Maybe I would. I guess I just don't know."

"It'd be pretty weird, I imagine. And it would be hard to feel grief-stricken about someone you really didn't know very well. The fact that you're related by blood might not make any difference."

"The only thing that comes up sometimes is anger."

Lucky looked at her friend quizzically.

"This is really going to sound horrible." Sophie leaned closer and whispered so low that Lucky could barely make out her words. "And if it weren't you I was talking to, I'd never say this, but I've just found myself getting angry at the thought that this could mess up our wedding day. What right did Rick have to show up here, not even respond to my e-mail, and die. Why now of all times?"

They looked up quickly as Nate's door opened. He

stepped out of his office and held the door for a tall older man with short-cropped white hair. The man wore a red-and-blue-checked cotton shirt and the young boy, his grandson, was dressed in a denim jacket and jeans. Holding on to his grandson's hand, Leonard Warner strode silently past the bench where Lucky and Sophie sat.

When he reached the front door, he turned and stared at Lucky. He took a few steps toward her, still staring, but said nothing. His gaze made Lucky uncomfortable. She knew who he was but couldn't imagine why he was looking at her.

Finally, he spoke. "Your Jack Jamieson's granddaughter, aren't you?"

"Yes." Lucky stood and held out her hand. "I'm so sorry for your loss."

Leonard stiffened and frowned at Lucky's outstretched hand. She let her arm drop when she realized he would not take it. He seemed to be struggling with a powerful emotion. Anger? Grief? She wasn't sure how to respond to him.

"You should talk to your grandfather."

"Sorry?" Sophie stood and moved closer to Lucky.

"I think he needs to admit what he's done."

Lucky was speechless for a moment. "What? What are you saying?"

"I'm saying your grandfather is responsible for my wife's death. For this little boy's . . ." He glanced down at the young boy next to him. "I think Jack Jamieson needs to step up and take responsibility for what he's done."

Lucky felt a hot flush rise to her face. "I think you're mistaken. I know what you're going through is terrible, but my grandfather didn't do anything wrong. He didn't make a mistake. He wouldn't."

Leonard nodded slowly. "You'll come around."

Lucky could feel her temper rising. "No." She did her best not to explode in anger. "I don't think I will. And I think you need to be very careful what you say about my grandfather."

Leonard didn't answer. His eyes had taken on a glazed look. He turned suddenly and pushed through the front door, grasping the little boy's hand.

Lucky continued to stare at the door Leonard Warner had just exited.

"Whew." Sophie let out a rush of air. "That was weird. Are you okay?" She placed a hand on Lucky's shoulder.

Lucky shook herself, returning to reality. "I'm fine. But I could feel my blood boiling. I don't like what he's saying, and I better not find out he's spreading any rumors about Jack in town, either." She turned back to Sophie. "I just put it together."

"What?"

"Who he is."

"We know who he is."

"I know, but I didn't really connect. When I first heard about it, the name Agnes Warner didn't mean anything to me. At least, I didn't remember who she was. But I remember her now, seeing her husband. From years ago. They used to come into the Spoonful. I'd see them whenever I came home to visit. But I haven't seen them since I've been back in town."

"You mean they stopped coming?"

"I guess so."

"Maybe they moved away—or at least moved farther out of town."

Lucky nodded. "Possibly. Just strange that I didn't really connect the names with the faces until now."

Lucky heard Nate call Sophie's name. He beckoned both of them over. They rose and followed him into his office. Nate stood in the doorway. "Our tech is in the back room grabbing a coffee, waiting until I was finished." He turned back to the front desk. "Bradley—go let the lady know we're ready if she can join us."

Nate entered and sat heavily in the armchair behind the desk. "How are you doing, Sophie?"

"I'm okay, Nate."

Nate looked at her dubiously.

"Really, I am," she replied. "Just . . . none of this seems real to me."

He nodded in acknowledgment. "I can understand that. I just want to cover all the bases here. Just need to make sure. There's something I should tell you, though. If your brother is a private investigator, I don't think he's licensed—at least not in New York State."

"Really?" Sophie looked puzzled. "Well, maybe he changed his mind. Maybe he never got his license."

"Could be," Nate replied.

At that moment, they heard a tap on the door. "Come on in," Nate called.

A young woman in her thirties, wearing jeans and a blazer, entered the office. Her bangs reached her eyebrows, and her hair was pulled up in a ponytail. Lucky was reminded of a kindergarten teacher she had liked very much. The technician smiled at them. "Are we ready?" she asked.

"Sophie?" Nate raised his eyebrows.

"I'm ready. What do you need?" she asked the technician.

The woman put on a pair of latex gloves, opened her case and pulled out a white pouch. She removed the covering to reveal what looked like a flat white plastic stick. She slid her thumb along the middle, revealing a covered section of the device. "With your permission, I'll just take a swab from the inside of your cheek. Nothing invasive. Won't hurt at all."

Sophie nodded and dutifully opened her mouth.

The technician was quick. She moved the end of the device across the inside of Sophie's cheek, slid the covering in place and then dropped it into a white collection pouch. She sealed the top with a self-adhesive strip.

"All done. That was easy, wasn't it?"

"That just looks like a paper pouch," Sophie remarked.

"You're right. It's for short-term transport with a desiccant inside. It'll keep the sample safe. The adhesive strip prevents anyone from licking the pouch closed and maybe contaminating the sample. It's very secure."

"Thank you," Sophie replied. She turned to Nate. "How long will this take?"

Nate looked up at the technician. She replied, "A few days. We send it to a larger lab. We'll have results then, and I'll give Chief Edgerton a call."

"Thanks for coming over." Nate stood.

"Not a problem." The tech smiled.

"Have all the paperwork you need?"

"Yes. Thanks. I'll be in touch." The technician left the office without another remark.

"Well. That's that," Nate said. "Thanks for coming by, Sophie. Glad this worked out. Didn't want you to trudge over to Lincoln Falls if you didn't need to."

"I appreciate that, Nate." She took a deep, shaky breath. "I just hope you're wrong."

"I hope so too, believe me."

Lucky followed Sophie through the waiting area. When they reached the front door, she heard Bradley call her name. She turned back. Bradley was waving her back to the front desk.

"What does he want?" Sophie asked.

"I don't know. I'll find out. You go ahead. I'll be out in a sec." Lucky walked back to the counter.

Bradley leaned across. "Lucky, would it be all right if I brought a guest, do you think?"

"A guest?" Was Bradley talking about the wedding? She cringed, imagining Sophie's reaction. "Uh, let me ask Sophie, if you don't mind." If Sophie agreed, at this rate they'd have to expand the party to Jack's next-door neighbor's garden.

Sophie was sitting in the passenger seat when Lucky finally emerged from the police station. She climbed behind the wheel. "Sure you don't want to drive?" Lucky asked.

Sophie shook her head. "No, you go ahead."

"I appreciate this, Sophie. I'm sorry the repairs are taking so long. Guy's had trouble getting some of the parts."

"Not a problem. You can use the car as long as you need it. Sage and I are fine with the one car." Sophie fastened her seat belt. "What did Bradley want?"

"He asked if he could bring a guest." Lucky glanced at her friend, as she revved the engine.

Sophie's eyes crossed. She groaned. "I can't think about that right now." She turned to stare out the window as Lucky drove down Green Street. Her jaw was clenched. "I have this terrible feeling that Nate might be right." She turned to Lucky. "But wouldn't I have recognized *something* about that man if it really was Rick? Something? The shape of his head or the color of his hair? Something . . ." She trailed off.

"How? How would you have recognized him? He was completely clothed and . . . Sophie, his face was gone. There was nothing to recognize." Lucky turned to face her friend. "I have an idea if you feel up to it."

"What's that?"

"Let's do a little investigating on our own."

Sophie smiled. "Okay. I'm game."

Chapter 16

LUCKY PULLED INTO a parking space reserved for employees of the Snowflake Resort. Sophie's employee sticker would cover them. She had been quiet on the drive, and Lucky was sure Sophie suspected what she had in mind.

"You're thinking there's some mistake, aren't you? That they might have given that room to someone else if Rick hadn't shown up to keep his reservation?" Sophie asked.

"That's exactly what I'm thinking. I'm sure it happens. I mean, they're not going to hold a room if someone doesn't show. Maybe the clerk let a friend stay there, for all we know. And maybe they don't want to admit that to Nate. You still have that picture with you?"

Sophie rummaged in her purse and retrieved a high school photo of her brother. She smiled and passed it to Lucky. "Will you look at the hair? Those school pictures are so awful, aren't they? The photographers even used to colorize them."

Lucky agreed. "It does look like something from another era. But it'll do. When you go in, I want you to check with the supervisor and see which maids were assigned to that area. We can show the picture around and see if anyone recognizes it. Nate's probably already done that, but these people know you. They might be a little more open."

"I agree."

They clambered out of the car and headed for the lobby entrance to the Resort. The clerk at the desk looked up as Sophie walked past and raised a hand in greeting. Sophie ignored him and, pushing through a door near the reception desk, descended a flight of stairs. They had entered another world. The aromas of steam and laundry detergent wafted up the stairwell. The uncarpeted stairs were concrete with safety strips at the edges. The walls and ceiling of the hallway and rooms below were painted glossy white. Sophie turned a corner and came to a closed door. She knocked once and entered quickly. A middle-aged woman with dark straight hair cut short looked up. A gray sweater was draped over her shoulders, partially covering a white uniform.

"Hi, Mary. Sorry to barge in like this. This is my friend Lucky."

Mary smiled. "Hello. Nice to meet you. Grab a seat, you two." She leaned across the desk. "Sophie. I heard. Nate Edgerton was here. I'm real sorry."

"Well, that's why we're here. We're not really convinced Nate's right."

Mary raised her eyebrows slightly, not sure what to say in response. Lucky could almost read the thought bubble over her head. She too was wondering whether Sophie was in a state of denial, but she said nothing.

"Can you tell me who had cleaning duty for the room this guy was in?"

"Oh. You want to talk to the maid?"

"Yes. We just want to show her the picture I have of Rick and see if she recognizes it."

"You might have more luck talking to whoever was on the front desk last week. They might remember or have gotten a good look, at least."

"That's true. Do you have that schedule? It would have been . . . Let's see"—Sophie glanced at Lucky—"maybe five or six days ago."

"Hang on." Mary opened a desk drawer and pulled out a manila folder. "They copy us with the schedules." She leafed through several sheets of paper. "It was Rosalie Baum on the morning shift and Davey Snyder afternoons and into the evening. But I'm pretty sure Rosalie's on vacation this week and I think Davey's out today."

"I'll catch up with them later, then."

Mary sat back in her desk chair. "Nate's already talked to everyone and shown that picture around, Sophie. Didn't he tell you?"

Sophie took a deep breath. "I'm sure he has, but did anyone recognize the man in the room from that picture?"

"Well, I didn't see the picture Nate showed them, and I don't really know firsthand what the maid told him." Mary's first instinct appeared to be to deny Sophie the information. Then her shoulders relaxed. "Okay, Brenda was also on duty in that section for the days your brother—I mean, whoever he was—had booked in. Let me see . . ." Mary checked her watch quickly. "You can probably catch her somewhere on the second floor right about now if you hurry. You'll see her cart."

"Okay. Thanks, Mary. Maybe I'm grasping at straws. I don't know. But I just need to know one way or the other if it was Rick. It's really starting to eat away at me."

"I can imagine." Mary's tone softened. "Listen, if there's anything I can do, anything at all, you'll let me know?" she asked.

Sophie nodded. "Thanks. I will."

They left Mary's office and waited at the service elevator at the end of the corridor. They passed a room where two workers were loading laundry into huge openmouthed dryers, and three others stood at a long table folding clean items. They exited the elevator on the second floor. Sophie walked purposefully down the hall, and as they turned the corner, they spotted a maid's cart loaded with cleaning supplies outside an open doorway.

"There she is," Sophie turned to say. She approached the open door and knocked. A very short woman peeked out from the bathroom. Her curly red hair was covered by a scarf knotted at the base of her neck. She had a cross expression on her face. Perhaps she assumed the inhabitant of the room had returned and would interfere with her schedule. When she saw Sophie, her face lit up.

"Sophie! Hi. What are you doing here?" As though just remembering her interview with the police, her smile faded. "Oh. Oh, Sophie, I'm so sorry." She walked toward them, wiping her hands on a towel. "I told the police everything I knew, which wasn't much."

Sophie retrieved Rick's high school picture from her purse. "I just wanted you to have a look at this and tell *me* if you think this was the man who was staying here."

Brenda's eyes traveled from Sophie's face to the photo. "That's the same one the police showed me." She shook her head. "I'll tell you the same thing I told them. I only saw him once. He was leaving the room and his back was toward me. I was coming down the hall with my cart. He looked at me quick and then walked away in the other direction. He had dark hair. Maybe in his forties somewhere. But I really didn't get a good look at him. It was just an impression."

"So you can't say one way or the other?"

Brenda shook her head. A stray curl fell over her ear. "I can't. I'm sorry."

"What about his suitcase and the stuff in his room? What happened to that?" Lucky asked.

"Oh, the cops took everything. I don't think it helped them very much. No tag on the luggage and just a bunch of clothes; that's all. Oh, one thing . . ."

Sophie looked hopeful. "What's that?"

"I saw a thick notebook, like the spiral kind you'd use in a class or something. It was on the desk. Other than the few toiletries in the bath, I didn't notice anything else at all." Brenda shrugged. "Sorry I can't be more help."

"That's okay. We'll find out one way or the other eventually. I was just hoping to speed up the process."

Sophie started to turn away.

"Hey, I meant to ask," Brenda said. "When's the happy day?"

Sophie smiled. "It's gonna be May twentieth."

"Great. I'll see you then." Brenda smiled widely.

Sophie's smile was pasted on her face. "Okay," she replied, casting a meaningful glance at Lucky.

Brenda glanced over Sophie's shoulder. Her expression changed; her smile disappeared. Sophie turned to look in the direction of Brenda's gaze. A large man with a heavy, barrel-chested build stood at the end of the corridor. He wore jeans and a Windbreaker. His arms were crossed in front of him, and he stared menacingly at the three of them.

"Who's that?" Lucky asked.

Sophie squinted briefly. "Ignore him. That's Lurch."

"Did you say Lurch?" Lucky hoped the man didn't have super hearing.

"That's what we call him," Sophie said quietly. "'Cause he's big and he lurks around a lot. His real name's Pete Manko, but we all call him Lurch." She smiled conspiratorially at Brenda, but Brenda wasn't smiling. If Lucky could have put a word to it, she would have said Brenda looked frightened.

"Are you all right?" Lucky was instantly aware.

"Fine," she muttered. "I gotta go."

"What's going on?" Sophie asked.

Brenda turned away and reentered the suite. When she was inside the room, she whispered, "I'll call you." Then she shut the door behind her. They heard the lock turn from the inside.

Puzzled, Sophie glanced at Lucky. "What's going on?"

"I have no idea. Come on, let's go." When they turned to leave, the man had disappeared.

"What was that all about?" Lucky asked in the elevator on the way down to the lobby.

"He's the company spy. Supposedly he's head of security but he spends a lot of time lurking around and watching the employees at the Lodge and all over the Resort." Sophie shrugged.

"Brenda looked frightened of him."

"I know. I didn't mean to put her in a bad spot. I hope

she doesn't get reported for talking to us. He scares a lot of people around here, believe me."

"He ever bother you?"

Sophie laughed outright. "He better not. Wouldn't do him any good, anyway. He can't ski. He'd never catch up with me."

Chapter 17

LUCKY PULLED INTO the gravel drive of her parents' house, the house that Horace Winthorpe now rented from her. The crunching of her tires must have alerted Horace. She saw his face surrounded by a halo of white hair at the kitchen window. She waved to him and climbed out of the car.

"Oh, my dear. How nice of you to visit," Horace said, opening the back door of the kitchen to allow her to enter.

"I hope I'm not interrupting Horace, but I wanted to pick up those boxes in the attic."

"Of course, of course. Come in. Glad of the company anytime." Horace was dressed in loose denim trousers with deep pockets on the legs and a dress shirt that had seen better days. He caught her looking at his outfit. "Pardon my appearance, but I'm planning to wear my old city clothes until they fall off of me—like this shirt."

"Very handsome shirt," Lucky responded.

"It was—once. Oh, that reminds me. I need your advice." Horace rushed down the hall to the main bedroom and returned with a hanging garment bag. He unzipped it and pulled out a dark suit. "What do you think?" he asked.

Lucky looked at him quizzically.

"It's too formal, isn't it?"

"For . . . ?"

"For the wedding, of course. Perhaps I should find something a little more casual."

"Hmm." *Things have gone too far,* she thought. She'd absolutely have to keep a guest list. "I think whatever you'd feel comfortable in, Horace. You could certainly wear that—it's very attractive—but it's just Jack's garden. You might want to dress down a bit."

"Exactly what I thought. I appreciate your opinion. I really do." He zipped up the garment bag and hung it over the door. "But come sit and join me for coffee. I just brewed an espresso in my little pot, but I'll make one for you. Just take a minute."

"Just what I need. While you're doing that, I'll go upstairs and drag those boxes down. I'm glad I remembered they were here."

"Need some help?"

"No, I should be fine. Be right back." Lucky slung her purse over the knob on the oak chair and headed for the front entryway of her parents' home. She loved coming here, especially to visit Horace, but hadn't once regretted that she had rented the house to him rather than sell it after her parents' death. When she had first returned to Snowflake, she hadn't been in a position to pay the mortgage on her own, and for Horace, retiring from the city, it had been a godsend.

She opened the small door in the front hallway that led to the attic. The house had been converted from a barn, the center portion revealing its origins, while the two small wings on either side had been added later. The dark red color of the exterior gave a hint of its past. The attic was in fact the original hayloft. Her father had finished and insulated it years before, but even when her parents were alive, it had been used only for storage space. Now only a few boxes remained, but she was sure one of them held the things her mother had squirreled away. Surely she'd find everything she needed to finish Sophie's wedding dress.

She ascended the curving narrow stairway to the second level and pushed through the hatch at the top. She climbed out into the attic. Dust motes floated in the air. A large square window gave a view of the front yard and the road. Three boxes stood in a corner, stacked one upon another. She lifted them one by one and carried them to the open hatch. They were surprisingly light. Holding on to the banister, she maneuvered each one down the narrow stairwell to the main floor. Then she returned to the second level, closed and locked the hatch, and shut the door to the stairway. She carried two of the boxes into the kitchen where the aroma of espresso filled the room.

"Smells divine, Horace."

"This gets me going in the morning. One cup of this, and I'm good to write for several hours. "So," he said, referring to the boxes, "did you find what you need?"

"I think so. I haven't looked through them yet. They're just too dusty. One of them should have sewing supplies but, to be honest, I'm not really sure what's there after all this time." She added some cream to her espresso and took a sip. "How's the book coming?"

Horace, a retired history professor, was finally doing the things he had never had time to do when employed full-time. His great interest was the Revolutionary War years in New England and, in particular, some of the lesser-known events and battles of the strife in Vermont.

"It's coming . . . slowly. Still have a long way to go, but it's taking shape nicely, I think." Horace chuckled.

"What's so funny?"

"Oh, I was just thinking about the famous Ethan Allen story. You've heard it, I'm sure. The one about his stay in England and the portrait of George Washington in the— what was it called then?—the necessary."

Lucky shook her head.

"Apparently Ethan Allen was supposed to have endured great teasing as an uncouth colonial when he was in England. He was asked what he thought about Washington's portrait hanging in the 'outhouse.' Allen is said to have remarked that nothing will make an Englishman—uh, you must insert a four-letter verb here—so quick as the sight of General Washington staring down at him."

Lucky laughed. "He had a very quick wit, I guess."

"Well, I'm not so sure it's true. Funny, yes, but accurate? I don't know. Abraham Lincoln was fond of telling the story a century later, but there's no record of Allen ever visiting England. He was imprisoned by the British, but that was in New York and he was later released. My hat's off to the man if he did say that, but I tend to doubt it. Might have been a fictional story that became an urban legend."

"Or a colonial legend." Lucky took a sip of her espresso. "I have one more box, Horace." Lucky walked down the hallway and retrieved the last cardboard box. She carried it to the kitchen and balanced it on top of the other two. "This one's heavier than the others. Do you mind if I take a peek and check what's in here?"

"Of course not. Take your time."

The top box held folders and files. Lucky leafed through the contents and realized they were old records from the Spoonful. The second box was full of fabric and sewing supplies. "Yay. Just what I was looking for," she remarked to Horace. She stacked both boxes to the side, then knelt and opened the third box. It was half full of old photos and enlargements. "Oh, look at this." She pulled a few out and passed them to Horace.

Horace pulled a pair of glasses out of his pocket and put them on. "This looks like the inside of the Spoonful."

"It is," Lucky replied. "My mother loved to take pictures. She took most of the ones hanging at the Spoonful. You've seen them I'm sure. It was her way to thank her best customers." Lucky rummaged in the box and pulled out a few more. "Oh, look. Here's my dad." She passed the large black-and-white photo across to Horace. "I forgot about some of these."

"This was your father?" he asked.

Lucky looked over his shoulder. "Yes. He's at the cash register, chatting with someone. And there's Jack in the background. Look how young Jack looks." Lucky was silent for a moment. "You just never think . . ." she said quietly.

"That one day they won't be here," Horace finished her thought.

She sighed. "The things we take for granted. Now it's like peeking into another world." Lucky leafed through a few other photos. Something caught her eye. "Look at this one. It's . . .Isn't this Agnes Warner? With her family? This must have been taken quite a while ago."

"Let me see," Horace said. "I don't think I ever met either of them."

"No. You wouldn't have. They haven't been at the Spoonful for several years. Actually, I had a rather unpleasant encounter with Leonard Warner earlier at the police station."

"Really? What happened?"

Lucky took a last sip of her drink. "Well . . . Leonard was very strange. He virtually accused Jack of killing his wife."

"Any special reason Agnes's husband was there?"

Lucky shook her head. "I guess to talk to Nate."

Horace asked. "Was he upset? Emotional?"

"He . . ." Lucky sighed. "It was very weird. He seemed perfectly rational, but he took me aside and pressured me. I don't know any other way to say it."

"Pressured you about what?"

"About Jack. He straight out said that Jack should take responsibility for what he had done and . . . That's all I can really remember because I almost lost it. I was so taken aback and I could feel my face turning red, and I told him in no uncertain terms what I thought of his ideas. I told him I better not hear that he's spreading any rumors about Jack around town. "

"Good for you. What a horrible thing to do to you."

"I guess I threatened him too. Now that I think about it, I wonder if he was there to pressure Nate to press charges against Jack."

"I can't really see Nate doing that. Not without proof of some wrongdoing. Warner's just angry, looking for someone to blame."

"My mother mentioned once that Agnes and Leonard

used to come to the restaurant a lot when their grandson was a little kid. Well, he's still young, but grown a bit."

Horace stared at a photo. "I don't see the little boy here."

"Let me see." Lucky took the photographs back. "That is strange. They're not smiling at the camera or anything. Mom would always ask people to give her a big smile. She was good at capturing a moment with her camera. You've seen some of the ones that are framed all over the walls. Leonard Warner has his back to the camera in this one and you can't see the little boy. Odd."

Lucky gathered up the loose photographs and returned them to the open box. "I better get going, Horace. Thanks for the great coffee."

"Anytime, my dear. Let me help you with those," Horace offered. He hoisted two of the boxes. Lucky slung her purse over her shoulder and grabbed the last one. Together they loaded them into the trunk of her car.

"That's a great little car you have there. They run forever. If you ever decide to sell it, let me know first."

"Oh, it's not mine to sell. This one belongs to Sophie. Mine's in the shop right now. Well, actually, that's Elizabeth's car, the one in the shop. She gave it to me for as long as I needed it when I first came back to Snowflake. That and half the furniture in my apartment. When I first came home, I was too upset and confused to focus on anything. You know, after my parents . . ." She slammed the trunk closed. "But I'm doing fine now. I've been saving, so hopefully I'll be able to get my own car soon." Lucky walked to the driver's door. "Thanks again, Horace. I'll let Sophie know you're interested in case she wants to sell."

"Thanks." Horace smiled. "I will see you later. I plan to pop by the Spoonful when I take a break this afternoon."

"See you then." Lucky started the engine and backed out onto the road, waving good-bye to Horace.

Chapter 18

LUCKY SAT AT her kitchen table under a bright lamp she had carried from the living room. She cut tiny circles of satin fabric and patiently positioned each one on the rounded metal top of a covered button. When she was sure the fabric was in the right spot, she quickly snapped the base of the button into place. So far she had made four covered buttons for the sleeves of Sophie's dress. She only needed two more, three on each bracelet sleeve. It was a tricky business and she wasn't an expert at it. The unsuccessful attempts were in a pottery bowl on the table. She was happy she had retrieved the sewing supplies from Horace's attic. She didn't anticipate working on any more wedding dresses, but the supplies she had recovered would last her a long time and save her many trips to the store, not to mention money. Once these buttons were sewn on, adding some pearls would be the final addition to the dress. After that, the only thing left to do was secure the veiling material to the circlet of pearls. She smiled, thinking how absolutely gorgeous Sophie would look in this outfit on her big day. Just a little more than two weeks now.

She snapped the last button base in place and put the

successful buttons in a separate bowl. "There," she said to herself. "Done." She heaved a sigh of relief and debated trying to disconnect the buttons that hadn't worked, the ones where the fabric hadn't caught properly. She finally decided to throw them away. If she tried to pry them open with a small screwdriver, it would only bend the metal base and they'd be unusable no matter what.

Tomorrow night she'd sew the buttons on the sleeves and finish the headdress. Her own dress hung in the closet ready to go. It was the color of pale lilac. Sophie was as crazy as she was about lilacs and decided that since she'd be married surrounded by her favorite flower, Lucky, as her bridesmaid, should reflect that color. Fortunately, it was a color that was flattering to Lucky's fair complexion. Like Sophie's dress, it was a simple, long, flowing gown with an empire waist, accessorized by a ribbon in the same color. She had discovered it on a sales rack at a department store in Lincoln Falls the month before, and just knew it would be perfect for the occasion. Her shoes had even been dyed to match.

Hopefully the weather would cooperate—not too warm and no rain. Spring weather could be so changeable. If it did rain and the wedding party was small, everyone could move inside the house. If Sophie and Sage decided to allow more guests, it might become a little crowded but not out of the question. Lucky wondered if perhaps they should rent a tent for the outdoor gathering, or at least a canopy for the back porch, but that could get very expensive. No matter what, she really wanted to pay for whatever was involved in hosting their wedding. It isn't every day a best friend gets married. Jack and Elias had offered to share the expenses with her, and Sophie and Sage were handling all the food and drinks. The least she could do would be to make sure all the rest was covered. It would be her wedding present to Sophie and Sage. If it became necessary to rent canopies, she'd just go ahead and handle it and not say a word to them.

She went into the living room and kicked off her shoes. She lifted the boxes with the photos onto the coffee table. The table wobbled and tilted, and the leg she had glued in place fell off. Photos spilled across the floor. She groaned. Not again. She gathered up the photos that had fallen and laid them on the sofa cushion. She went back to the kitchen and grabbed the tube of glue and a few paper towels. Returning to the living room, she flipped the table over and squirted generous amounts of glue into the opening where the table leg would connect. Then she carefully slid the wooden leg into the opening, pressing hard, and wiped off the excess glue. She moved the table away from the sofa to give herself more room. If this didn't work, she was ready to drill screws into it, or take it to the dump if it refused to behave.

Lucky reached into the box and pulled out the rest of the photos. Leafing through the stack, she smiled at the pictures taken at the Spoonful. The wide pine floors and wainscoting hadn't changed since her parents had started the business. The old yellow gingham curtains, replaced now with new ones, cast a soft light over the room. The older photos were black-and-white, but the more recent ones were in color. Her mother, Martha, was behind the counter, smiling at the camera. Undoubtedly a picture taken by her dad. She gently touched the face in the photo, imagining the feel of her mother's cheek and the scent of her soap. Another showed Jack—a younger Jack—at the corner table with Hank and Barry. She gasped when she came across a photo of herself and Sophie, sitting on the back steps of the Spoonful. It was summertime. They were dressed in shorts and sleeveless cotton blouses, with sandals on their feet. Sophie held a melting ice cream in her hand. How old were they then? Ten? Eleven? She decided she'd make a copy for herself and have this one framed as a gift. She knew Sophie would love it.

Lucky stacked several of the most special photos on the sofa cushion, ones she knew she'd never part with. She turned back and continued to dig through the box. A large brown envelope secured with a clasp was at the bottom. She felt the thickness inside of it, undid the clasp and tilted it upside down. Another stack of enlarged photos fell out. These were in color. They were all photos of the Warner family. The skin on her arms prickled as she leafed through them. There were more loose ones in the box. Methodically she went through its contents. She culled several more photos in which the camera was aimed at the Warners and placed them in a separate pile.

Why were there so many photos of the Warners? And why had they been kept separately in the envelope? She sat on the floor and leaned back against the sofa, spreading the pictures across the carpet. They were similar to the other photos, but they were all poor attempts to capture the same three individuals. Only one photo caught Agnes Warner's face. She was glaring at the camera. Leonard was standing next to his young grandson and reaching across the table. His arm blocked the boy's face. There were ten photos total, and in all of them, their grandson wasn't visible. In some of them, Leonard stood in front of the boy with his own back to the camera. Agnes was turned away in one, and in another, her head was down as though rummaging in her purse for something. Were these just rejects? Then why would her mother have kept them?

Lucky let out a sigh. She hadn't realized she had been holding her breath as she stared at the photos. What was her mother thinking of, to take these unusable photos and keep them all these years? On an impulse, she turned them over. A few were dated on the back in pencil, all the dates within the same month. One date was followed by an exclamation mark. What did it mean?

As far as she knew, her mother had never bothered to put dates on photos. And Martha Jamieson was thrifty. She never would have bothered developing or enlarging photos she didn't intend to use. She took them only to memorialize their restaurant and their customers. But these customers didn't seem to be cooperating. The date was in autumn—October 10 five years earlier. For some reason this date was significant. But why? *Mom*, she thought, *what were you doing? What was on your mind?*

A chill ran up her spine. Had her mother known something about Agnes Warner? Or suspected something about the whole family? But what was it? And why was this date significant? Maybe Jack knew something about this. She'd have to have a talk with him.

Chapter 19

WHEN LUCKY ARRIVED at the Spoonful the following morning, she heard a clatter of pans in the kitchen and two voices. Sophie was there. She hurried down the hall, tying on her apron, and entered the kitchen. Sophie was seated on a stool, watching Sage as he chopped vegetables for his Asian tofu soup. A big-band CD heavy on the horn section was playing.

"You're here early," Lucky remarked to Sophie.

Sophie turned on the stool and smiled. "I came in with Sage. Woke up so early. Maybe it's wedding nerves; I don't know."

Lucky smiled in sympathy. "But exciting, right?" She caught Sage's eye.

He nodded to acknowledge her statement, but said, "I don't know about exciting. Maybe for women, but for guys it's a fearful thing. We worry about money and getting ahead in life."

Sophie sat up straighter. "We worry about that stuff too. It's not all a male domain."

"I didn't mean it like that." Sage looked up quickly. His hand swept a pile of green onions into a pot.

"Yes, you did," Sophie replied with an edge to her voice.

Sage was silent, staring at Sophie. "Hey . . . what's wrong?" he asked.

Sophie sighed. "I'm sorry. Didn't mean to bite your head off. My nerves are on edge, I guess."

"Look, enough, you two lovebirds. We've got a restaurant to open." Lucky peeked through the hatch. "You haven't seen Jack, have you?"

Sophie was immediately serious. She shook her head. "No, not yet. I'm sure he'll be in soon. He's taking all this very hard, isn't he?"

"He is. I can't fault him for that, but I just think everybody's wrong." Lucky sighed and pushed through the door. She grabbed a pile of place mats and started setting up the counter. She heard a sharp rap on the front door and looked up. A solidly built man stood on the threshold. The sun was behind him, making it impossible to see his face. She hesitated, then walked to the front door. Pointing to the CLOSED sign, she indicated ten minutes by holding up two hands. The man shook his head and held a large envelope close to the glass. Puzzled, Lucky unlocked the door and opened it. When she was able to see the man's face, she realized this was the same man she had seen in the corridor of the lodge. Up close, his complexion was beefy and pockmarked. His sandy hair was cut so short, he at first appeared bald. Muscles bulged under the sleeves of his jacket.

"Is Sophie Colgan here?"

Sophie had watched the exchange through the kitchen hatch. She entered the front room and approached the door. "I'm here."

"Delivery for you," the man replied and handed the envelope to Sophie. He immediately turned away, heading south on Broadway.

Sophie raised her eyebrows. "Personal delivery? It must be from the Resort. How would Lurch know where to find me?"

"Open it."

Sophie ripped open the envelope. Inside was a letter on

thick bond paper engraved with several names. She scanned it quickly and looked up. "It's a letter from the same lawyers— the lawyers for the Resort. They're requesting a meeting to discuss purchasing my mother's property."

"When?" Lucky asked.

"Tomorrow at one o'clock at Tom Reed's office."

"Reed . . . I remember him. I don't think he likes me very much after the time I suspected him of being involved with that winter tourist."

"I could care less what he likes. I'm to call to confirm. What should I do, Lucky?"

Lucky shrugged. "Give them a call and see what they have to say. You can always say no to whatever they offer."

"I don't want to go alone." In spite of Sophie's occasional brashness, Lucky knew she could be easily intimidated at times by those she perceived in authority. "Will you drive me up there?"

"You only have to listen to what they say, but I'm happy to go with you if it makes you feel better."

"Thanks!" Sophie reached over and squeezed Lucky's arm. "Sage would come too, but if he sees me get upset, he'll get upset. Besides, it's easier for you to get away on a break."

"I hope so. Hopefully Jack will be here to cover for me."

Chapter 20

LUCKY SPREAD THE photos across Jack's kitchen table. She had walked over after closing time, partly to talk to him about the photos she had found in the box but mostly to check in, hoping he was on an even keel. In a way, she was relieved that Jack's being at home had given her an excuse. For some reason she couldn't quite put her finger on, some instinct, she wanted to keep the photos private. She didn't want anyone at the Spoonful to see them yet or ask her what they meant. A good thing, because she herself had no idea what they might represent.

Jack rubbed his chin. "Don't have a clue," he said. "Your mother just liked to take pictures—pictures of the family, of you when you were little and growing up. She wasn't any expert at it, but she had this knack, I guess you'd say. She could capture a moment. I sure could never do it. I'd hit that button too late and it was gone. But your mother—she had a real gift for that."

"So you have no idea why she would have taken all these photos of the Warners and kept them?"

"Nope, none at all, my girl." Jack poured his beer into a

chilled glass. "They were regulars for a while so a photo or two would make sense, but I guess she never got one good enough to hang up. Now they never come in anymore. Musta been something, but it was so many years ago. Seems like your mom was on about something, but I'll be damned if I can remember."

"I do recall seeing the Warners on occasion when they used to come to the Spoonful," Lucky said. "But since then they've dropped off the radar, haven't they? I haven't seen them once since I've been back in town. Did anything happen at the restaurant to upset them?" She remembered her conversation with Leonard Warner at the police station, but she had no intention of repeating that to Jack.

Jack shook his head. "I don't think they argued, not that I remember. They just didn't show up anymore. I don't remember them much after that time when your mom was taking all those pictures.

"Look, Jack. She even put a date on the back of some of these. Somehow this time period was significant." Lucky turned the photos over. "You're sure she never said anything about these?"

"To me? No. But she woulda talked to your dad. I remember one time your dad was"—Jack hesitated—"like he thought she was snooping where she shouldn't be snooping."

"I think maybe I inherited that trait from her because this is really bugging me, Jack."

"What's bothering you about it?"

Lucky paused to marshal her thoughts. "Nate's asking questions about the herbs you gave the women, as if somehow you made a mistake and that caused Agnes's death. Or she had an allergic reaction to something and maybe that caused it. But what if it wasn't an accident or an allergic reaction? What if there was something about her that made her a victim? Something about her life that made someone want to harm her?"

"I hope you're right about me not making a mistake with those plants. I'm not so sure I convinced Nate and that professor."

"Why do you say that?"

"Turns out, where I picked the woodruff leaves, there's some water hemlock growing. The Professor spotted it, and I'll bet she's thinking I made a mistake." Jack shook his head. "But I can't imagine doing that. I know water hemlock. Looks completely different. But I could tell from the expression on her face, she wasn't so sure." Jack took a sip of his beer. "But what you're saying is somebody might have changed something or added something else to that drink that shouldn't have been there." He shook his head. "That may be pretty far-fetched. Assuming some kinda poisonous plant caused her reaction and maybe that caused something more serious, like a heart attack, wouldn't somebody have had to know she was allergic or that she would be the first to drink that concoction?"

Lucky sighed. "That's true. That's a lot of what-ifs. We don't have any results as to what was in that drink yet. The wine could have been perfectly fine and she just had a heart attack. And now that she's dead, we have no way of knowing if there was something Agnes was violently allergic to. Well, unless Nate can find out from her doctor or her husband."

"Well, if they turn up something bad in the autopsy, how could anyone have fooled around with that basket I gave Cecily? You don't think Cecily . . . ?" Jack left his statement unfinished.

"No. I don't. Not Cecily. She's the dearest person on earth and she'd have no reason to want to hurt anyone. And Cordelia . . . Well, she's not my favorite person, but why would she want to harm Agnes? I can't imagine. And Emily Rathbone? I can't see that either. But there were two other women there that night. What if one of them . . . ?"

"Who were the others?" Jack asked.

"I don't know all their names. I can ask Cecily. She might remember, if I can talk to her without Marjorie overhearing, or maybe Emily or even Cordelia if I have to."

"I guess I've done nothing but cause you a lot of trouble."

"Don't say that, Jack. I'm sure you haven't done anything

wrong or made any mistakes. And you haven't caused me any trouble. We're family. We look out for each other."

"You be careful what you go poking your nose into, my girl."

"That sounds like something my dad would have said."

"Yes. And I'm giving you the same good advice. If there's somebody in town evil enough to poison another human being, they're not to be trifled with."

Chapter 21

SOPHIE IMPATIENTLY FLIPPED through the pages of one after another of the magazines. Lucky glanced over. The magazine cover Sophie held in her hand displayed an attractive couple happily schussing down a snow-covered slope. Sophie's foot was wiggling in an ever-increasing rhythm. They were seated in the reception area of the executive offices of the Snowflake Resort. Lucky had changed into a skirt and jacket to appear more appropriate for a business meeting. Sophie had refused. She wore her jeans and a T-shirt, the type of outfit she wore to the Spoonful on a day when she'd be working in the kitchen with Sage.

In the stillness of the waiting room, the slapping of glossy magazine pages seemed unnaturally loud. Once or twice the heavily made-up receptionist glanced over at them irritably.

"How much longer are we supposed to wait?" Sophie hissed in a stage whisper.

"I don't know. Just be patient."

"If they're trying to make us nervous, they're succeeding."

"I'm not nervous."

"Of course not. You don't have to talk to them."

"Sophie." Lucky reached over to still her friend's hand. "There's nothing to be anxious about. We're just going to listen to what they have to say, what they're offering, and you can always say you'll give it some thought for a day or two, and then leave. It's not a firing squad."

Lucky looked up. It was the man Sophie called Lurch. The same man who had been watching them in the corridor of the Resort, the same man who had delivered the letter to Sophie, stood at the entrance to the waiting room. He locked eyes with Lucky but made no effort to approach. Lucky regarded him carefully. She noted his square jaw and small eyes in a tanned, rough face. Today he wore black jeans, work boots and a black T-shirt under a casual jacket. He turned his head and gave a slight nod to someone in the corridor behind him, someone out of sight. Then he returned the way he came. A moment later, a man in a dark gray business suit entered the waiting room and approached the reception desk. He spoke a few inaudible words to the receptionist and then turned and walked toward them. Lucky recognized Tom Reed, a man she had had an unfortunate exchange with a year or more before. She groaned inwardly.

"Ms. Colgan?" He smiled and held out his hand.

"Yes." Sophie stood, tossing the magazine on the table.

"Thank you for meeting with us today." He smiled, but slid a sideways glance at Lucky. She was certain he vividly remembered her last visit to his office.

Sophie caught his look and turned. "This is my friend Lucky Jamieson. I've asked her to come along."

"Oh yes?" he replied.

"Hello." Lucky quelled her own anxiety. She hoped any ill will he harbored toward her would not be directed at Sophie. "I believe we've met before."

"Oh?" Reed's face took on an uncomprehending look.

He was putting on a very good act. Obviously, he wanted nothing to interfere with this meeting. Sophie's parcels must be quite important to their development plans. "It's not relevant." She smiled.

"Let me take you to the conference room." As an after-thought, he asked, "Would you like a coffee or tea?"

"No, thanks," Sophie replied.

Reed didn't wait for an answer from Lucky. He turned back to the archway he had just passed through and led them down a corridor to the end. They followed him in silence. He turned to the left where a glass wall separated the corridor from a spacious conference room. Inside was a large round table at which two men and a woman, all in black business suits, were seated. One of the men was focused on an open laptop as they entered.

"Ms. Colgan . . ."

"Call me Sophie, please."

"Sophie. I'd like you to meet Paul Rudnick, Gary Mercer and Pamela Kittridge. This is Sophie Colgan."

The two men rose and reached across the table to shake Sophie's hand. The woman, a severe-looking blonde, nod-ded. Something akin to a smile almost made her lips move.

"These gentlemen and Ms. Kittridge are attorneys with the firm of Leahy and Robertson in New York. Their firm represents the business interests of the Snowflake Resort." He pulled a padded chair away from the conference table and held it for Sophie. She sat, a stony expression on her face. Reed made no move to offer Lucky a seat. She sat on a duplicate padded chair next to Sophie.

One of the attorneys cleared his throat. Lucky tried to remember his name. Was he Paul or Gary? Already it had fallen from her mind.

"Ms. Colgan . . . Sophie, you may not be aware of this, but the Resort is interested in extending the ski run on the east side of the mountain. We hope to create a black diamond run there. I don't know if you're familiar with all the runs the Resort offers . . ."

Sophie tried to speak. "I'm very familiar—"

Tom Reed interrupted quickly. "Ms. Colgan works for the Resort as a ski instructor. She's an excellent athlete and very familiar with all the trails."

"Oh. Oh, thank you, Tom. I wasn't aware of that history."

He gave a twinkling smile to Sophie. "Well, then, you can understand how popular the Resort has become and how necessary it is for us to offer more to our guests. I'm sure you'd appreciate a new run."

Lucky noticed Sophie's jaw clenching. These people were getting under her skin. "Could we get to the point?" Sophie asked abruptly.

Paul—or was it Gary?—sat back in his chair. "Of course. Of course." He rifled through a few of the papers that were on the table in front of him. "The Resort is interested in making you an offer for several acres of land that are currently in the name of Marguerite Colgan, your mother, I believe. And you are, of course, one of her heirs."

"I have a brother who inherits as well," Sophie replied.

"Yes . . . uh . . . Yes, we are aware of that. Richard Colgan is your brother; is that correct?"

Sophie nodded wordlessly.

"We plan to meet with him as well."

"I see," Sophie responded grimly. She flicked a glance in Lucky's direction.

"The Resort is willing to make you an offer for all of the parcels now in your mother's name. However, the company is particularly interested in the acreage on the east side of the rise. If we were to be able to purchase that, we could extend runs in that area."

"I'm not interested in selling the land the house is on. Not at all."

"But you would be open to selling the acreage on the other side of the hill?"

"Possibly," Sophie answered, squirming a bit.

The man looked over at his two colleagues and quickly glanced at Tom Reed. "In that case, we could offer you and your brother . . ." He named a sum that caused Lucky to gasp inwardly.

Sophie's chin drew back. "Have you already spoken with my brother?"

"Uh . . . no, not as yet. We'll be meeting with him . . .

Tom." He glanced at Reed. "I believe you're meeting with him initially?" he asked.

Reed nodded but said nothing.

"I see." The attorney turned back to Sophie. "Why don't we get together again, in that case, after we've spoken with your brother? You can take your time deciding. Consider it a standing offer."

"And if my brother isn't interested in selling?"

"Well . . ." He trailed off. "We *might* consider purchasing your half interest in any event. But I'm sure your brother will be pleased with our offer."

"We'll see, then," Sophie said and stood.

The two men rose to their feet. One of them passed a business card across the conference table. "Give us a call at any time if you have any questions or concerns. We'll be here at the Resort for the next few days, but our office can conference any of us in if you should call."

Sophie nodded. "Thank you." She turned and left the room, Lucky following in her wake. Neither of them spoke a word as they retraced their steps to the waiting room and stepped out into the parking lot.

Sophie gripped Lucky's arm. "Did you hear that? I thought I would collapse right then and there."

"I heard it. It's a complete windfall, Sophie. The only problem is . . ."

"My brother. I know. Sophie linked her arm through Lucky's as they walked slowly back to Sophie's car. "Like where is he? Why hasn't he answered my e-mails? And do we even know if he's alive?"

They had reached the car. "Can you drive back?" Sophie asked.

"Sure. What's wrong?"

Sophie laughed. "Believe it or not, my legs are wobbly."

Lucky smiled. "No problem." She took the keys from Sophie's hand. "Just remember, you can sell it if you want to. My question is why are they willing to fork over money without a guarantee that a second party will sell?"

"It does seem strange." Sophie climbed into the passenger seat. "Maybe they figure if he's not interested now, they can eventually whittle down his resistance. They must want that land awfully bad, Lucky." Sophie stared out the window. "I still can't get over how much they're offering. They've made it very hard to say no."

A chill ran up Lucky's spine. She wondered whether the lawyers knew that Rick could already be out of the equation. "Sophie, we need to know who that man was in the creek. That could change everything."

Chapter 22

LUCKY FLIPPED THE sign over on the front door. The Spoonful was closed for the night. Jack sat at a table by the window, staring out into the darkening evening. Lucky slid a harp instrumental into the CD player. She heard the murmur of conversation from the kitchen as Sophie helped Sage clean up for the night. Finally, the whir of the dishwasher.

"Jack," she called to her grandfather.

"Huh?" He looked up quickly, as though caught in a reverie.

"Would you like a beer?"

He nodded. "Sounds good, my girl."

"Hang on," she said as she headed for the kitchen. The Spoonful never served alcohol, but Lucky and Sage always made sure there was a supply in the refrigerator for nights like this—nights when the work was done and everyone needed to relax.

"You having a beer?" Sophie asked when she saw Lucky open the refrigerator.

"No. Just getting one for Jack. How 'bout you and Sage?"

Sophie glanced over at Sage as he washed his hands at the sink. "Sure. One for both of us."

"You got it," Lucky replied. She grabbed a small tray and loaded three tall chilled glasses from the freezer and three bottles of beer.

"You're not having one?" Sage asked.

She smiled. "No. Wine's my drink of choice. Just never liked beer particularly."

"You know, in the time I've known you, I guess I never noticed that," Sage said, walking over to the large refrigerator. "Hang on. I've got a few bottles of white wine stashed in the back here. I've been saving them in case I wanted to try them out in some recipes. I'll open one."

"Just for me?" she asked.

"Sure. If we're all having something, you can't be odd man out."

Sophie had carried the tray out to Jack's table. Sage poured a glass for Lucky and handed it to her with a flourish.

"Thank you, kind sir." She laughed. "Let's join the others. I think Jack needs a little cheering up."

Sage nodded but said nothing. He followed her out to the front of the restaurant and sat at the table with Jack. Lucky moved around the room and turned off all the lamps but one. It cast a pool of light over their table and the blue and yellow neon sign in the shape of a bowl of soup glowed in the window.

"Best time of the day," Sage said, breathing a long sigh and rubbing the back of his neck.

Sophie turned to them. "I was just reminding Jack that no results are in yet and he shouldn't be worrying about anything."

"She's right, Jack," Sage added. "We don't have any answers about anything." He looked at Sophie. "Anything— not even about Sophie's brother."

"You're right," Jack said. "Here I am worrying myself to death about those herbs, and you're up against something big. I've been a self-centered old man."

"You couldn't be self-centered if you tried," Sophie

answered. "Besides, if that was Rick in the water . . ." She shuddered involuntarily. "If that *was* Rick, I would have known . . . Wouldn't I?" Sophie looked around the table.

"I honestly don't know," Lucky said. "I think there should have been something about that man's body that at least struck you, or reminded you of your brother. His hairline, his hands, something."

"Well," Sophie replied ruefully, "to be honest, I didn't look too hard. I was so repelled when I realized it was a human, I couldn't take everything in."

"That's understandable," Jack said. "The eyes and the brain can only take in so much before everything shuts down in shock. I'm a living example of that. If I'd seen that . . ." Jack trailed off. They all knew Jack was referring to his occasional bouts of PTSD from his wartime service in the Pacific. Jack called those times his "spells." He took a sip of his beer. "Not sure I can finish this. I think I'll take off. Can you kids batten down the hatches?"

"We'll take care of everything." Lucky followed him to the front door and gave him a hug. She locked the door behind him and watched him through the glass as he turned in the direction of Birch Street and home. She returned to the table and sipped her wine.

"You're worried about him, aren't you?" Sophie asked.

"I am, yes. He's been so distracted and down since this thing happened. I don't know why but he's taken it all upon himself. And I just can't believe he made a mistake that caused a death." Lucky watched her friends carefully. "There's another possibility."

Sophie looked across the table at her friend. "What's that?"

"Something I've been thinking about." She hesitated. "Maybe it wasn't a mistake. Maybe it was deliberate. Maybe somebody wanted Agnes dead."

"You mean somebody messed around with that basket that Jack gave Cecily?" Sage asked.

Sophie had a doubtful expression on her face. "Agnes Warner? Why would anyone want to kill a harmless woman like that? Besides, how would they know Agnes would be the first one to drink the wine?"

"That was Jack's point too. But what if one of them knew she was terribly allergic to something? Maybe what she drank wasn't deadly, but harmful enough that it could have caused her to have a heart attack or something."

"Possible." Sophie turned that thought over in her mind.

"It's a theory, Lucky," Sage offered. "But have they analyzed the wine or what's left in any of the containers or bowls or done the autopsy yet? If not, there's nothing to back it up."

Lucky was about to respond when Sage turned his head. "Did you hear that?"

The two women looked at him. Lucky was just about to say she hadn't heard a thing when a loud rap came from the rear corridor.

"You expecting anyone?" he asked.

"No," Lucky replied. "I'll go see who it is."

"Uh-uh. You two stay here. I'll see who's there." Sage rose from his chair and went through the swinging door to the corridor.

They heard a low murmur of voices and then Sage reappeared at the doorway. Lucky and Sophie turned to look at him.

"It's someone for you, Sophie," Sage said.

"For me? Who?"

"He says he's your brother."

Chapter 23

SAGE STEPPED ASIDE and held the door open. A rugged-looking man in his midforties with a weather-beaten complexion and a few days' growth of beard stepped into the restaurant.

"Hi, Sis. I was told I'd find you here."

Sophie stared, her eyes wide. She didn't utter a word.

The man took long strides toward the table. He wore work boots, jeans and a green khaki jacket. His hair was dark and curly, like Sophie's, and something about the shape of his forehead and eyes struck Lucky. The family resemblance was visible.

"You don't seem very happy to see me."

Sophie stood, almost knocking over her chair. "Rick!" she cried. "They told us you were dead."

He raised his eyebrows. "I wasn't informed." He laughed. "What are you talking about?"

Sophie walked to him and reached out to hug her brother. He returned the affection but each of them stood slightly awkwardly, as though not sure how to respond to each other.

Sophie, remembering Sage, who stood nearby, said,

"Rick, this is Sage—Sage DuBois—my fiancé. Sage, my brother Rick." She turned and indicated Lucky. "And Lucky. You remember her, don't you?"

Rick turned, then nodded to Lucky and shook Sage's hand. "Nice to meet you." He gave Sage an appraising look. "And congratulations." Rick nodded to Lucky. "I do remember you, Lucky. Nice to see you." He took a seat at the table.

"Would you like a beer?" Sage asked.

"That'd be great. Thanks," Rick answered. "So, Sis. What's going on? What do you mean you thought I was dead?"

Sophie took a deep breath. "Actually, I really didn't believe it myself. Lucky and I went up to have a look at Mom's house and down in the creek we found . . . we found a dead guy floating in the water."

Rick's jaw clenched. His eyes narrowed. "When was this?"

"I think . . . five days ago."

"Did you call the cops?"

Sophie narrowed her eyes. "Of course we did."

"Do they know who he is?"

She shrugged. "No. The police came. Nate Edgerton's the Chief of Police now; did you know that? He told us there was no identification on the body. The only thing they found on him was one of those ballpoint pens they leave in the rooms at the Resort. So they checked up there."

"What did he look like?" Rick was completely alert now. Sage returned with a bottle of beer and a chilled glass and placed it on the table for their guest.

"That's just it," Lucky said. She had remained quiet until now, sizing up a man she hadn't seen since she and Sophie were children. "His face was gone."

"What do you mean 'gone'?"

"Battered beyond recognition." Sophie shuddered. "It was pretty awful. At first we thought maybe he was somebody who fell in farther up, you know, where the current's stronger and just got banged around and drowned. Or maybe animals. The police don't know much yet at all."

Lucky could see the wheels turning behind Rick's eyes.

It was hard to believe the man sitting at the table with them was the same teenager she remembered who used to play a beat-up guitar on Sophie's mother's front porch.

"Why are you asking?" Lucky asked.

Rick stared at Lucky for a moment. "I haven't been able to reach my partner for several days."

"Your partner?" Sophie asked. "What kind of business are you in? I told Nate you were working on getting your investigator's license, but he said he couldn't locate you through the state listings in New York."

"I did that for a while, true, but I never bothered to get my license. We . . . uh . . . My partner, Eddie, Eddie Fowler and I . . . We set up a small operation together."

"To do what?" Lucky asked. Already she was feeling that his explanations were sliding away.

"We find people."

"Like missing people?" Sophie asked.

Lucky glanced at Sage, who sat quietly, watching Rick.

"Yeah, like that—people who don't want to be found."

"People hiding from the law?" Lucky asked.

"Sometimes. But mostly it's just personal stuff or family disputes like an ex-spouse that took off and stopped paying child support. The system's so overburdened nobody has the resources to keep tracking, but we do—for private parties."

"Is that why you're here? Why your partner was here?"

"Sort of. I got a letter from a lawyer about Mom's property."

Sophie stared at her brother. "How did they find you? I don't even have your address."

Rick smiled. "Guess they have people who do what I do. Besides, Sis, I'm never home. I move around a lot. E-mail is best if you ever want to reach me."

"I tried. Did you get my e-mail?"

He nodded. "Yeah. I did."

"I got a letter from the lawyers too. I met with them today."

"What did they have to say?" Rick's face seemed to have closed down.

"They offered a ton of money. They'll buy everything, but what they really want is the acreage on the other side of the hill. They want to extend a ski run."

Rick's jaw tightened but he didn't speak.

"So you didn't answer my question," Sophie said. "Why was your partner coming here?"

"We . . . uh . . . Well, Eddie's pretty knowledgeable about real estate. I asked him to have a look at the house and the land around it to kind of give me an idea what it's worth."

"Nate told us you were registered at the Resort but no one had seen you . . . or whoever was in your room for the last few days."

Rick fell silent. "Eddie came on ahead of me. I couldn't get away and I'm supposed to meet him here."

Lucky and Sage exchanged a glance. "You think he went out to have a look at the property, Rick?" Lucky asked.

Rick nodded. "I hope to hell that wasn't him you found in the creek." He looked at Sophie. "You say Nate Edgerton's the Chief of Police now?"

Sophie nodded.

"I remember him. I'll go see him first thing in the morning."

"Was he registered at the Resort under your name?" Lucky asked.

Rick shot a look across the table. "I, uh, I made a reservation after I got the letter from the lawyers, but then I had to finish up a job. Eddie was planning to come with me, but he decided to go on ahead until I could catch up."

No one spoke. Lucky was sure they all shared the same thought. If Rick's partner went out to the property and met his end, and he was staying in the room Rick had reserved, what were the odds the man in the creek was Rick's missing partner?

"So what do you think, Rick?" Sophie got right to the point. "Sage and I want to make you an offer for your share of the house and the land around it. I want the fireplace that Granddad built. I don't want to see it bulldozed for a ski run or cabins. We can sell them the other land. That's what they really want—another ski run."

"Uh-uh." Rick shook his head. "I don't think I want to sell that."

"What? Why not?" Sophie's voice had risen.

"I'd just like to hang on to that." Sophie's face fell. Rick stood and nodded to Sage. "Thanks for the beer. I'll see you around, Sis."

"Wait," Sophie said. "We need to talk about this. Where are you staying?"

"Up there." He indicated the general direction of the Resort. "I'll be in touch." Rick turned away and unlocked the front door. He shut it firmly behind him and disappeared in the night.

Sophie sat, a stunned look on her face. Lucky and Sage waited for her to speak.

"He's always been like that. Here one second, gone the next. But I'm not gonna let him get away with it, not this time," she vowed.

Chapter 24

LUCKY PICKED UP the boxes she had left on the living room floor the night before and stacked them in the hallway closet. She planned to organize them when she had more time, maybe after the wedding. Some of them tugged at her heart and brought up so many memories. Photographs could freeze a moment in time and bring it back so sharply it hurt, moments that would otherwise be lost to memory.

She wiggled the table leg gently. It seemed to be holding firm. She righted the coffee table and spread the Warner photos across the surface. It was too much of a coincidence that not one face was clear in any of the pictures. Either one of the two adults moved at the right moment to blur the photo, or one of them stood in the way to block the picture.

Her doorbell rang. She jumped involuntarily. She wasn't expecting anyone and her only visitors at night were either Sophie or Elias. But she knew Sophie was at home tonight and Elias was in Lincoln Falls seeing patients and might stay there overnight. She walked to the hallway and called out, "Who is it?"

"House call." She heard Elias's voice. Laughing, she hurried down the hallway to open the door.

He stepped over the threshold and enveloped her in a hug.

"I thought you'd be at the hospital tonight."

"I did too, but I managed to get away early."

"Have you had a chance to eat?"

"I'm fine. I'm hungry only for you." He made a fierce growling sound and pretended to gnaw on her shoulder until she collapsed in laughter.

"You are a silly man!"

"Silly about you," he replied, smiling, showing the dimple in his chin that Lucky loved.

"Come on in. I'll pour you a glass of wine."

"That would be very welcome. Thanks."

Elias shrugged off his jacket and slung it over a chair in the living room. Lucky returned from the kitchen carrying two glasses of red wine. She sat next to Elias on the sofa and they clinked their glasses together.

"What's all this?" he asked, indicating the array of photographs.

"I haven't had a chance to tell you about this. They came from a box that was up in Horace's attic. I picked the boxes up the other day. One of them was full of photos my mother used to take at the Spoonful. But these—the ones you see here—were in an envelope and they're all of the Warners from years ago."

Elias picked up one of the photos.

"Notice anything strange about these?" she asked, not wanting to plant her suspicions in his head.

"Your mother took these for the restaurant? Is this the dead woman and her husband?"

Lucky nodded. "And their grandson, Mike."

"Well, these must have been the rejects because no one is exactly smiling or looking at the camera. Are there any others?"

"This is all there is. Notice anything else?"

"Hmm." Elias leafed through the photographs. "Someone

is either turned away or looking down or standing in front of the boy. Is that what you meant?"

"Yes. My mother used to ask people to look up and smile at the camera. She was always looking for great photos to hang on the wall. I'm sure she did the same here, but they obviously ignored her."

One of the photos slid off the end of the table. Elias reached down to retrieve it. He turned it over and saw the date on the back of the picture. "Date mean anything?"

"No. Not that I can recall, and none of the others in the box were dated. But a few of these are. These dates are all within the same month. And one of the dates has an exclamation mark after it."

Elias leaned back on the sofa and pulled her close. "Uh-oh. I know that look. What are you thinking?"

"I'm thinking that Agnes and her husband didn't want to be photographed. I'm thinking they were keeping their identities secret."

"Lucky, I know you're concerned about Jack—that he might have made a mistake."

"Jack didn't make a mistake. I'm sure of that."

Elias took a deep breath but didn't respond.

"What? What's that big sigh about?" she demanded.

"Look. I came by tonight because we need to talk."

She felt her stomach clench in a knot. This didn't sound good. "Okay," she finally said.

"The autopsy was completed. Agnes Warner died of a heart attack. She had severe arteriosclerosis and occlusion of the coronary artery."

"Well." Lucky breathed a sigh of relief. "That's good news, isn't it?"

Elias watched her face carefully. "The cardiac event could have happened at any time, but the apparent immediate reaction indicates it was brought on by what she drank. The stomach contents were examined carefully and they've found traces of what they believe might be a toxin. They haven't identified it yet.

"A poison? I don't understand."

"Many plants are poisonous; some contain alkaloid poisons. They're still going over everything: the wine, the utensils, just trying to narrow down what it might be. It's a difficult job if they don't know what they're looking for."

Lucky felt her heart sink. "That couldn't be. Jack knows his plants. He couldn't have made a mistake like that!"

"I certainly hope you're right. I just wanted to tell you first before you or Jack heard from Nate."

Lucky put her head in her hands. "I can't believe this. Jack will be devastated." Suddenly she looked up. "Could Jack be charged with anything?"

"That I don't know. The question is, did the contents of the wine cause the heart attack? Would someone else who drank that wine have remained unaffected? Still more questions to answer. There might have to be a hearing or an inquest. No one would suspect Jack of anything premeditated. At worst, it's a case of a mistake leading to an unfortunate death. It does happen. People have died from botulism eating badly preserved foods prepared by a loving relative." Elias continued, "I just wanted to tell you myself. Nate will probably get the autopsy report tomorrow at the earliest. Identifying the exact toxin will take longer."

"Poor Jack. He's been depressed enough already, but this could send him into a tailspin."

Elias pulled her close and held her in his arms.

"Can you stay with me tonight?" she asked. For the longest time it was she who had been unwilling to spend the night with Elias at either his house or her apartment, afraid of wagging tongues and any gossip that would hurt his reputation most of all. But tonight she knew she didn't want to be alone.

"Of course, if you want me to."

"Elias, if anything was wrong with that wine the women brewed, then somebody had to have tampered with Jack's basket of herbs. He would never have made that kind of mistake. This goes way beyond an accident or an allergic reaction."

"Yes," he agreed.

"What if one of those women knew Agnes would be the first person to drink? Maybe somebody wanted her dead."

"Or somebody wanted all of them dead."

Lucky groaned. "I can't think about this anymore. I'll have to worry about it tomorrow." She sighed and leaned against his shoulder. "Just hold me in your arms tonight."

Chapter 25

THE MORNING RUSH was in full swing by the time Lucky arrived at the Spoonful. Elias had left in the wee hours to go home and change before starting his day at the Snowflake Clinic. She had no memory of doing so, but she must have turned off her alarm clock and fallen back into a dreamless state. She woke in a panic, aware she'd be late. When she rushed through the back door of the restaurant, she realized no harm was done. Unlike her, everyone else had arrived either early or on time.

She dropped her purse in the office and pulled a fresh apron from the closet. The Spoonful's aprons were yellow with the outline of a steaming bowl of soup in blue. Her mother had created these and her dad had followed suit with the neon sign in the front window of the restaurant. She pushed through the swinging door into the front room. Meg was taking orders from new customers and Janie was manning the counter. Jack was at the cash register and handing out flyers for the library drive as each customer paid.

"Thanks, Janie. I'll take over. I'm running late today."

"No worries. Everything's under control. By the way, you

just missed Marjorie. She left a few minutes ago," Janie whispered.

"Oh?" Lucky's eyebrows rose. "Was Cecily with her?"

"Uh-uh." Janie shook her head. "I think they're still spatting."

"Oh dear. Poor Cecily."

"I think it's terrible the way her sister keeps her in the doghouse. She always seems so disapproving."

"She does, I know. But she's the older sister, and I think she's always played mother with Cecily."

"Cecily's a grown woman. So what if she wanted to take part in that ritual? I think it's kinda cool. I wouldn't have thought that old bat Cordelia could have dreamed this up."

"Shh. Someone will hear you." Lucky suppressed a laugh. "I know she's a terrible snob, but actually I suspect she's very vulnerable. Who knows? Maybe she was just bored and thought this would be exciting."

"Exciting, all right," Janie said in a stage whisper. "Dead body and all." Janie wiped her hands on a dish towel. She glanced over at Meg, who was starting to look a little harried. "I'll give Meg a hand." She pulled an order pad from her apron pocket and ducked under the hatch of the counter. Lucky watched her as she moved between the tables. Janie was planning to start college in the fall. Lucky was excited for her but knew they'd all miss her terribly when the time came.

The bell over the door rang and Lucky looked up to see Cecily, on her own. Lucky waved her over, and Cecily took a stool at the counter.

"How are you today?" Lucky asked as she placed a napkin and fresh silverware on the counter.

Cecily smiled, but she seemed to have lost her usual exuberance. "I'm all right, dear. As you can see I'm on my own today—again."

Lucky nodded sympathetically. "Tea and croissant? The usual?"

"Yes. Please."

Sage had spotted Cecily at the front door and had already

prepared her order. It was waiting on the hatch. Lucky carried it to the place mat. "Here you go."

"Thank you, dear." She looked up. "I assume my sister has already been and gone?"

"So I've been told."

"Hmm. Good. She's been so crabby since all this happened in the woods."

"I'm sure she'll get over it soon. And I'm sure she just worries about you."

"I know she does. But it's ridiculous. I'm not a child anymore; nor am I an idiot."

Lucky noticed two customers leaving. She hurriedly cleared away their dishes and delivered fresh place mats and napkins to the empty seats. She refilled the coffee cups of the three remaining patrons and moved back to the spot where Cecily sat.

"Cecily . . ." Lucky leaned closer. "I wonder if I could talk to you about the day you picked up those herbs from Jack." She glanced over at the cash register where Jack sat, hoping he hadn't overheard her question.

"Of course. You can ask me anything."

"Let's step into the corridor, if you don't mind."

"Of course not." Cecily placed her napkin next to her teacup and rose from the stool.

Lucky glanced over the counter. This would take only a minute, and everything was handled for the time being. She pushed open the swinging door for Cecily and followed her into the hallway.

"I don't mean to bug you. I just want to make sure of this because Jack's been torturing himself about the plants he picked. And . . ." Lucky hesitated, not willing to share the news that Elias had given her the night before.

"He shouldn't. I'm sure whatever happened to Agnes had nothing to do with him," Cecily replied.

"I agree with you. I just wish Jack felt the same way. Tell me again how all this was arranged."

"Well, I was appointed to ask Jack for the things we needed for the May wine. I spoke to him one day—oh, maybe a couple of weeks ago—and he said he'd be happy to pick the plants for us. He said to just give him a call the day before I needed the herbs. I called him . . . Let's see, the morning of the twenty-eighth, two days before our ceremony. As far as I know, he picked the plants the same day and I stopped by his house after we closed the shop that evening. And he gave me the basket. It was probably more than we needed, as it turned out, and then I drove up to Cordelia's house and dropped it off."

"Was she there to receive it? Or did you leave it on the stairs or anything?"

"Oh no. She opened the door right away and thanked me and took it in."

"Would there be any herbs left over, by any chance? Maybe Cordelia didn't use them all, or maybe she saved them?"

Cecily shook her head. "I don't think so." She thought a minute. "No, I'm sure there wouldn't be. I remember her saying she put them all in the wine."

"I see."

"I don't think Jack had anything harmful in there at all. I think Agnes . . . Oh, it was terrible to see, Lucky. Agnes had a terrible reaction. She seemed to become dizzy and then she clutched her throat and started gasping. She couldn't breathe, her chest was heaving and then she fell on the ground and just lay gasping like a fish out of water." Cecily shuddered. "I really don't want to think about that anymore."

"I don't mean to make you relive it, Cecily. My only motive in asking is to find out if someone could have added anything dangerous to that basket."

"I understand, dear. But be patient. Everything will eventually come out."

Lucky heard a crash from the front of the restaurant and a man's raised voice. "Uh-oh. What was that?" She felt an adrenaline rush as she pushed the door open and hurried to the front of the restaurant. Cecily was right behind her.

Leonard Warner stood in the middle of the restaurant. He had pushed a table, crashing some dishes to the floor and knocking over a chair. His face was beet red. He looked enormous. He was over six feet tall and probably weighed two hundred pounds. He was shouting at Jack. "You killed her. You killed my wife." Tears were streaming down his face. The restaurant was completely silent. No one dared to breathe. Lucky heard Sage's footsteps as he rushed out of the kitchen in defense of Jack.

Jack's complexion had turned a ghastly white. He stumbled to his feet behind the cash register, knocking over his stool. His mouth opened and closed as if he wanted to speak, but no words came out. He stared speechlessly at Leonard, shaking his head.

Lucky stepped in front of the cash register in an effort to protect Jack from further abuse. She had to crane her neck to look up at Leonard Warner. She spoke quietly but everyone in the restaurant could hear. "He did no such thing. He never harmed anybody in his life. You'll have to leave. Now. Before I call the police." Sage had moved to Jack's side, ready to take action if needed. Hank Northcross and Barry Sanders were on their feet, also ready to rush to Jack's aid.

Lucky felt a moment of compassion for Leonard, but her first priority was to protect Jack. "This isn't going to bring your wife back."

Leonard Warner seemed to collapse into himself. He raised a shaking hand and pointed at Jack. "You'll pay for this, old man."

Barry moved swiftly. He was next to Lucky before she realized it. "You heard the lady." Barry stood with his legs apart. "You better get out now."

Lucky's face was as red as Leonard's. The damage had been done, she knew. Jack could go into an emotional tailspin. She stabbed a finger in Leonard's chest. "You have no idea what you're talking about." She wondered whether Leonard had received the report of the autopsy yet. Did he know as much as she had learned from Elias? "Her death had nothing to do with Jack."

Leonard took a step backward. He wiped his face with the back of his hand.

Lucky could feel her anger mounting. She moved closer to Leonard and stared directly up into his eyes. She spoke quietly. "I better never see you anywhere near my grandfather again. Never."

Leonard stumbled through the front door, shooting a last glare in Jack's direction. Lucky caught a glimpse of Greta on the sidewalk. She held an armful of books, a terrified expression on her face. She had been heading to the restaurant but stopped when she heard the shouting. She turned and hurried away before Leonard reached the sidewalk.

Lucky took a deep breath. She looked around the restaurant at the shocked customers. "Okay, folks. It's over. Everything's under control. Sorry about this."

Janie stood in the doorway to the kitchen with a broom and dustpan in her hands. "I'll take care of this," she whispered to Lucky as she passed by. Lucky signaled to Meg to take over the cash register. She put her arm around Jack's shoulders. "Come into the office for a minute."

He nodded mutely and followed her down the corridor. She forced him into a chair and shut the door behind them. She took both his hands in hers. "Are you okay?"

Jack was shaking. She knew this had been a terrible blow, as terrible as if Leonard had physically battered him. She was afraid Jack would lose his grip on reality and think he was back in the Pacific trying to rescue screaming men from the sea.

"I . . ." He couldn't speak.

"It's all over now. Nothing to be afraid of, Jack."

"I didn't know. I must have picked the wrong things." He looked up at her. Tears had filled his eyes. Lucky thought her heart would break.

"You did not pick the wrong things, Jack. I know you didn't." She clung to that belief in spite of what Elias had told her the previous evening. "You're too knowledgeable. Leonard is just in terrible grief. He's angry, and he wants to blame somebody. You're a very easy scapegoat. Please trust me on this." She said a silent prayer that she was right, that whatever might have triggered Agnes's reaction would be discovered and if anyone had added anything toxic to the wine, that person would be revealed.

"I know you mean well, my girl, but . . ."

"But what?"

"It's my fault." His chest shook as he stifled a sob.

"What is?"

"It's my fault . . . your mom and dad. If I hadn't been . . ."

What was Jack trying to tell her? "If you hadn't been what?" she whispered.

"That night . . . they shouldn't have been driving." Lucky knew he was referring to her parents' car accident. "They were supposed to stay in Bennington 'cause the roads had iced up. I *told* them not to drive with the weather like that but they wouldn't listen. I was sick with the flu, real sick, and they were worried about me. They were trying to get home because of me."

Lucky's heart fell. "You're saying you're the reason they were on the road that night?" she asked quietly.

"Yes." Jack could barely form the word. "I'm sorry, my girl. I've wanted to tell you for a long time, but I didn't know how."

"Jack, that wasn't your fault. You didn't cause anything. They made the decision to try to get home. You can't blame yourself for that. They knew the dangers, and they made a terrible decision. It's *not* your fault."

"Do you know how many times I've told myself that? But it won't let go of me. There isn't a day that goes by that I don't think about it. My only son and his wife. And you, left all alone now."

"I'm not saying don't grieve for them. I do. But it was an accident. It shouldn't have happened, but it did. And it was terrible for them and for you and me. But we can't turn back the clock. And you should not be beating yourself up about it either."

"Easier said than done. This . . . I'm sorry, my girl. This has brought it all back." Jack rubbed his forehead as if to chase the images away. "What if they find something that proves I picked a poisonous plant? What then?"

"I don't know, Jack. I don't have an answer to that one. But if they do find anything, there's got to be another explanation. We'll have some answers soon. I know we will." She cringed, knowing that Nate could very well be on his way with the news of the autopsy findings.

Jack nodded and took a deep breath. "It's only three bells, but I think I might call it a day, if that's okay with you."

"That's fine. This has been pretty upsetting, and I'm so sorry. You didn't deserve this. Want me to walk with you?"

Jack rose to his feet. "No. You're needed here. I'll be all right." Jack stood slowly. He opened the office door and headed down the hallway to the back entrance. Lucky watched him from the doorway. His shoulders had slumped. His head was downcast. She hated to see him leave the Spoonful in such a state, but she couldn't think what more she could say to erase the scene that had just transpired.

Chapter 26

LUCKY HEARD HER name called as she walked toward Elm Street and the library. Pastor Wilson from the Congregational Church was hurrying toward her. His thin sandy hair, blown by the wind, stood at attention. He wore a faded corduroy jacket with patches on the elbows and carried a stack of books.

He was breathless as he caught up. "Lucky! How are you? Are you on your way to the library, by any chance?"

"Yes. I'm taking a quick break from the restaurant. Are you headed there too?"

Pastor Wilson always had the air of having forgotten something essential and being on the verge of remembering what it was. He reached up and plastered his thinning hair over his head. The breeze immediately blew it up again.

"Could I ask a favor of you? I'm late for an appointment with a parishioner but I wanted to bring these books over to the library for their drive."

"I'm on my way to see Emily, but I'm happy to take them."

"Phew. That's a relief. Thank you, my dear." He lifted the stack into Lucky's arms. "They're heavy, I'm afraid."

"No problem at all."

"I'm not myself these days. Not after hearing about those women in the woods. A terrible thing! I don't know what they were thinking. It's not right. It's just not right that they—and Cordelia of all people—should be dabbling in paganism. I was horrified when I heard about it! It's an insult to organized religion! It's downright . . ." Pastor Wilson looked as if he were about to splutter, becoming more agitated the more he spoke of it. "Barbaric. That's what it is. Don't you agree?" He looked intently at Lucky.

"Well, I think they were inspired by the travelers who were here last fall. I don't think any of them were thinking of undermining anything."

"Hmm. Well, I plan to have a word with Cordelia Rank in the very near future." He drew himself up to his full height. Lucky tried to imagine Pastor Wilson arguing with the formidable Cordelia Rank. Unless she had underestimated his agitation on the subject, she didn't think he'd stand a chance against Cordelia.

"Sorry, Lucky. I didn't mean to bend your ear. I've just been so upset about all this. I do have to run, though." He started to turn away and then turned back. "Oh, one other thing . . . Please remind Sophie and Sage they shouldn't wait until the last minute to book my time. I need to arrange my schedule in advance, you know."

"Oh." Lucky sighed. Pastor Wilson must be certain he would be asked to perform Sophie and Sage's wedding ceremony. She didn't have the heart to tell him Sophie had arranged for a justice of the peace from Lincoln Falls. It had never occurred to Lucky, but now that she thought about it, Pastor Wilson would be devastated he hadn't been asked to officiate. "I'll mention it to both of them as soon as I can."

"Thank you. Thank you. Must run." He turned away and half walked, half ran down the street, his jacket flapping behind him. Lucky watched his loping stride until he turned the corner.

She shook her head, imagining Sophie's reaction to this conversation. Why did weddings have to get so complicated?

Shifting the stack of books in her arms, she turned around and walked the length of the block to the Snowflake Library. The small cottage home had been left to the town by its former inhabitants. Emily Rathbone, a retired teacher, manned the library most days with the help of various volunteers, the industrious Greta Dorn being the most recent of Emily's helpers.

She entered and spotted stacks of gently used books on the long table in the front hallway. She called out, "Emily?"

"Back here," came an answering voice.

Lucky followed the hallway to a rear room, once a bedroom, used now as a storeroom and mending workshop. Emily was seated at a table with glasses halfway down her nose, working on a torn binding under a strong light. She looked up quickly.

"Oh, Lucky! Hello. Good to see you." Emily smiled.

"You look busy."

"Not a problem. Come on in and have a seat. Just struggling with gluing this binding together." She waved a hand in front of her nose. "So pungent, this glue. What can I do for you? Are those donations you have?"

"Yes. These are from Pastor Wilson. I ran into him on my way over. He was running late and had to head back."

"Wonderful! Just give me a second and I'll take them off your hands."

"I actually came by because I was hoping you could spare a few minutes to talk about the other night in the woods."

"Ugh." Emily grunted. "Not that again." She looked up. "I'm sorry. That's not aimed at you. It's just that I've gone over it and over it several times with Nate. And it was such a shock, I can tell you."

"I can imagine." Lucky heard a footstep behind her and turned to see who had come into the room. Greta stood on the threshold.

"Hi, Greta," Lucky said. "I haven't forgotten the drive. I've gone through some boxes in my closet and I'll bring over some books you might be able to use." Lucky stood. "These are from Pastor Wilson."

"Oh, thank you," she breathed. "That's very generous of you." She hesitated. "Anything else I can do today, Emily?"

"No. Thanks so much for organizing all that stuff. I'll be around for a few hours, so you go on ahead. I'll see you tomorrow."

Greta seemed to waver in the doorway as though unsure she could trust Emily's decision. Finally, she said, "All right. Tomorrow, then." She turned away, her footsteps echoing down the hallway. The front door closed behind her.

"She's such a big help. This library drive has been a lot of work, but we've added to our inventory. People have been wonderful about donating. Greta's done most of the work. Trudging around town with flyers and picking up books." Emily secured the book she was working on with a clamp. "There. That should do it. Lovely binding. What did you want to talk to me about?"

"It's not just idle curiosity, Emily. My grandfather has been very worried that he might have made a mistake, giving Cecily the wrong plant that could have caused Agnes's reaction. I'm positive he didn't, but he's been torturing himself with the thought. I just wanted to ask you if you know how the wine was brewed."

Emily sighed. "Nate's been asking the very same thing. You see, this was all Cordelia's idea, really. And it did seem like something novel and fun to do. She had found a recipe for May wine which is used in May Day celebrations and she wanted to pass that around during our festivities." Emily shot a quick look at Lucky. "Nothing really pagan, mind you—no bonfires or orgies—just rather a women's gathering. We've been meeting here and reading up on goddess-based religions, so that's sort of how the idea started. I think we were all inspired by the travelers and all the stories about the ancient stones."

Lucky sat down on the chair by the worktable. "Did it seem as though Agnes was reacting to an allergen or poison of some sort?"

Emily stared off in the distance. "At first, I did think so. Her behavior seemed to have the earmarks of some sudden reaction. But then, I know stroke victims sometimes suffer vomiting. I'm not a scientist, so I really can't say. I don't even think the police or coroner knew for sure, although they were suspicious of it."

"They're analyzing the wine, aren't they?"

"Oh, yes, I'm sure they are."

"How was it made, do you know?"

"Cordelia took care of that. She soaked the herbs in the wine overnight and then brought it with her to our . . . ritual. No one else, just Cordelia. I think the police took what was left of the wine that night. Cordelia's very upset about this, as you can imagine."

"But Cordelia . . . Wouldn't she have been the first to drink?"

"No. I can't remember the order we were supposed to be in. I was after Cecily and before Willa."

"Willa?"

"Willa Persley. You might not know her. She lives up in Lincoln Heights." Emily continued, "Anyway, we were all assigned our places so the cup would move clockwise. Cordelia decided she should be the"—Emily blushed slightly—"high priestess. This all sounds rather silly when I actually put it into words, but at the time, it seemed to fit the occasion."

"So Agnes was the first to drink the mulled wine?"

"Yes. But, Lucky, no one could have planned to hurt Agnes. We were all prepared to drink the wine. Whatever plants Cecily brought were what Cordelia put in the wine to flavor it."

Lucky sighed. This was getting her nowhere. Every question she asked seemed to get her right back to square one. No one but Cecily and Cordelia had access to Jack's herbs, and she was sure neither woman would wish to harm Agnes Warner. She rose from her chair. "Thanks, Emily."

Emily looked at her sympathetically. "I wish I could give you a better answer. Jack shouldn't take this upon himself. It's much more likely she had a reaction to some medication."

Lucky turned to go and hesitated. She turned back. "One more question, Emily."

"Yes?"

"Who were the other women there that night?" Lucky was afraid she was straining the librarian's patience.

"I gave all the names to Nate." Emily sighed. "Let me get you our roster. I guess there's no harm in giving you one of these. All the women got one. This has all our names and addresses and phone numbers. Cordelia originally wanted twelve women plus herself to make thirteen, but unfortunately, we couldn't get enough women interested in the group. So, it was only myself, Cordelia, uh, Cecily and the other four." Emily turned and opened a side drawer in her desk and pointed to the names.

Lucky read it over Emily's shoulder. In large lettering at the top it stated "*Snowflake Coven*." Underneath that in slightly smaller lettering, "*Beltane Eve Celebration*." A brief description of the rituals of May Day and Walpurgisnacht followed by a list of seven names, including Cordelia Rank at the top; the rest were alphabetized.

Lucky glanced over the information. Other than Emily, Cordelia, Cecily, Agnes and Greta, there were two other women whose names she didn't recognize. "So Greta was also part of your group?"

Emily smiled. "She was. But under duress, you might say. She was commandeered to make a seventh. She really had no interest. I'm sure she thinks we're all crazy."

"And Willa is the one who lives in Snowflake, I see."

"Yes. Lucinda Nolan's from Lincoln Falls. She drives over occasionally for our meetings. I'm sure after this, we'll never see *her* again."

"Was Agnes close or particularly friendly with any of these people?"

Emily shook her head. "I don't believe so. I'm not even sure I ever saw her chatting with anyone. And I'm sure Agnes never knew them before we all got together. I doubt she had time to make anyone's acquaintance. That husband of hers was always in his car outside when the meeting drew to a close, and poor Agnes seemed terrified that she might be late and keep him waiting. Why are you asking?"

Lucky shook her head. "I don't know, really. Do you think any of *them* could have tampered with the wine or with the herbs?"

"Oh, heavens, no. None of us touched anything. Cordelia brought the wine in a container and poured it into the cauldron herself. You're thinking one of them might have had some ax to grind with Agnes?"

"I just think it's strange, Emily. Agnes lived right outside of town for years, but I don't know anyone who really knew her or was friendly with her."

"Between you and me, I think that's why she came to our women's group. I think she was lonely. Looked to me like her husband ran a very tight ship. She always seemed afraid of her own shadow. She was out there with a little boy and her husband and nothing really to do all day except cook and keep house." Emily thought for a moment. "Actually, I think there was something odd between Willa and Agnes. Willa made an effort to strike up a conversation with Agnes at one meeting, but Agnes was rather cold to her. I don't know what that was about."

"Interesting. Maybe I'll try to have a chat with her."

"What are you hoping to find out?"

Lucky ran her finger down the list of names. "I'm not sure. But I am curious."

Chapter 27

LUCKY HAD RETURNED to the Spoonful with more questions and fewer answers. If Emily was correct, none of the women present had a prior relationship with Agnes Warner. If she excluded Cordelia and Cecily, and Emily herself, that left three women who may have had access to the wine in spite of what everyone had sworn. And one of those might have had a grudge against Agnes. Lucky folded the flyer and stuck it into the pocket of her slacks. She grabbed a fresh apron and took over the counter from Janie.

"I just don't get it, Lucky." Sophie sipped her iced tea, twisting her legs around the stool at the counter.

"What's that?" Lucky asked as she cleared away dishes and wiped down the counter.

"Why Rick was so squirrelly last night. I can't help but suspect he's working some deal with the Resort and I'm gonna get left out in the cold." Sophie had arrived earlier that morning and had been helping Sage prepare orders all day. The dinner rush had just ended and now she was taking a well-earned break.

Lucky leaned over the counter. "Well, he can't cut you

out. You're both heirs to that property, right? Any deal the Resort made would have to include you."

"Yeees," Sophie replied hesitantly. "But what if the Resort offers him a lot of money for the parcel the house is on, more than Sage and I could offer him?"

"Well . . ." Lucky thought for a moment. "Let's say he sold his fifty percent interest in that parcel to them. In order to completely own it, you'd have to buy them out, right?"

"And they'd demand way more than I could pay." She heaved a sigh. "This is making me very nervous. Rick is up to something."

"You're making this far too complicated. You could always trade for the land they want. They just want to extend the ski run; that's the crux of the matter."

"Right. Believe me, I know those ski runs like the back of my hand. And they need that land. They don't need the acreage the house is on."

Lucky leaned across the counter. "Sophie, what do *you* want to get out of this?"

"I just want to buy Rick out of the house and the land around it. I really don't care about anything else. I want to be lighting a fire in my very own fireplace that my grandfather built. I couldn't care less about what ski runs the Resort wants to carve out. And if I could get Rick to see reason, selling that would give both of us money. Sage and I could buy Rick out and we'd have plenty of money to remodel that house. The way things are, I'm stuck. Rick won't give me a definite answer about anything. Why, I don't know. It just doesn't make any sense. And I refuse to sell the house and the land around it. Right now it's a stalemate. Rick says he won't sell that portion and I won't sell the other."

"Has he explained why he's so adamant about that?"

"No. That's just it. He shows up, no warning—after we think he might be dead. He disappears again and won't return any calls. I've left messages for him up at the Resort. He's ignoring me. I know he is."

Lucky sighed. She didn't want to voice an opinion, but Rick struck her as a very practical, no-nonsense sort of man.

He must have a reason for his decision. Was he holding out for more money? Maybe there was some way she could talk to him—away from Sophie. Maybe she could get to the bottom of this and help a friend. He just might be more open with her than he would be with his own sister.

"Oh, I almost forgot to tell you," Lucky said.

"What?"

"I ran into Pastor Wilson on my way to the library earlier. Sophie"—Lucky leaned across the counter—"he thinks he's doing the honors at your wedding. He reminded me that you have to talk to him because he doesn't want his schedule to fill up."

"You are kidding me! Where did he ever get that idea? I haven't even talked to him for months and months. I never even see him around. And I certainly don't go to church." Sophie groaned. "I can't believe this. I'm getting a headache. Sage . . ." she called out. She spun off the stool and headed for the kitchen. A moment later Lucky heard murmurs from the kitchen. Sage was trying to calm Sophie down.

Lucky glanced up as the bell over the door jingled. Nate Edgerton. Her heart sank. Nate entered and glanced around the restaurant, his eyes lingering on Janie, who was at the cash register. Was he expecting to see Jack at his usual spot? Realizing he had Lucky's full attention, Nate stepped in and took a stool at the counter.

"What can I get you, Nate?" Lucky did her best to smile. "We have a really nice carrot ginger soup, a chicken tortilla with a tomato base, and a shrimp tofu today."

"Nothing, thanks, Lucky. I'm on my way home right now. I just stopped in hoping to see Jack. Is he here?"

Lucky shook her head. "He's been at home all day. We had a little . . . episode this morning with Leonard Warner. Jack was pretty upset; he left right after."

"What?" Nate looked concerned. Nate cared a great deal for Jack. They had become close when Nate's father had died. Lucky knew he wouldn't stand for anyone treating Jack badly. "What happened?"

Lucky grimaced. "Leonard came in and knocked some

things over and accused Jack of killing his wife. It was a pretty bad scene."

"Want me to have a word with Leonard?"

Lucky shook her head. "No. No need. We all jumped down his throat. Me and Barry. And Sage and Hank were ready to get involved if need be. Leonard finally left. I'm sure he's all torn up. In spite of what happened today, I feel really bad for him."

"Well, let me know if you change your mind. He had no business doing that."

"I will, but I honestly don't think he'd dare come back now."

"About the autopsy, Lucky. I should probably tell you first before I go see Jack."

"I know already, Nate," she admitted. "I haven't had the heart to tell Jack."

"How . . ." Nate looked at her questioningly. "Oh, never mind. Elias?"

Lucky nodded. "He came over last night to give me a heads-up. Nate, I just can't believe it. Jack really knows his plants. I just don't believe he could have made any kind of a mistake. I'd be willing to bet somebody tampered with those plants."

"We have nothing definite yet, so I'm not sure what to think either. Bottom line is Agnes died of a heart attack, but we still need to identify any possible toxin. If somebody wanted to harm Agnes, then we're looking at a premeditated action."

"You don't think Jack . . ." Lucky didn't continue.

"No, of course not." Nate spluttered. "No way. But, Lucky, I've talked to everyone involved, and they all swear no one had a chance to touch that basket of herbs from the time it left Jack's house until the time Cordelia poured the wine."

"I know. I've heard the same thing."

"But you don't believe it?"

"I can't believe it. If that's true, that no one else touched it, and a toxic substance is found, then Jack has made a terrible mistake that might have led to someone's death, and I don't know how he'll live with that."

Nate nodded. "It could hit him hard. But don't jump to any conclusions yet. First thing is to identify what the lab turns up; then we'd have to know if it could have been fatal. Maybe it led to her heart attack, but wouldn't have caused a problem with a healthy person. I'll be very kind, Lucky. Jack's house will be my next stop." He glanced at the kitchen hatch. "Is that Sophie I see?"

Lucky turned and looked into the kitchen. She nodded.

"Could I use your office for a few minutes? I'd like to talk to her in private."

"Of course."

Nate pushed through the swinging door to the corridor and gestured to Sophie to follow him.

Sage caught Lucky's eye as if to ask what was happening. Lucky shook her head and shrugged to indicate she had no idea why Nate wanted to talk to Sophie.

A few minutes later, Sophie returned to the kitchen and Nate waved to Lucky as he left by the front door. Sophie leaned through the hatch. "Come in the kitchen for a sec, Lucky."

Lucky nodded and pushed through the door. Sophie stood at the worktable. "I might as well tell you both at the same time. Nate got the DNA result. It was no match, of course, but Rick has identified his partner's body."

"How?" Lucky asked.

"Eddie had a unique tattoo. Rick was with him when he got it. That's how he could be sure."

"Whew," Sage remarked. "That's tough."

"I know," Sophie said. "Maybe that's why he hasn't gotten back to me."

OVER THE NEXT few hours, Lucky filled several more orders at the counter, keeping an eye on the clock. As the sun set, she felt a mounting sense of anxiety. The restaurant wasn't busy right now, although several customers still lingered.

Hopefully Sophie could help her out. She had a gut instinct that she should head for Jack's house and make sure he was all right. She walked into the kitchen where Sophie was seated on a stool, watching Sage add spices to a pot.

"What's up, Lucky?" Sophie's mood seemed much lighter. Sage had obviously calmed her down.

"Can you cover the counter for me in a little while? I want to check on Jack."

"Oh, sure," Sophie answered. "Are you worried about him?"

"I am." Lucky took a deep breath. "I haven't had a minute to talk to either of you today, but you should know." She filled them in on the results of the autopsy to date.

"Oh no!" Sophie exclaimed. "That can't be."

"It's not looking good, but there are no firm results yet. Don't get me wrong. I still don't believe Jack made a mistake. But Nate went to his house earlier, and if Jack hears this, it could just do him in. He was in tough shape after what happened with Leonard Warner this morning."

Sophie climbed down from the high stool. "Go now. Don't worry about the restaurant. Everyone's here, except for Jack. We can take care of closing up if you need us to. We'll be fine."

"She's right, Lucky. You go on. We'll cover everything," Sage said.

"You're the best—both of you. Thank you!" She pulled off her apron and hurried down the hall to the office. She flung her apron over the chair and grabbed her purse, slinging it over her shoulder, then hurried out the back door.

WHEN LUCKY REACHED Birch Street and Jack's front porch, she was dismayed to see the windows dark. Nate had undoubtedly come and gone, but where was Jack? She peered down the driveway. Jack's car was parked in front of the garage, so he hadn't driven anywhere. Could he have gone for a walk and not come back yet?

She rang the doorbell and knocked on the door. No answer. She peered through the glass of the front door but

could see no light at the rear of the house. She kicked herself
for not going back to her apartment where she kept an emergency key to Jack's house. She didn't want to intrude on his
privacy, but if he was out, he'd never know she had used her
key. There had to be another way. She hurried down the
front steps and walked around to the rear of the house. She
thought she heard noises as she stood on tiptoe and tried to
peek through the kitchen window. The curtain was still open
but the room was dark. She wasn't able to see anything
inside. Then she heard it, thumps and banging and Jack's
voice crying out. He was inside, somewhere in the dark. She
had to find a way in.

*Jack knew it was happening . . . again. This time he couldn't
seem to block out the screams. He was on the boat, rising
and falling in the sea. The water was purple with blood and
the smell . . . It was in his nose, in his eyes; he'd never be
able to get rid of it. A hand reached up from the dark waters.
Jack grasped it and held on with all his strength. Then the
swift rush of a sleek monster, the quick glimpse of the
shark's fin, and the man was gone. He was grasping a dis-
embodied arm. Jack screamed. The sharks! The sharks!
While all around him were the cries of men being torn to
pieces. He sobbed. He couldn't help them, no matter how
quick he was, no matter how strong. He wasn't fast enough
to save them.*

Lucky hurried back to the window closest to the kitchen
table. She knew the lock was broken. The window was shut
tight, but if she could reach up, she was sure she could gain
entrance. She pushed with all her strength. It wouldn't
budge. She didn't have enough leverage from this position.
She needed to get higher and closer to the window. She
needed something to stand on.

She ran to the back garden and dragged a heavy wooden
lawn chair around to the side of the house. Two windows
and French doors looked out to Jack's rear deck, a recent
renovation, but Lucky knew those windows were secure,

and she hoped not to have to break a windowpane to get in. Once the lawn chair was in place, she climbed onto the heavy arms. She was able to stand almost at the same height as the window. She reached up and pushed. The window resisted. Using the heel of her hand, she banged heavily on the wood frame. Moisture had caused it to stick. She pushed hard again and this time it shot open all the way. Balancing carefully on the back of the lawn chair, she threw her purse in ahead of her and climbed up. She slithered head first through the kitchen window, landing on her side on the floor. She stood and flicked on the kitchen light.

Jack's moans were louder now. She reached the hallway and called his name. He was in the bathroom. She hit the light switch and knocked on the door. "Jack. It's me. Open the door."

The moaning continued. Lucky jiggled the knob. He had locked himself in. A sob caught in her throat. He must have realized what was happening and barricaded himself in, in an effort to control the memories. The door was an old-fashioned wooden one with a flimsy lock. She had to get it open and try to calm him down. The sound of glass shattering came from within. Then a heavy pounding. What if Jack hurt himself? There were so many dangerous things in a bathroom.

She hurried to the kitchen and grabbed a small thin knife from the wooden block next to the stove. Running back, she knelt in front of the door. Sliding the edge of the blade into the doorframe, she wiggled the knife back and forth carefully to release the latch. A heavy thud hit the door and Lucky fell back in shock, the knife falling from her hands. Her heart was racing and her hands were sweating. She wiped her hands on her slacks and pushed the knife into the crack again. Wiggling the blade, she felt the metal tongue that held the door. The lock released. She dropped the knife and cracked the door open a few inches. She saw a shadow, seated on the floor next to the old claw-foot bathtub. Jack's hands covered his face. He was sobbing. She reached around the jamb and flicked on the light, illuminating the room.

Jack shouted and jumped to his feet. He made a lunge for the doorway where Lucky stood. He didn't realize who she was. He was lost in his nightmare. She pulled the door shut quickly and felt it shudder as his body hit the other side of the wood. There had been blood on the floor and Jack was bleeding profusely from a cut on his arm. He continued to shout and pound on the door. She raced to the front hallway and with shaking fingers dialed Elias's number at home. He answered on the third ring.

"Can you come over to Jack's house right away?"

"What's going on? What's that noise?"

"It's Jack. He's having an attack. I can't reach him. And he's cut himself somehow."

"Be there in five minutes. I'll stop at the clinic for medication."

Lucky returned to the doorway. Jack was quieter now. She knelt on the floor and called his name.

"Jack. It's me. Lucky. You're okay. You're home. You're in Snowflake. All that's gone away now. There's nothing to be afraid of."

She could hear murmuring from within. Maybe it would be safe to open the door again. Light spilled through a space at the bottom of the door. Erring on the side of caution, she turned on the outside light and unlocked Jack's front door. Elias would be able to walk right in when he arrived. She returned to the bathroom door and opened it slowly. Jack was seated on the floor. Blood had dripped into the bathtub and a small pool had formed on the floor. It was smeared across his face where he had rubbed his head. Broken glass was everywhere. The contents of the medicine cabinet had spilled onto the floor. Lucky carefully picked up the larger pieces and tossed them in the sink. She grabbed a small towel from the rack and wrapped it around the cut on Jack's arm.

"It's okay now, Jack. It's over. You're safe. You just have to stay still."

He looked into her eyes, confused. "Lucky?"

"Yes, I'm here."

"What happened?" he whispered.

"You had a spell, but you're okay now. Elias is on his way."

Tears spilled down Jack's face. "I'm sorry. I'm so sorry."

"Nothing to be sorry about. Everything's going to be all right now." She prayed her words would make it true.

She heard Elias's car pull into the driveway and, a few seconds later, his steps across the threshold and down the hall.

"Let me give you a hand," he said. Lucky stood aside while Elias helped Jack to his feet. He glanced sympathetically at Lucky, as if to acknowledge how badly she had been frightened. "Let's get him into the bedroom and I'll patch up his arm. Can you make some tea with lots of sugar?"

"Sure," she replied and hurried to the kitchen to put the teakettle on. When the water had boiled and the tea was ready, she carried it to the bedroom on a tray with some cookies she had found in the cupboard. Elias sat in the chair next to Jack's bed. He had helped him undress. Jack was now in his pajamas and the cut on his arm was bandaged. He was sitting up, propped up with two pillows, but looking very pale. Lucky sat on the other side of the bed and rested the tray on Jack's lap.

"I'm sorry, my girl. I didn't mean to frighten you. It just came over me."

"I know. I walked over 'cause I was worried. I know Nate's been here." She glanced at Elias. "Nate told me he was coming round to see Jack. I should have come with him. It's my fault. I knew this would hit Jack hard. I shouldn't have waited so long."

Elias shook his head slightly to indicate it was best not to talk about anything just yet. "I gave Jack a sleeping pill. And I think if he has trouble sleeping over the next few nights, it might be a good idea to take one before bedtime. It'll help him relax, which is what he needs right now. That and those cookies and tea. His blood sugar's probably low too—that's not going to help."

Lucky supported the heavy cup as Jack sipped it slowly. He broke off a piece of the cookie and placed it in his mouth. "I don't wanna be a burden to you two."

"You're never a burden, Jack. Don't even say that."

"It's no trouble," Elias replied. "We're all vulnerable. It's okay to ask for help. That's what family and friends are for."

Jack finished the cookie and almost all of the sugary tea. His eyelids were closing. Lucky took his cup and placed the remaining cookies on a napkin at the bedside table. She turned on the night-light on the bureau. It was a small white porcelain lamp of a man and woman waltzing. She smiled to see that Jack had kept it all these years, the silly lamp her grandmother had loved. She turned off the lamp next to the bed and covered Jack with a light blanket and spread. She eased one of the pillows from under his head. He was fast asleep already. Elias stood and carried the tray out to the kitchen.

Chapter 28

LUCKY COLLAPSED IN a chair at the kitchen table. She was completely drained and emotionally exhausted. She rubbed her temples and finally rested her head on her hands. She heard Elias's steps behind her and then felt his warm hands on her shoulders. He massaged her neck until her tense muscles began to relax. She breathed deeply. He leaned over and kissed the top of her head.

"Can I get you something? A glass of wine?"

She felt laughter burbling inside her.

"What's so funny?" Elias's hands were still.

"Don't stop. That feels wonderful." She sighed. "Jack wouldn't allow a bottle of wine in his house. He thinks it's for sissies. I'll make us some more tea." She rose from the chair and added water to the kettle.

"That's even better." Elias watched her carefully as she moved around the kitchen. "It was bad tonight?"

She turned and nodded. "Very."

"I'm sorry. I wish I'd been with you."

"It's okay, really. I was worried about him all day and especially after Nate turned up. I sort of had a feeling all this recent stuff, Leonard attacking and threatening him like that . . ."

"What's that?" Elias looked concerned.

"It happened this morning at the Spoonful." She filled Elias in on the confrontation. "Then Nate talking to him about the autopsy results. I had a feeling this might happen—might set him off. I was able to talk him down a bit before you got here." She turned and smiled. "Thank you."

"For what?" he asked.

"For being there. Being there for me—for both of us."

"Of course."

They fell silent as Lucky poured the boiling water over the chamomile tea. She carried the mugs to the table and passed the sugar bowl to Elias, knowing he liked to sweeten his tea.

"Can I walk you home?"

She shook her head. "I think I should stay here tonight—just in case."

"I'll stay with you."

"I appreciate the offer." She reached over to touch his hand. "Really, I do, but you'll feel better if you get a good night's sleep. I can crash on the sofa. Jack has a second bedroom, but he uses it as an office, so there's no extra bed."

"Ah. Rejected again."

"Stop that." Lucky laughed.

"That's better—you're smiling." He studied her face.

"Oh, I totally forgot."

"What?"

"I left the lawn chair by the window outside. That's how I got in. I should drag it back."

"I'll get it. You stay here." Elias left by the kitchen door. She heard him outside the window, grunting as he lifted the heavy chair. A minute later he returned.

Elias took a sip of his tea. "Jack will be fine. This has been a bad time for him, but I'm sure he'll get over it."

"Not if he thinks he gave those women something poisonous, he won't. And I know he didn't. He doesn't trust himself as much as I trust him. He wouldn't make that kind of mistake."

"What do you think happened, then?"

Lucky glanced at him quickly to reassure herself he wasn't being dismissive. She was afraid he might laugh at her suspicions. "I think someone tampered with that basket of herbs. I think Agnes was a target; her death was not an accident."

Elias stared at her. "What? Why?"

Lucky leaned across the table and took his hand in hers. "You saw those photos my mother took. I think the Warners were deliberately avoiding the camera. And the dates that were written on the back—one was October tenth with an exclamation mark."

Elias nodded. "I remember."

"Look, I don't know what it means, but it means something. Jack remembers that my mother was going on about something at one point in time. When she got an idea in her head, she wouldn't let it go. And he said that my dad told her to leave it alone, to mind her own business." Lucky tested her tea. It had finally cooled down enough to drink. "I think she knew something, or she suspected something about the Warners, but I don't know what it was."

"Well, maybe the date is significant. Something happened on that date that she connected to that family. How we'd go about figuring out what that was, I don't have the slightest idea."

Lucky was heartened to hear Elias use the word "we." He hadn't dismissed her suspicions but was giving them a fair hearing.

"I've been thinking about it a lot and maybe I'm on to something—something that might clear Jack. It might not explain how some toxin ended up in that wine, if it really did, but at least it would prove that Agnes was a target. I just know there's an explanation that doesn't involve Jack."

"Right now, you need to get some rest. Come on, I'll help you make up a bed. Maybe it's a good idea for you to spend the night, in case Jack wakes up or feels confused." He followed her down the hall and helped her lift blankets out of the linen closet. Grabbing one end, he spread one out over the sofa cushions and watched as she kicked off her shoes. "Since you're kicking me out, at least walk me to the door and give me a good-night kiss."

Lucky smiled. "Of course." She wrapped her arms around his neck and clung to him as he kissed her tenderly.

"Good night. Sleep tight and lock the door after me."

Lucky watched him as he walked down the path to the drive where his car was parked. He gave her a quick wave, then climbed in and drove away.

Lucky walked through the house, making sure all the windows and doors were locked. She rinsed out the mugs that she and Elias had used and then remembered the mess in the bathroom. No rest for the weary, she thought. Once all the medications had been replaced in the cabinet and the broken glass cleaned up, she scrubbed and rinsed the tub and mopped the floor, cleaning up any trace of glass and blood. Tears threatened to come as she thought of Jack and how much he still suffered. How much did he keep to himself and not tell her? When she finished and the bathroom and its contents were back in place, she peeked in the doorway of Jack's bedroom. He was fast asleep and snoring gently. She breathed a sigh of relief and collapsed on the sofa in Jack's office, kicking off her shoes.

She was still too wired to sleep. She picked up a book from the shelf. It was one she had read years before but she didn't care. She opened it to the first page and started to read. Before she knew it, her eyes had closed and the book had fallen to the floor. The sound caused her to jump. She reached down and put the book on the table next to her. She should take off her slacks and blouse and try to get some sleep but a feeling that there was something left undone bothered her. She tiptoed through the house. Everything seemed fine. A night-light burned in the kitchen. She shivered, and closed the curtains at the window. She felt plagued by an unsettled feeling. She walked the length of the hallway to the front door. The hallway was dark and the outside light was off. With a hint of moonlight she could clearly see the sidewalk in front of Jack's house.

Someone stood there. A shadow. The hairs on the back of her neck rose. She reached over to the hallway table and quietly slid a drawer open. She grasped the flashlight that Jack kept there. She carefully turned the knob of the front door and stepped outside. She flicked on the light and shone it at the man who stood there. Leonard Warner's face was clearly lit. He blinked and turned away from the light, then turned back to stare at her. Their eyes locked. She could feel the red anger that emanated from the man. She took a step forward, wanting him to know she wasn't afraid of him and wouldn't stand for his behavior. Leonard turned away and walked quickly down Birch Street. She shuddered and breathed deeply, aware now that she had been holding her breath. Perhaps she would have a word with Nate after all.

Suddenly the night closed in and a wave of anxiety tinged with loneliness swept through her. Did Jack ever feel like this? Living all alone in his cottage, his wife gone, his only child dead? She was all her grandfather had to live for. She had to make sure he was looked after. She stepped back inside the house and locked the door behind her.

Chapter 29

"I SWEAR, THIS is the last time I'll put you through this," Lucky said.

Sophie stood patiently as Lucky lifted the gown over her head and zipped up the side of the elegant dress. Sophie wiggled her shoulders to ease the gown on. The material whispered softly as she moved. "You're not bugging me. I love you for doing this. You know I'd never find anything I'd like, much less spend the money on. An expensive dress is just not me. I'd rather buy outdoor gear." She jiggled her legs. "I want to look in the mirror. Let me see."

"Not yet." Lucky planted her foot firmly in front of the bedroom door so Sophie wouldn't push it closed, revealing the full-length mirror on the inside. She propped it open with a doorstop. "Close your eyes," Lucky ordered.

Sophie obediently squeezed her eyes shut.

"Now wait!" Lucky moved to the bed and pulled the cover off the hatbox. Lifting out the circlet of pearls, she gently fitted it on Sophie's head, sweeping the length of veil away from her face.

Sophie continued to squeeze her eyes shut.

"Okay. Now you can look." Lucky pushed the doorstop away and closed the door, revealing the full-length mirror. Sophie opened her eyes.

Her face fell as she gazed at her reflection. She was silent, her eyes wide.

Lucky watched her closely. "What's wrong?" she whispered. "Don't you like it?"

Sophie shook her head. Tears came to her eyes. "It's so beautiful. And it's all so real now." She shivered involuntarily.

"Of course it is," Lucky answered. "It's really happening."

Sophie turned and flung her arms around Lucky, hugging her tightly. "How can I ever thank you?"

Lucky laughed. "No need. Just seeing you looking absolutely gorgeous is thanks enough. And you do. You look incredible."

"Is this really happening? Sage and I will be married? And we'll have a family if we're lucky? And it will all turn out perfectly for us?" she asked in all sincerity.

"Yes. It will. You both deserve a happy life. With all the blessings."

"Oh, Lucky, we've both come from such terrible poverty as children. I want to believe we can create everything we weren't given. I think I'm just afraid to believe that."

Lucky took her friend by the shoulders. "Look at me." Lucky stared directly into Sophie's eyes. "You can. You have that chance now. Don't let fear get in your way."

Sophie nodded mutely.

"So?" Lucky turned Sophie back to the mirror and smiled. There was no doubt in her mind that the dress couldn't have turned out better, and the circlet of pearls and the veil against Sophie's hair added just the right touch. "What do you think?"

"I love it. I never in a million years ever thought I would wear something so beautiful."

"I can't wait till Sage sees you on your wedding day. He'll faint." Lucky laughed. "Okay. Let's get you out of it, shoes and all, and I'll bring it over to Jack's house the day before with everything you'll need. It's best, I think, for you to change there and get ready before Sage arrives." Lucky thought for a moment. "Are you superstitious? Do you think Sage should spend the night before somewhere else? You know the old saw about not seeing the bride on the wedding day until the ceremony?"

Sophie shook her head. "Nah. I don't believe in any of that stuff. Not seeing the dress, okay, I agree with that. But I think I'll be a lot calmer if we're together the night before."

"Okay. Fine with me. It's whatever you want. It's your day." Lucky hung the dress on a padded hanger and then, over it, a protective garment cover. She carefully replaced the circlet of pearls and the veil in the hatbox.

"And speaking of tying the knot, what about you and Elias?" Sophie watched her friend carefully as she pulled her jeans back on.

"Oh, I don't know." Lucky could feel the blush creeping up her cheeks. "We haven't really talked about anything like that."

"Why not?" Sophie persisted.

"Well, neither one of us has actually brought it up. Don't forget, we were on the verge of a total breakup a few months ago."

Sophie quickly counted on her fingers. "Seven months ago. That's a huge amount of time."

Lucky smiled. "Not really."

"Aren't you the one always telling me not to let fear get to me? Is that what it is? You're a scaredy-cat?"

"I don't know." Lucky shrugged. "I know how Elias feels about me, and I feel the same way about our relationship. I think there must come a point when it just happens naturally; don't you think? That moment when you know it's the right thing to do?"

"Sure. But you maybe need to talk to each other about it. Maybe you're just too comfortable with the way things are. Maybe you're afraid of making a big change in your life."

"I'm not afraid," Lucky replied defensively. "That's silly."

"Oh yeah?" Sophie responded sarcastically.

"I just can't picture it, Sophie. Is that strange? I mean, Elias and I love each other, definitely, but being *married*? That's such a big step. It feels so . . . responsible."

"You're very *responsible*. I don't get what the issue is. The only thing that would really change in your life is you'd have to give up your apartment. And maybe you'd change your last name. You'd be Mrs. Letitia Scott."

"That's what I mean. It's like morphing into another identity. Maybe there are more things that would change in my life that I wouldn't like. And besides, who are you to stand there and lecture me? Mrs. DuBois-to-be?"

"You're right. I'm nobody to lecture anybody. I'm sort of scared myself. But I guess we all hope and pray for the best when we make these decisions. And hope it turns out all right."

"Well, I'm thrilled you and Sage have taken that step. You're my two favorite people in the world, along with Jack and Elias." Lucky tied the cord around the hatbox and placed it on top of the bureau. "You up for a glass of wine?"

"Absolutely."

"Finish getting dressed and I'll get some cheese and crackers ready."

Lucky went to the kitchen and prepared a tray with a variety of crackers and two different cheeses. She carried the tray with a chilled bottle of wine and two glasses down the hallway into the living room and placed it on the coffee table.

Sophie followed a moment later. She spotted the cardboard box next to the table and peered inside. "Are these the photos you mentioned? The ones your mom took?"

"Yes." Lucky was glad she had brought the photo of the two of them to the pharmacy to have it sent away and copied. She didn't want to give away her surprise bridesmaid's gift. "Have a look," she said as she uncorked the wine and poured two glasses. "The ones in the large envelope are the photos of the Warners. I want you to see them. Tell me what strikes you."

Sophie glanced at her quickly. "Is this a test?"

"Sort of."

Sophie popped a piece of cheese into her mouth and took a sip of wine. She laid the envelope on her lap and shook the enlargements out. Leaning back on the sofa cushions, she slowly reviewed each one. She reached over to the coffee table and moved the tray to the side, laying the photos out in a long line.

"What do you think?"

"I think . . ." Sophie heaved a sigh. "I don't know what to say. They just look like photos that didn't turn out."

"Sophie, it would be very difficult to take so many unusable photos. You can see there was movement as the shutter clicked, see the blurriness here and here," Lucky said, pointing to two different photos. "I know what my mom used to do. She'd pick out a table or two and ask the people to look up and smile. She was never rude or intrusive. So I'm sure that's what she did here. She wouldn't just snap a candid shot, so they must have ignored her or deliberately looked away just in time."

"How long have the Warners lived here?" Sophie asked.

"I'm not sure. Just guessing, I'd say five or six years. I remember them from trips home. I don't think they ever lived in town. I can't be sure, but I think they bought a house a few miles away. Remember the small farmhouse out on the main road, before you get to the turnoff to Bournmouth?"

"A yellow house, set back a bit?"

"That's it. The owner had been a farmer and he couldn't work anymore so he started selling off the land. And I think the Warners bought it from him before he died. Or maybe they bought it from his kids after he died. The man's children weren't going to farm the land and they had already moved away to the city. I remember somebody talking about the owner years ago."

"Where did the Warners come from?"

Lucky shook her head and shrugged. "I have no idea. I think Leonard might have done some kind of handyman work, or he might have been retired by then. And they were raising Mike, their grandson."

"Where were Mike's parents?"

"They were gone. I assumed they were both dead. If I recall, there was a lot of sympathy toward the Warners. Their son had died or been killed, maybe in an accident or something, and his wife, the boy's mother, had died of some illness. But that's all I know. No one really knew any more details about their past."

"So Mike must be about what now? Ten? Older?"

"Maybe. Look at these pictures. He's a little kid here, looks like about five years old? So he must be ten or eleven by now. There's not one photo where you can actually see the little boy's face. You can see his arm, or a piece of him, but he's blocked in every single photo, either by his grandfather reaching across the table for something or standing right in front of him. And you can tell these were taken on different days; the clothing is different. They're only wearing the same outfits in two of these pictures."

"I noticed that too."

"My mother must have been determined to get their picture. She had to be suspicious of something. Suspicious of who they were, maybe, or do you think it could have been something criminal? Or did she think they were fugitives of some sort?"

Sophie shrugged. "I have no idea. But it's pretty hard to be fugitives with a five-year-old kid in tow, don't you think?"

"There's something else."

"What?"

Lucky described finding Leonard standing outside Jack's house in the dark.

"That's unbelievable!" Sophie exclaimed.

"I feel sorry for what happened. I really do. Even though I'm sure it wasn't Jack's fault. But last night . . . it was intimidation. I think he was hoping Jack would see him, not me. It's like he's trying to drive Jack around the bend, and last night . . . he almost succeeded."

"Poor Jack. I can't imagine what that must be like. All alone in the house, and he must have been aware it was coming on. It must be like a migraine or a—I don't know—like something happening to you that you can't control. So frightening." Sophie turned the photos in her hand over. "There are dates on the back."

"I know. All within the same month. But there's an exclamation point on one of them—October tenth. Somehow that date must have been very significant."

"What do you think it means?"

Lucky shook her head. "No idea. But it must mean something. Maybe there was something in the news on that date that sparked my mom's interest?"

"Hey, let's boot up your computer. Let's search that date. Maybe it is significant in some way. We would have been . . . what? Twenty-four, twenty-five then. I don't know about you, but I wasn't paying much attention to what went on in town."

"Me neither. I was a couple of years out of college and still living in Madison. I didn't even make trips home that often." Lucky walked across the room to the small desk where her computer sat. She clicked it on, and a few seconds later the screen came to life. She sat down in the desk chair. "Hey, why don't you grab the stool that's in the kitchen so we can do this together."

Sophie dashed to the kitchen and returned a moment later with a wooden stool. She moved closer to Lucky and watched as Lucky typed the date into her search engine. Immediately a link popped up offering popular stories of the *Lincoln Falls Sentinel*. Lucky clicked the mouse and scrolled through the highlights.

"Here's what we have: 'Court Adds Case to Census Review,' 'Signs of Hope Seen in Diplomatic Deal' . . ." She continued to read aloud the major international and national stories run by the newspaper.

"Nothing criminal?"

"Not that I can see. But that's only Lincoln Falls. And stories of state or national interest come from wire services, don't they? Maybe we should try farther afield. A larger city . . . maybe Boston or New York?"

"Okay, give it a shot. Their archives might be better." Sophie waited patiently while Lucky scrolled down the list of links. "Here we go . . . 'Deputies Crack Alleged Theft Ring.' 'Man Killed Wife with Friend's Help.' Lovely!" Sophie commented. "Oh, look," she said, pointing to the screen. 'Police Bust Drug Ring.' Maybe Leonard is a crook? Maybe Agnes was selling drugs?"

Lucky shook her head. "Can't really see that. But who knows? Truth is often stranger than fiction." She finished scrolling down the links to the stories in the newspaper. "October tenth could mean anything. Maybe my mother wrote it down because she heard a news story on the radio. Maybe she made a note of it because it wasn't in the local or national news."

"Let's Google their names. Agnes Warner and Leonard Warner."

"Okay." Lucky cleared the browser and began again with Leonard. "Well, here we go. There are fifteen profiles of men named Leonard Warner. Here's another reference to a Leonard Warner, internist."

"Oh," Sophie said. "Maybe he was a doctor and he was driven out of the medical profession for some crime?"

Lucky smiled at her friend. "You have a very active imagination!"

"Go down some more. There are images of Leonard Warner."

Lucky patiently clicked over each photo. "Any of these look like the Leonard we've seen?"

Sophie shook her head. "Nope. Maybe it's an alias."

"Well, they bought that house outside of town when they first arrived. It's a little hard to do that with an alias these days."

"Not if they bought it from the owner and paid cash, and never applied for a bank loan."

"Good point. They maybe wouldn't even have had to show identification if it was all done privately."

"Right. Why would the seller care? He's getting what he wants for his house. He wouldn't wonder if he was selling it to a criminal, for heaven's sake." Sophie sighed. "Let's try Agnes and Leonard Warner together."

"Okay." Lucky typed the names quickly and waited. "Hey, look at this."

"What?"

Lucky stared at the screen. "It's some kind of cemetery search. I never knew there was such a thing." She turned to Sophie. "We found an Agnes and Leonard Warner. They're both buried in Michigan if you can believe that. And they'd be over a hundred years old if they were still alive." Lucky shook her head. "This is getting us nowhere. They could really be Agnes and Leonard Warner and completely legitimate people. We're chasing our tails."

"I thought you wanted to do this for Jack," Sophie said.

"I do. I've just been so worried about him. And I really believe he did not make a mistake, but this is haunting him."

Sophie nodded in sympathy. "Let's try just Agnes."

"Okay," Lucky agreed. They sat silently in front of the computer screen as Lucky exhausted all the links that promised information on that name. Finally she sat back in her chair and heaved a sigh. "Nothing. Nothing that looks promising, anyway."

"Well, it was worth a try," Sophie replied, standing and carrying her stool back to the kitchen. "I better get home. Sage will be wondering what happened to me."

"He's not coming over?"

"No, but I promised to call him when I was ready to leave, and he'll meet me halfway."

"He's really worried about you, isn't he?"

"Too much so," Sophie answered, clicking open her phone. It rang immediately. Sophie stared at the caller ID.

"What's wrong?" Lucky asked.

Sophie shook her head. "Not a number I recognize." She hit the button. "Hello?" she said.

Lucky listened to one half of the conversation.

"Yes. What's wrong?" Sophie held up a finger to get

Lucky's attention. "I'm at my friend's apartment. Do you want to come here?" Sophie listened a moment and then said, "Okay. Let me write this down." She grabbed a pen and a pad of paper from the desk and made a quick note. Then she hung up.

"What's up? Was that Sage?"

Sophie shook her head. "It was Brenda. Remember her? We met her at the Resort."

Lucky nodded.

"She wants to talk to me. She says there are things I need to know before I come back to work."

"She didn't want to come here?"

"She says she's afraid. She thinks she might be followed."

"Whaaat?" Lucky asked. "By whom?"

Sophie looked troubled. "She wouldn't say. She sounds very wound up and said it was important."

"She gave you her address?"

Sophie nodded.

"Well, let's go see her. If something weird's going on, you shouldn't go alone."

"Okay. I'll call Sage on the way, let him know where we're going."

Chapter 30

LUCKY DROVE, FOLLOWING Sophie's instructions. Brenda rented a cabin with two other roommates near Ridgeline. Her roommates were both out of town and she was alone in the house. Sophie called Sage to tell him where they were headed. Following the one-sided conversation, Lucky was sure Sage was advising her to pick him up on the way if she was insistent on visiting a friend so late in the evening. Sophie reassured him that all would be fine and she would call him on their way home.

When they arrived at the address and pulled into the drive, the front door light came on. Brenda was waiting for them. They climbed out silently and approached the front door. It swung open immediately.

Brenda looked relieved. "Thank you for coming up here. And I'm sorry to be such a ninny, but I'm really nervous."

"What's going on?" Sophie asked.

"Come into the kitchen and I'll explain." They followed Brenda through a small living room filled with two over-stuffed sofas and several small tables. "This place came furnished," Brenda explained over her shoulder. "It's a nice little house, but I'm always nervous when I'm alone here. Have a seat," she said, indicating two stools at the counter. "Would you like a coffee . . . beer, anything?" she asked.

Lucky and Sophie both shook their heads negatively." Okay," Brenda said, taking a nervous breath. "I wanted to talk to you the other day at the Lodge, but when I saw Lurch hanging around in the hall watching us, I got nervous. He scares me."

"Has he ever threatened you?" Lucky asked.

Brenda shook her head. "No. Not directly. When he's around, there's something about him that's like . . . I guess an implied threat. You see, you might not be aware of this, working kinda independently as you do"—she addressed Sophie—"but we don't get overtime pay, and we're under pressure to work a lot of double shifts, especially when it's the busy season. Under state law, retail and service places, like hotels or restaurants, are exempt from having to pay time and a half, even though under federal law that's not the case."

"Really?" Sophie asked. She turned to Lucky. "Did you know that?"

Lucky nodded. "It doesn't affect us at the restaurant, but I was aware of it."

Brenda continued, "We've been lobbying the hotel to change that policy. The Resort's owned by a big corporation and they can afford it. One of the guys in our little group— we're keeping it small for now—is looking into forcing the issue under federal law, but something happened to him. I just found out today. One of the waiters. He lives closer to Lincoln Falls. He came home to find his house burning to the ground."

"That's awful," Sophie said.

A chill ran up Lucky's spine. "They suspect arson?"

Brenda shook her head. "They're claiming it's a faulty propane heater. That something happened to it to cause the fire."

"Is Nate Edgerton looking into this?" Sophie asked.

"I don't think that's within his jurisdiction," Lucky offered.

"Anyway, I've had the feeling of"—Brenda looked across the counter at them—"please don't think I'm crazy, but I swear I keep feeling like somebody's watching me. I keep looking over my shoulder like I'm gonna catch someone. That's why I didn't want to leave the house and then have to come back alone. I just feel safer staying inside. I wanted to give you a heads-up about all this weird stuff before you come back to work this summer."

"If what you suspect is true, who do you think is behind all this?" Lucky asked.

"I haven't got any proof, but I think it's Lurch. I don't know if he's the only one or if he's got guys working for him. But he gives me the creeps. I make sure I'm never in a place where I'm alone, or if I am, then I lock the door and make sure the security bolt is on if I'm working in a room." Brenda's forehead was creased in worry. "Anyway, that's not the only reason I wanted to talk to you away from work."

Lucky and Sophie sat in silence while Brenda marshaled her thoughts. "I overheard them talking about you."

"Me?" Sophie asked. "Who was talking about me?"

"I was clearing away cups and stuff from a conference room. You know that big one on the mezzanine level? The one they can partition into two separate rooms?"

Sophie nodded.

"One of the lawyers and Tom Reed were in the other room. I heard Lurch's voice. It sounded like he was reporting to them about something. I couldn't make out the words but my ears went up. Then I heard them say your name. They didn't realize I was right next door, and that partition's real thin so you can hear some of what's being said in the next meeting room. So I just stayed still and listened."

"What did they say?" Sophie asked.

"I couldn't catch it all. Just words and phrases here and there. First it was that lawyer talking. I don't know his name. The one who's always really friendly and smiling. Then I heard Lurch talking and then either Reed or the other guy—I think it was Reed—said something like, 'She'll come around.' And I think it was the lawyer who said, 'And if she doesn't?' Then Reed laughed and said, 'The less you know, the better. But you won't have to worry about her.' "

"You're sure it was me they were talking about?"

"Oh yeah, that's what made me listen. I heard one of them say your name just before all that."

Lucky and Sophie exchanged a look.

"It had to be you they were talking about. Why would they take an interest in you?"

Sophie hesitated, then decided to confide in Brenda. "They want to buy several parcels of land that belonged to my mother. They want to extend a ski run and they need to buy me and my brother out."

"So why were they talking like you were a problem?"

"I don't know. They've made a very generous offer but I haven't gotten back to them. Besides, it's my brother who doesn't want to sell, not me. So why they would see me as a problem, assuming they do, I don't know," Sophie continued. "But please don't pass this around. I really appreciate your telling me this, but keep the stuff about my mother's land under your hat. Please."

"I will. Don't worry. It's nobody's business but yours. I just thought you should know what's been going on and that you're a subject of discussion up there."

"Thanks, Brenda. I don't know what it all means but I'll keep quiet about it."

"Have you told Nate Edgerton about all this stuff?" Lucky asked.

Brenda nodded. "I didn't say anything about Sophie. But I called Nate today 'cause I wanted him to know what's going on at the Resort, and I told him about the man whose house burned down. I don't know what Nate can do about any of it, but I thought he should know anyway."

"I agree," Lucky said. "And hopefully his house fire won't be judged as arson."

"I guess you're right. It's terrible for him no matter what caused it, but the idea that somebody could do that—too awful to think about," Brenda replied.

"We better get going, but thanks for talking to us." Sophie picked her purse up off the floor.

Brenda led them back to the front hallway. "Wait a second," she said. She turned off the interior light and peeked through a curtain in the front hallway.

"I'm not crazy." She turned to them. "Look at that." She pointed at the window.

"What is it?" Lucky asked.

"There's a flatbed truck parked across the street. I think someone's in it watching the house. I've seen that truck before." Brenda's fear was palpable.

"Really?" Lucky said. "We'll see about that." She opened the door and stepped out.

Sophie tried to grab her arm. "What are you doing?" she hissed.

"Putting an end to this cloak-and-dagger stuff. Let's see who's inside." She hurried down the drive and marched across the street toward the driver's side of the vehicle. The engine came to life.

"Hey! You!" Lucky shouted. Before she could reach the truck, the engine revved and the truck barreled down the hill. Lucky stood in the middle of the road watching the red tail-lights grow smaller. Brenda and Sophie ran across the road to her.

"Did you get a license number?" Brenda asked.

Lucky shook her head. "Only a few numbers. He took off so fast." She turned to Sophie. "Six-seven-three. That's all I caught. At least that's what I think I saw." She turned to Brenda. "You go back inside and make sure you're locked in. If that guy comes back or you see that truck again, call Nate right away. Obviously whoever's doing this doesn't want to be caught out."

Brenda nodded, rubbing her arms against the chilly night air. "Thanks again for coming," she said and hurried back across the road. Lucky and Sophie watched her until she was in the house and heard the locks click.

They climbed into Sophie's car and Lucky started the engine. She drove slowly down the hill, keeping her eyes out for the truck. "Sophie, I think we should tell Nate about this too. Maybe if he hears about the labor dispute at the Resort from Brenda and then hears about your name being mentioned . . ."

"Yeah, I could talk to Nate, but what could he do? I can't claim my life's been threatened or anything like that. He'll say it's perfectly normal for them to be discussing me in regard to their offer for the land. He'll want something solid that he can move on. We can't even swear, even though we know it's true, that someone is watching Brenda's house."

"I think she's got a stalker too. But now whoever's keeping tabs on Brenda will wonder why you're visiting her. I don't want you to be any more of a target than you might already be."

Chapter 31

LUCKY TOSSED HER purse under the desk in the office and hung her jacket on a hook. She walked down the corridor and grabbed a fresh apron from the closet, tying it around her waist. She felt as if she hadn't slept well, even though she'd been unconscious for a full eight hours. In her dreams she remembered hearing the engine of a truck revving but when she tried to find the source of the noise, there was nothing there.

"Hey, Lucky," Sophie called out when she heard Lucky's footsteps in the corridor.

Lucky peeked around the doorway of the kitchen. Sage was scooping chopped vegetables into a large pot and Sophie was clearing off his worktable.

"Hi, guys. What's on the menu today?"

Sage looked up. "I'm doing an onion soup today, and something kind of different—watercress and pear. What do you think?"

"Sounds very different."

"I thought it might be a good choice for a spring soup. I'm trying to decide on a couple of others. I can do the potato kale again—I know you like that one—and then maybe a sausage and pasta stew or. . . . How about a chicken pot pie soup with dumplings?"

"Mmm. That sounds great, so comforting, chicken pot pie with dumplings. Great range of choices," Lucky replied as she joined them at the tall butcher block and pulled up a stool.

"Okay, I'll do that one today, then."

"Save me a big bowl."

"Isn't he brilliant?" Sophie grinned from ear to ear as she turned to Lucky.

"I think he is," Lucky replied seriously.

Sage whacked Sophie's arm gently with a dish towel. "Stop that. I'll get a big head."

Sophie laughed in response. "Just kidding. Don't be so serious."

Sage looked across the worktable at Lucky. "Sophie told me about Brenda and what she had to say last night. I don't like this one bit."

"Me neither," Lucky offered. "No way to prove it but it looks like real down-and-dirty intimidation to me."

"The more I mull this over," Sage said, angrily slamming his knife into the worktable as he chopped, "the more I really don't want Sophie going back there."

"To the Resort?"

Sage nodded.

"Hey." Sophie reached over to touch his shoulder. "I know you worry about me but I'm a big girl. I'm not afraid of those goons."

"One goon. At least from what I've heard. And I'll tell you what I'm gonna do to him if he even says one word to you. If he even looks at you or breathes funny around you. Around either of you," he said, indicating both Sophie and Lucky. "In fact, I may not even wait for him to make a move. Maybe I'll just have a word with him now."

"Better you don't, Sage," Lucky said. "We don't know anything for a fact yet. There could be a reasonable explanation for everything. We only have suspicions, and you might be escalating a situation that could hurt Sophie."

"Look, I really don't give a damn about the Resort or how much overtime or not they pay. That doesn't affect Sophie anyway. But I don't like their making remarks about how she's gonna come around. What the hell does that mean?"

"I agree with you," Lucky said. "But, and I'm just playing devil's advocate here, Brenda didn't hear the whole conversation, only bits and pieces. And it was thirdhand. It could be put in an entirely different context if she had heard the whole conversation."

Sage took a deep breath and struggled to calm down.

Lucky continued. "Besides, she's willing to sell the land they want. They made her a great offer. She just can't do anything about her brother's stubbornness."

Sage looked up, a dark glint in his eye. "Somebody killed Rick's partner. Did that happen because they thought he was Rick Colgan? Think about this—if Rick were out of the picture and, God forbid, if anything were to happen to Sophie, they could pick up that land for pennies on the dollar." He shook his head and moved a pile of chopped vegetables to the side with his large bladed knife. "All I'm sayin' is . . . be careful. And next time you want to visit a strange house, please, please take me with you. I just don't feel like anything is safe right now."

"Good point. And you might be right," Lucky offered.

Sophie had remained quiet during this exchange. She reached over and squeezed Sage's arm in sympathy.

Lucky turned and peeked through the hatch into the front room. "Is Jack in yet?"

"He called a little while ago. Said he wasn't coming in today." Sage hesitated. "He's not doing well, is he?"

Lucky sighed. "He's a little better, I think. I can understand he's upset, but I'd feel better if he was here with us. I'll give him a call later." The morning before, Jack had felt groggy from the medication and had made his apologies. Lucky urged him to stay home and not come back to work until he felt better. She turned to Sophie. "I think I should talk to Nate about those photos we were looking at."

"Photos?" Sage asked.

"I told you," Sophie said. "The ones Lucky found in her mother's attic. All those blurry photos of the Warners."

"Oh, right. I remember now."

"Maybe I'm crazy." Lucky leaned over the worktable. "But whatever was in that wine, or whoever tampered with the basket before or after Cecily picked it up, wasn't just making a mistake. Someone in that group must have known Agnes would be the first to drink. I think whatever happened was deliberate."

"That's assuming something bad was in the wine, isn't it?" Sage replied.

"Yes," Lucky grudgingly admitted. "That's true. They don't have a result yet. But if that's what happened, wouldn't it have had to be someone who was part of the plan, someone who was part of the library group?"

"But how would they know Agnes had a heart condition?" Sophie asked.

"They might not have known that. Maybe whatever was in that drink was enough to take out an army. Agnes had an immediate reaction. And maybe if she hadn't had an immediate reaction, whatever it was might have killed her eventually, just a bit more slowly. I think somebody tampered with it, but how, I can't figure out. Jack harvested the herbs; Cecily picked up the basket and brought it to Cordelia's house. No one could have touched it other than Cecily or Cordelia."

"What does Cordelia have to say?"

"I haven't talked to her—yet. But I intend to."

Sophie shuddered. "Leave me out of that!"

"What about the other women?" Sage asked. "Do you know who they are?"

"Besides Cordelia and Agnes, there was Emily from the library, Cecily and Greta, and two other women: one from Snowflake, who lives up in Lincoln Heights, and one from Lincoln Falls. Emily was certain that none of them had any prior connection with Agnes. She seemed fairly certain none of them had even met Agnes prior to this women's group forming. Although she did mention there was some . . .

coldness, she said . . . between Agnes and the woman from Lincoln Heights. I do want to talk to Cordelia, though. You never know what you'll find out if you push hard enough." Lucky slid off her stool. "I better get busy before we open. And I do think I should talk to Nate about those photos. He'll probably laugh at me, but I think they're significant."

"If you're going to see him this afternoon, I'll go with you. Maybe if we both show up, it'll make more of an impression," Sophie said.

"Good idea. I'll zip home and grab those photos before we go."

Chapter 32

LUCKY AND SOPHIE sat on the hard oak bench against the wall of the waiting room, hoping that Nate would be available soon. Lucky held the envelope containing her mother's photos close to her chest.

Bradley, Nate's deputy, glanced at them occasionally, but when Lucky had refused to state her business with Nate, he sniffed audibly and told them Nate was busy with someone in his office and to take a seat.

Finally, they heard a sound, and Lucky leaned forward to catch a glimpse of Nate's office door. She nudged Sophie. Rick Colgan was leaving Nate's office. They watched him as he approached the area where they sat. His face was pale and he gave them no notice as he passed by.

"Rick!" Sophie jumped up as her brother passed them. "What are you doing here?"

He shook his head, unable to speak. "Can't talk now."

Sophie's jaw tightened. "Then when?"

Rick walked out the front door and Sophie followed him. Lucky glanced at Nate's door, but Nate hadn't come out. She followed Sophie out the front door of the station and watched as Sophie attempted to halt Rick's progress.

"Why won't you talk to me, Rick? Why haven't you returned my phone calls?" she demanded.

"Sophie." Rick turned to her and grabbed her by the shoulders. "Get off my back. Please. I had to identify my partner's body a couple of days ago, okay? I had to sign a statement and go over everything with Nate again. Eddie's dead. I just don't want any more hassle today."

Sophie fell silent. "I heard. I'm so sorry, Rick. Does Nate know how he died?"

"Get a grip, will ya. Somebody killed him. Animals didn't do that to his face. Wolves didn't remove his wallet. I asked Eddie to have a look at that property. He . . . Never mind. I might as well have sent him to his death."

"Who would have done that to him?"

"I don't know. I really don't. But I'm not hanging around much longer." He turned and started to walk away.

Sophie ran a few steps to catch up to him. "Rick!"

"What?" He turned back.

"You say you find people, right?"

"Yeah. What of it?"

"I want you to find our father." Sophie seemed to be holding her breath.

"What?" Rick laughed bitterly. "What the hell for?"

"Because. Because he's my father, and yours too, I might add. Because I'm getting married and starting a new life and I want to find him."

Rick shook his head. "He was a no-good son of a bitch, Sophie. He took off years ago. He didn't give a damn about us. Why would you want to bring him back into your life now?"

"That isn't how I remember it."

Rick's jaw clenched. "What the hell did you know? You were a baby when he left."

"But I remember him, Rick. I remember him sometimes, and I missed him. It was awful for mom and you guys after that. You were all older . . ."

"That's right. We were all older and we remember better. I think you're in some kind of a fantasy world where you had the perfect dad, except . . . Gee, where is he?" Rick replied sarcastically.

"I have some money. I can pay you. I know you could find him if you'd just try."

"Sorry, Sis, no can do." Rick turned on his heel and walked away.

Sophie covered her face with her hands. Lucky walked down the steps of the station and put an arm around her friend's shoulder.

Sophie took a deep breath and reined in the tears that were threatening to flow. "S'okay. I'll be okay. Let's go talk to Nate."

NATE REMOVED THE photographs from the envelope. Lucky and Sophie sat silently on the two armchairs in front of Nate's desk while he slowly examined each of them. He heaved a sigh and looked up. "I don't know what you want me to make of these. They just look like rejects."

"Nate, I'm sure my mother had a reason for taking those photos. And she wouldn't have had them enlarged if they were rejects. She wouldn't have bothered. You know how she used to like to take photos of the regular customers. But these were segregated from all the others. They were in an envelope, and on the back you'll see that there are dates on some of them."

Nate turned the enlargements over and spotted the handwriting. "Okay. I see that. But what does it mean?"

"I don't know. These photos and these dates were significant to her in some way. I admit, I don't know how or why, but I do think it's important."

Nate looked at her with what she could only interpret as pity in his eyes. "Lucky, I realize Jack is very upset about what happened to that woman. I don't blame him. If it were me, I'd feel the same way. And—"

"That's just it, Nate. Jack shouldn't be feeling the way he's feeling. I know he didn't do anything wrong."

"Let me finish, okay?" he continued. "I know you're reaching for some motive that somebody has for doing Agnes Warner in—"

Lucky interrupted him again. "I'm not reaching." Her statement came out far more vehemently than she had intended. She took a deep breath and tried to calm down. "I'm sorry. I don't mean to be upset with you, but I'm convinced Agnes's death wasn't an accident."

Nate's eyebrows rose. "You're saying Agnes Warner's death was murder. Is that right?"

Lucky nodded.

"Fine. But unless something presents itself to prove that, I have to operate on the assumption that she died of a heart attack and might have been poisoned. Maybe these ladies had no idea what they were brewing and, quite possibly—no, more than likely—it *was* Jack's mistake."

Lucky could feel her anger rising. Her face had turned beet red. "I thought you cared about Jack. I thought you considered him a friend!"

"I do." Nate's temper flared. "Don't you go accusing me of not being Jack's friend. I'm the best friend he has in the world. You know that, Lucky. But I'm the law here and I have to operate accordingly. If the toxicologist does find something, there will probably have to be an inquest."

"So you're not going to do a thing about this, are you?" Lucky demanded, pointing at the photos on Nate's desk.

Sophie touched Lucky's arm gently to warn her to stay in control.

"I'm sorry, Lucky. This . . ." He indicated the photos spread out in front of him. "This tells me nothing."

"Fine." Lucky reached over and snatched the photos off the desk. She shoved them back into the envelope. "Thanks for your time." She stood and walked out of Nate's office.

Sophie gave Nate a look that silently asked him to cut Lucky some slack.

Nate leaned forward in his chair. "Uh, Sophie, before you go. I guess you know your brother was just here."

"I saw him," Sophie replied noncommittally.

"Any idea what he's doing in Snowflake?"

Sophie sighed. "He says he came to talk to the people at the Resort about our mother's land."

Nate regarded her silently. "And that's all he's told you?"

"Yes, that's all. Why? You think there's more he's not saying?"

Nate shrugged. "Just asking."

"But you suspect there's more?"

"Seems odd that he and this Fowler guy'd come all this way to talk about land he doesn't want to sell. Don't you think? I just thought he might've told you more," Nate replied.

"Yeah, right. I can't even get a straight answer out of him, much less get him to open up a little. Believe me, you'd stand a much better chance of that than me."

Chapter 33

LUCKY WOKE TO the sounds of birds fluttering and chirping in the trees outside her bedroom window. The flowered curtains billowed softly in the early-morning breeze. It promised to be a perfect spring day, warm at midday and cool at night. Winter was banished and every tree and bush was covered with pale green buds.

All the worries of the preceding week came back in a rush. If only there was something she could do to allay Jack's fears. The only thing that offered any promise was to learn more about Agnes Warner. Lucky held a growing certainty that the cause of Agnes's death, whether by poisoning or cardiac crisis, lay in the woman's past. Lucky's own mother was no one's fool and she had been focused on Agnes and her family five years earlier. What had her mother thought? What had she known or suspected? If only she had left a note in a time capsule that Lucky could retrieve in present day.

She heaved a sigh and swung her legs out of bed. She padded out to the kitchen in her nightgown and put the kettle on to boil for coffee. On her way, she rubbed the nose of her folk-art kitchen witch for luck. The witch, with its black hat and carved face and skirt of straw, had been a present from Elizabeth Dove when she first moved into her apartment. Elizabeth had told her it would bring her luck and she was right. In more ways than she could count, it had. Now it was Jack who needed a little luck.

She pushed up the window in the kitchen. When the coffee was ready, she set her mug on the windowsill and looked down at the back garden behind her building. The rosebushes were just sprouting their first swollen pink buds, soon to erupt in fragrant blossoms. Beyond her fenced-in yard she had a clear view of the Victory Garden where Snowflake's fortunate residents were marking out plots and tilling the soil for spring plantings.

She drank the last of her coffee and headed for the bathroom to shower. A loud knock at the front door stopped her in her tracks. Before she could respond, a second knock came, this one even louder. She ran back to the bedroom and grabbed a bathrobe from the closet. She tiptoed down the hall. Who would be knocking at her door this early in the morning? Jack or Elias would have called out to her. So would Sophie.

"Who's there?" she said.

"Rick. Rick Colgan," a deep voice replied.

Wrapping her robe around her, she undid the lock and opened the door. Rick's face seemed even more strained than the day before when she had seen him at the police station. She couldn't imagine why he was on her doorstep.

"Come on in, Rick." She led him down the hall to the kitchen. "Coffee?" she asked.

"No. No, thanks. I apologize for showing up this early. I just wanted to talk to you in private—away from Sophie."

"How did you know where I live?" she asked.

Rick shrugged, as if to say it wasn't hard to find out. "I saw Sophie and Sage leaving your apartment the other night."

"So that was you that Sage spotted on the street?"

Rick nodded. "I didn't mean to scare anyone. Just wanted

to get the lay of the land. It's been a long time since I've been here."

"Okay," Lucky replied hesitantly. "What did you want to talk about?" She sat on a kitchen chair, wondering what was on Rick's mind and how long this conversation would take. She needed to get moving and get to the restaurant. "Have a seat, Rick."

He nodded but didn't sit. He stuck his hands in the pockets of his jacket and began to pace back and forth in front of the stove. "You've gotta get Sophie off this kick about selling any land to the Resort."

"Why? What's going on?"

Rick opened his mouth as if to speak and hesitated a moment. Finally, he said, "It's just not a good idea."

"She just wants the house and the land around it. That's all she really wants, and she and Sage are prepared to buy you out. It hasn't been easy for either one of them to save all that money."

"I know that. At least, I figured that."

"Then what's the problem? Do you want the house for yourself?"

A dark look flashed across his face. "Good God, no. I don't give a crap about that house or the land it's on."

"So . . ." Lucky felt like her head was spinning.

"I just want to make sure Sophie doesn't sell her interest in the other acreage to the Resort."

Lucky remembered that possibility had been raised by the attorneys for the Resort and that she and Sophie had discussed it. "What's to stop her doing that? You just keep saying you won't sell, but maybe they figure they can buy out her interest and eventually wear you down until you agree."

His face darkened. "Or until I'm dead."

Lucky looked up at him quickly. "What are you saying?"

"Come on, Lucky. Don't be dense. Why do you think my partner was floating in the creek with his face bashed in?"

She didn't want to admit it, but the thought had occurred

to her and to Sophie. For Sophie's sake, she hadn't wanted to explore that suspicion.

"They thought it was me."

"They?"

"Those thugs at the Resort." He laughed bitterly. "Especially the ones that wear suits. When they saw my partner check in, they thought the same thing the cops did. That he was me. They figured I—I mean Eddie—was up there to check out the property . . . And he was, but I had already told them I wasn't interested in selling the land they want for the ski run."

Lucky took a deep breath. Tom Reed had always given her a bad feeling. Was that because he harbored a grudge toward her since the day she had asked him whether he was having an affair with a murder victim? Or was it because he truly was a man with bad intentions? Could Rick be right? Was his partner killed because of mistaken identity? "That's an incredible accusation, Rick. They may be anxious to get that land, but you're accusing Reed and his lawyers of murder."

"What other reason could there be? Eddie didn't know a soul here. He had no connection to the Resort or to the town."

"So Eddie came here just to help you out?"

"That's right."

The full impact of what Rick was telling her hit. "But you're saying Sophie could be in danger if she *isn't* willing to sell."

"Maybe. But I'm warning you. She can't sell. She can have the damn house, but she can't sell her interest in those other parcels. If she holds firm, we're both safe. And I'm asking you to make sure she does hold firm."

"What do you mean *safe*?" Lucky had no idea what this conversation was really about. "And how am I supposed to do that?" She was frustrated. What was it that Rick wasn't telling her? "Rick, what are you really doing here if you have no interest in selling? You didn't need to come to Snowflake to check out that property. And even if you were thinking about selling, you could have called any Realtor and gotten an idea."

Rick stared at her but didn't respond.

"Did you come here because you were on a job? Were you hired to find someone?" She waited for him to respond but he said nothing. "Was that someone Agnes Warner, by any chance?"

His jaw tightened. "I can't tell you that."

"Maybe Eddie's murder had nothing to do with the land. Maybe it had something to do with the job you were working on."

"I doubt that."

"Then who were you hired to locate?"

"Look." Rick heaved a sigh. "We were hired to locate a woman named Alice Washburn. That's all you need to know. It's really not any of your business."

"So, that's the real reason you're here now? Did you locate her?"

"In a way, yeah."

"Then tell me who hired you and your partner."

Rick had stopped pacing. "I can't tell you that either."

"Well, if it's all so secret, why would you assume the only reason your partner was killed was because the Resort wants that land? Surely there could be another reason. Why won't you tell me everything?"

He glared at her. "Just make sure Sophie doesn't cave."

"And if I can't?"

"Then I'll stop her any way I can." He turned and stormed down the hallway. Lucky heard the door slam as he left the apartment.

Lucky poured a second cup of coffee and sat at the kitchen table. She rubbed her temples. Her conversation with Rick Colgan had left her with a pounding headache. What was it all about? He said he wanted no part of the house, and that Sophie could have it, yet he wouldn't give his own sister a definite answer. Why couldn't he tell that to Sophie himself? He had been hired to locate a woman named Alice Washburn. The name meant nothing to her and he wouldn't reveal the name of his client. And he was convinced his partner had been killed by unknown people employed by the Resort. Anything was possible if a greedy corporation wanted land. Who knew what sort of dirty tricks they might stoop to if a land grab was involved, but murder? She sighed and finished her coffee. She had to get moving or she'd really be late. She rinsed out her cup in the sink and headed down the hall to the bathroom. She heard a light knock at her front door. *What now?* she thought. Puzzled, she walked the length of the hall to the door again, hoping it wasn't Rick Colgan returning.

"Who is it?" she called out.

"Hello. It's me . . . Greta."

Lucky opened the door. "Oh, hi, Greta. You surprised me."

Greta's carryall hung from her wrist. "I heard you walking around. I thought maybe I could pick up the books you mentioned. I'm on my way to the library now. I didn't want to bother you at the restaurant."

In the commotion of the past days, Lucky had completely forgotten she had promised to deliver the books to Greta. "I'm so sorry. It slipped my mind. Come on in."

"Thanks." Greta smiled.

Lucky led Greta into the living room. "Here they are. This box is kind of heavy. Would you like me to carry it downstairs?"

Greta stood next to the coffee table. She held one of the photos in her hand and was staring at it intently. "What's this?" she asked.

The night before, Lucky had spread the photos out on the coffee table and stared at them as if they would offer some new inspiration. She kicked herself for not putting them away from prying eyes. She certainly didn't want to explain her thoughts or theories to a stranger. "Oh, just some of my mother's photos from years ago. She always used to like to take pictures of our customers."

"Ah. I've noticed some of the pictures around the restaurant. I'll have to have a closer look one of these days." Greta reached out for the box Lucky held in her hands. "I'll take that." Greta was a very slight woman; Lucky wondered whether she was strong enough to handle the heavy box.

"You're sure you can manage?"

Greta nodded. "Oh yes. Not a problem. Thanks again. Sorry if I came at a bad time."

"No. It was perfect."

Lucky closed and locked the door after watching Greta descend the stairway, carefully lugging the heavy box. She returned to the living room, mentally kicking herself again for not putting the enlargements away. She really didn't want just anyone looking at them. She picked them up one by one and slid them into the envelope. Something was different. There had been ten photos. She was sure of it. She opened the envelope and counted them again to make sure. Now there were only nine. She glanced around the room and checked under the sofa and coffee table. She checked each one. There was definitely one missing. The one of Agnes, her face turned away from the camera, holding the little boy, his face not visible, his head snuggled against Agnes's shoulder. She was sure of it. She shivered. Had Greta taken it? But why? Lucky rushed out to the corridor and leaned out the hallway window. She saw a glimpse of Greta's brown skirt as she turned the corner on Spruce.

Chapter 34

"I CAN'T BELIEVE he did that!" Sophie exclaimed. She shook her head. "What is wrong with him? And why is he so adamant about not selling those parcels? And how come he won't name his price for the house? I'm ready to scream!"

It was a few minutes before opening time and Lucky and Sophie sat in the office. Lucky had taken her aside to tell her about Rick's visit. "I don't know why Rick wouldn't know that I'd tell you about his visit straightaway."

"I know," Sophie agreed. "And even if I had made up my mind, what were you supposed to do about it? Talk me out of it? For no reason at all?"

"You have any idea what's behind it all?"

"None whatsoever. Granted, Rick doesn't know me at all, not really, but if he did, he should know it would only make me dig my heels in deeper and do it in spite of what he wants."

Lucky leaned across the desk. "My advice? Don't pick a fight with him over something you don't care about. Focus on what you do want—getting him to agree to sell you and Sage the house."

"What did he have to say about that?" She laughed

mirthlessly. "I love it that he'll talk to you about it, but won't get back in touch with me."

"He was very clear he wanted no part of the house and never wanted to be in Snowflake longer than he had to."

Sophie looked up, her face flushed. "Well, then, what's he doing here? He's had time to talk to the lawyers at the Resort. He's identified his partner's body. As long as he gives Nate a way to get in touch with him, he doesn't have to be here at all. He can go back to New York or wherever he's been all these years, for all I care."

Lucky shook her head. "I don't know, but he did tell me one thing. The woman he was hired to find was someone named Alice Washburn. That name mean anything to you?"

Sophie's face took on a blank expression. "Never heard it."

"There's something else. Greta turned up right after Rick left."

"The library volunteer?"

Lucky nodded. "I forgot to put the photos away. They were on the coffee table and she was staring at one of them."

"So?"

"After she left, I picked them up to put them back in the envelope. Sophie, I could swear there's one missing."

Sophie looked at her dubiously. "You must have counted wrong."

Lucky shook her head. "I really don't think so." She glanced at the clock. "Oh, look at the time. I need to get out there and open. But, Sophie, just so you know, I intend to keep sniffing around. I'm not willing to accept that Jack could have caused anyone's death."

LUCKY PRESSED THE doorbell. Somewhere inside the house, it chimed. She shifted her weight from foot to foot and waited. Nothing. She pressed the doorbell again. This time she heard footsteps approaching and the door was flung open.

Cordelia Rank stood in the doorway. "Yes?" she asked, as if Lucky were a total stranger. Cordelia was dressed in a

matching green blouse and light wool skirt. Lucky immediately felt self-conscious in her wrinkled cotton slacks and
T-shirt. Cordelia was always perfectly turned out even on a
day at home. She suspected Cordelia still harbored anger
toward her from the year before when Lucky had been a
witness to Cordelia's humiliation. Cordelia, a proud member
of the Daughters of the American Revolution, had stolen a
Colonial-era lead ball, fired by a rifle, that would have
proven her ancestor to be a traitor to the Revolution. Under
duress, Cordelia had been forced to admit her theft and
return the artifact.

"I wonder if I could talk to you for a minute?" Lucky
asked.

Cordelia made a show of checking her watch. "I have a
minute." She did not offer to invite Lucky in.

Lucky felt a wave of irritation rise, but quickly pushed it
down. "It's about the herbs that Jack picked."

Cordelia rolled her eyes. "Not that again."

Lucky gritted her teeth. "Yes. That again. Perhaps you
don't think it's important that someone died in the woods
the other night—"

"How dare you, you impudent—"

Lucky forged ahead, ignoring Cordelia's threatened rant.
"But I happen to think it's terribly important. I'm sure Nate
Edgerton has asked you all about this, but I'm here because
of my grandfather."

Cordelia's nostrils flared slightly. "Fine. What is it you
want to know?" she said with thinly veiled irritation.

"What exactly did you do with the basket of herbs that
Cecily Winters brought you?"

Cordelia's back straightened. "I certainly hope you're not
accusing me of anything!"

"I'm not accusing you of anything. I'm merely asking,
Cordelia. What happened after Cecily delivered the basket
to you?"

Cordelia heaved a sigh, demonstrating her impatience,
and spoke slowly as if to a mentally challenged child. "I
washed all the leaves and added them to a large pot to which

I then added white wine. Jack had picked a bit more than we asked for, but I used them all. The wine was purchased at a local market and I opened the bottles myself. The mix steeped overnight, and I transferred it to a large, tightly lidded container and, with a small cauldron and bowls I washed myself, transported it to our . . . meeting." Cordelia's mouth twitched slightly.

"Did anyone else have a chance to touch it or add anything?"

Cordelia pursed her lips. "I know what you're getting at. But no. No one laid a hand on it before we started or after. And I certainly didn't add anything harmful to the wine, so the only possible conclusion is that your grandfather is getting senile and my only mistake was in trusting him to do something right."

Lucky felt another surge of anger rise in her chest but she kept her voice level. "Cordelia, don't you *dare* accuse my grandfather. He knew what he was doing when he picked those herbs. Somebody had to have tampered with it. I know that's the only explanation."

A slow smile spread across Cordelia's face. It didn't reach her eyes. "Why don't you tell that to Nate Edgerton? See what he has to say? Your grandfather is obviously dotty and you'll just simply have to accept that."

"Look . . ." Lucky did her best to quell an angry retort. "Jack is anything but—"

"If that's all, then, I'm very busy . . ."

"No, Cordelia. It's not all." Lucky edged her foot over the threshold. "I didn't drive over here to be treated rudely or have a door slammed in my face. Under the circumstances, I would think you'd have the common courtesy to at least talk to me."

Cordelia had the good grace to blush slightly. She took a deep breath. "Fine. What is it you'd like to know?"

Lucky struggled to marshal her thoughts. Her reaction to Cordelia had caused logic to fly to the winds. "Was Agnes friendly with anyone in your group?"

"Not particularly."

"Did she know any of the women before the group formed?"

"I would have no idea." Cordelia pursed her lips.

"Did she have any disagreements with anyone there?"

"Certainly no . . ." Cordelia hesitated. Lucky was sure she had hit upon something.

"Yes?" She waited.

Cordelia pulled herself up to her full height, standing straighter if such a thing were possible. "There was something. I don't know if it was an argument. I wouldn't say that, but there seemed to be a bit of distance, or discomfort, if you will, between Agnes and one of the women. I have no idea what it was about."

"Which woman?"

Cordelia looked as if she'd love to deny Lucky an answer but must have finally decided the sooner she answered, the sooner Lucky would leave her alone. "It was Willa. Willa Persley."

"I see. Thank you."

Cordelia made no pretense of courtesy. She stepped back. Lucky managed to move her foot a second before Cordelia slammed the door firmly.

"I'll show you who's dotty," she muttered to the closed door. She gave it a swift kick before she turned away and headed down the stairs.

Chapter 35

LUCKY CLOSED HER eyes and took a deep breath, willing herself to be calm. Her confrontation with Cordelia Rank had caused her blood to boil. The woman was insufferable and patronizing and rude. It wasn't for her own sake that she was tempted to give Cordelia a black eye; it was her remarks about Jack that cut her to the quick. Cordelia couldn't possibly have been more cruel. Lucky turned off the engine and pulled the flyer that Emily had given her out of the pocket of her pants. She checked the address again. Willa Persley's house was a two-story white Colonial half-way up the hill. Lincoln Heights was an enclave of those the village of Snowflake termed "newcomers"—people who hadn't been born and lived in the village for the past hundred years or more. It was a wealthy section, just above the town, and most of the people who lived there were in some way connected with the Snowflake Resort, executives and middle-management people who had moved here from other places, pursuing well-paid employment.

Lucky climbed the stairway to the front door. The house was built on a rise with no space for a front lawn, but a rock garden of trailing plants and flowers was beginning to bloom. Lucky caught whiffs of lavender and mint as she ascended the brick stairway. A flowered wreath hung just below the small windows in the upper part of the heavy door. She took a deep breath, remembering the frosty reception she had received at Cordelia's home. She mentally prepared herself for the same.

She rang the bell and heard it chime inside. A few moments later, the door swung wide and a small plump woman in an apron decorated with butterflies stood in the doorway. Splotches of flour covered the front of her apron, and under it she wore loose cotton pants and a print blouse. The woman smiled. Lucky wondered how long the welcome would last once she stated her business.

"Hello."

"Hi. I'm Lucky Jamieson. We've never met but I was hoping you could talk to me for a minute about Agnes Warner."

"Oh." The woman's eyes opened wider. "Oh. Of course, please come in. I'm working in the kitchen right now, but follow me." She spoke over her shoulder as Lucky followed her down the main hallway toward the kitchen.

"Please have a seat. Would you like a cup of coffee?" Willa bustled about the kitchen, clearing off a space at the tall butcher block that dominated the center of the room.

"No, thank you, though. I'm fine. I'm just taking a break from work and I hoped to find you at home."

"Oh, where do you work, dear?" Willa asked, smiling.

"I own the By the Spoonful Soup Shop."

"How wonderful! I've been hearing about that place." She leaned over the worktable. "I don't get out very much. I'm a widow, you see, and I live with my son and daughter-in-law. They both work at the Resort and they've talked me into coming to live with them. I've only been here about six months, so I haven't had a chance to get to know the town. I don't drive and I need to be here when the children come home from school. And, of course"—she waved her arm, indicating the kitchen—"I spend most of my time here. I do love to cook, though."

Lucky smiled, warmed by Willa's reception. "Well, we have a wonderful chef. I'm sure you'd enjoy his recipes."

"I may just take you up on that offer." She sat on a stool on the other side of the butcher block. "Now, what can I help you with?"

Lucky cleared her throat. "My grandfather is Jack Jamieson, the man who provided the herbs for Cordelia's May wine."

"Ahh, I see." Willa's gaze became very focused.

"I know that everyone thinks Jack may have picked a poisonous plant that could have led to Agnes's death, but I don't believe so."

Willa nodded. A serious look came over her face. "You're thinking that something else killed poor Agnes or that the answer isn't that simple."

"Exactly." Lucky took a deep breath. "I've been told that there might have been an altercation between you and Agnes, and I wanted to find out more about that, if you're willing to talk about it."

"Oh no." Willa's eyes widened. "Not at all. There was no argument, nothing like that." She shifted her weight on the stool to be more comfortable. "You see, being new here, I heard about the women's group that was meeting at the library and I thought it would be a good way for me to get to know some people. My son was willing to drive me down there in the evenings, so I decided to go. As time went on . . . well . . . Cordelia Rank—do you know her?" Willa asked.

"Oh yes." Lucky did her best to reply noncommittally.

Willa pursed her lips. "Well, Cordelia is quite an imposing—is that the word I want? I guess it is—an imposing figure, and the meeting began to morph into something else. It wasn't quite up my alley, but I thought, well . . . The other women were quite nice, so I thought I'd give it all a little more time." She looked directly at Lucky. "I never in a million years thought it would end *that* way!"

"I can understand." Lucky had heard all this before, but she felt it best to let Willa rattle on. She suspected the woman had no one to talk to all day and was grateful for the company. "But you got along fine with Agnes?"

"I thought so. I don't quite know what happened. It was very strange." Willa took a sip of coffee from the mug at her elbow. "Ugh, it's cold now. Oh well." She took another swallow. "We got chatting about where we were all originally from. Agnes happened to mention that she and her husband had lived in Pennsylvania before they moved here years ago, when her husband retired. You know she was raising their grandson?"

"Yes, I had heard that."

"Agnes said they had lived in a town called Greenville. Well, there are lots of towns with that name all over, even one in Massachusetts . . . or maybe it's Greenfield in Massachusetts. I'm not sure now. But I happen to know Greenville, Pennsylvania, quite well. I grew up there. My family moved away when I was young, but I still remember the place. It's a lovely town. I was excited to find out that someone in our little group knew the place."

"How did Agnes react to that?"

"Fine. She smiled and agreed with me that it was a lovely town. But . . ." Willa trailed off.

Lucky waited, unwilling to break Willa's train of thought.

"I told her how much I remembered and loved Snowden's Ice Cream Shop and asked her if she used to go there too." Willa shrugged. "That was it. She said yes, she remembered it." Willa paused a moment. "Then, the next time I saw Agnes, it was the following week. She gave me a cold shoulder. She acted as if . . . Oh, I'm not sure how to put it into words. It made me very uncomfortable. She . . . acted as if I had done something to offend her. I tried to address it, but she said it was nothing. There was no argument or anything like that, but Agnes just chose to ignore any friendly overtures. I was a little taken aback. Enough to think over anything I had said to her, but I couldn't imagine that I had done or said anything to upset her. There wasn't much more I could do about it. So I just had to ignore it. I don't think anyone else really noticed. Maybe they did, but if they did, they never said anything to me about it, so I just let it lie."

"I see. You have no idea what caused the change in her behavior?"

Willa shook her head. "No. To be honest, I was more than a little hurt. Maybe I was being oversensitive because I'm so new here, but there wasn't anything to be done about it."

"And it happened after your mention of the town you grew up in?"

"That's right, dear. I wondered if that had something to do with it. Maybe she wanted to avoid any talk about Greenville. Although I can't imagine why." A timer on top of the kitchen stove went off. "Oh, hang on." Willa jumped up and pulled out a cake pan. "Got it just in time." She laughed. "I get talking and I can't shut up. I'd burn the house down if I didn't have this little thing."

"I better get going myself, Willa. It was a pleasure meeting you and I hope you decide to visit the Spoonful soon. Maybe you could take a night off and come with your son and daughter-in-law."

"I will. We'll do that. We all need to get out of the house sometimes."

"Thanks for your time. I really appreciate it."

Willa followed her to the front door and opened it for her. "You must be concerned for your grandfather," she said.

Lucky nodded. "I am."

"And you're thinking that Agnes had some secrets?" Willa asked, her eyes sharp and clear.

Lucky nodded. "I don't know what they are, but I don't want to see my grandfather railroaded."

"You just call on me if you ever need a friend to talk to." Willa touched her arm gently.

Lucky felt tears starting to threaten. Other than those closest to her, this was the first person she had talked to who understood what drove her. "Thank you. I can't tell you how much I appreciate that." She stepped outside to the brick entryway and Willa closed the door behind her.

Lucky walked slowly back to the car. She turned the key in the ignition and started down the steep hill toward town. She mulled over her conversation with Willa. Had Agnes turned her back on Willa because she hadn't wanted any questions asked about her life in Greenville? Had Agnes known that Willa's family had moved away when Willa was young? Or was the story about Greenville, Pennsylvania, a complete fiction? If Agnes had lied about where the family had come from, she might have been afraid Willa would start asking more questions and she would be caught out in a lie. Perhaps she feared Willa was still in touch with people from the town who would have known that there had never been an Agnes or Leonard Warner in Greenville. That had to be the explanation. Agnes was afraid of being exposed for telling a lie, and what better way to deflect questions than to behave as though Willa had offended her in some way? A good defense to forestall any more questions from being asked.

She was halfway down the hill when she realized something was terribly wrong. Sophie's car began to shudder, its movements more and more violent. Was it the road? Had a tire blown? She hit the brakes as the sharp turn at the bottom of the hill came into view. The car gave a frightening lurch. She heard the shrieking of metal. Sparks flew from the road. The steering wheel spun out of her hands. She fought to gain control as the car neared the edge of the paving. A tree trunk loomed in front of her. Lucky screamed. Breaking glass was the last thing she heard before all went black.

Chapter 36

THERE WERE VOICES far away in the distance, a murmuring. Lucky strained to make out the words. Someone was touching her face, and a blinding light filled her vision. She groaned.

"Stay still." It was Elias's voice. "Don't move."

She tried to speak but only a croak came out. She tried again. "Elias."

"It's me. You're at the clinic. I had them bring you here."

"What happened?" She struggled to sit up.

"Don't move," he said more firmly. "You're going to be fine. I don't even think it's a concussion, but you did hit your head and you blacked out. Good thing you were wearing your seat belt, though. Hold still, now. I want to check your pupils." The light moved to the other eye, as Elias gently pulled her eyelid up.

"The car . . . Sophie's car . . . What happened?"

"You went off the road. You lost a tire."

"Help me sit up." She grasped his hand.

"Take it very slowly. You're going to be dizzy." Elias gently helped her to a sitting position. "You're one lucky woman. You've got a cut on your cheek, but I think it'll heal without a scar. And you'll have a very large egg on your head and a bad bruise."

Lucky shook her head and the room spun around. "I'll be fine." She looked up into Elias's concerned eyes. "Really, I'm fine."

"Damn." Elias took a sharp breath. "People die from stuff like this. The only reason you're still here is the road was flat and your car went straight into the bushes. You narrowly missed a tree. And you're not fine, by the way. I'm ordering rest for a few days. I'm serious. No running around at the restaurant. And I will check on you, so don't tell me one thing and do another."

Lucky realized he'd never let her out of the examining room if she didn't agree. "The car?"

Elias shook his head. "Totaled, I'd say. I didn't see it, but I heard about it."

"But why? How did this happen?"

"The lug nuts must not have been tightened properly. At least on the front passenger side, or so I've been told. That's why it swerved so badly and you lost control. Do you know who serviced it last?"

"No idea. But Sophie or Sage would know."

"Dangerous not to check the wheels. Guy Bessette's a good mechanic. I can't imagine he'd make a mistake like that." Elias cleared away the implements on the rolling tray and tossed the used sterile gauze into the wastebasket. He moved to the sink to wash his hands. "Everyone's outside in the waiting room, worried sick about you. You feel okay to stand?"

Lucky nodded.

"On second thought, you stay here. I'll tell them to come down." He kissed her lightly on the lips. "I'm pretty upset about this. I intend to get to the bottom of it." Elias stepped out to the corridor, and a few moments later Lucky heard voices. The door opened and Jack rushed in.

He gripped her hands. "Oh, my girl. You coulda been killed." His face was flushed and his hands were shaking.

Lucky reached up and touched his cheek. "But I wasn't. I'm fine, Jack. It was an accident." She looked over his shoulder to see Sage and Sophie with serious expressions on their faces. Elias had come back into the examining room.

"It was no accident," Sage said. Sophie watched Lucky's face carefully.

"What do you mean?" she asked.

"I changed both front tires for Sophie a couple of weeks ago. Believe me, I know how to tighten lug nuts. It's not a mistake I would ever make. Somebody tampered with that wheel."

They all turned to stare at Sage. Finally Elias spoke. "I think we need to report this to Nate."

"But why?" Lucky spoke. "You're saying someone deliberately wanted to hurt me?"

"Either you or Sophie. It's Sophie's car, after all. We had it towed to Guy's Auto Shop. He's going to have a look at it. I think someone wanted to take one of you out of commission. If I ever find out who did this . . ." Sage was so angry his face was white. He couldn't seem to find the words to express his outrage.

Sophie touched his arm gently. "Let's talk about this later," she said softly. She turned to her friend. "Come on, Lucky, we're taking you home and you're going to lie down. And I'll stay with you to make sure you do."

"Not so fast," Elias said. "She needs an X-ray. I want to make sure there are no fractures. Won't take long."

No one spoke a word as Elias stepped out to the corridor. Jack grasped Lucky's hand and held it tightly.

Lucky's eyes locked with Sophie's. She knew they each thought the same thing—if Rick was right and his partner, Eddie, was killed because of a case of mistaken identity, Sophie's life was truly in danger.

Chapter 37

NATE WAS SILENT, listening to the hydraulic whir as the damaged car was lifted from the concrete floor of the Auto Shop. Guy Bessette released the lever as soon as the front passenger wheel was directly in his line of sight. He moved closer to examine what was left of the rim and the mangled undercarriage. At a worktable near the wall of the shop, Guy picked up a hubcap that had miraculously survived the impact with very little damage. He clicked on a nearby work light and examined it. Then he picked up two of the lug nuts that had been retrieved from the accident.

"Have a look at this, Nate."

Nate approached the bench and peered over Guy's shoulder.

"Now, here's the two we were able to find after the accident." Guy held the metal parts in a hand coated with black grease and turned the work light around to illuminate them. "See these scratches and marks on the metal? You can tell somebody just wrenched these in a hurry. They weren't too careful. Didn't even use the right tool. Maybe they did it with a pipe wrench or something like that. And you can tell they scratched up the hubcap pretty bad too."

Guy was hunched over the worktable. He looked up at Nate. "Now come over here and look at this." He led Nate to the driver's side wheel and pulled a flashlight out of his back pocket.

"Here, the axle's been damaged, but look at this front wheel. The lug nuts have held just fine."

Nate nodded.

"And you don't see those scratches, like on the other ones."

"I see," Nate agreed. "Funny the hubcap popped off like that with no damage from the accident," Nate remarked.

"Not really. Wasn't much holdin' it on. First big bump she hit, it could've popped off and rolled away. If Lucky had seen that happen, she might have stopped and realized something was wrong."

"I don't like the sound of this."

"Me neither. She coulda been killed. Believe me, it's something Harry drilled into my head when I was learning about fixing cars. He used to say never ever forget to double-check the lug nuts. No matter what." Guy referred to his mentor, the original owner of the auto shop who had left his business to Guy. "It's a real easy mistake to make and it happens, believe me. But I've never forgotten Harry's lectures. It's a real good way to kill someone."

"How long could you drive a car with the lug nuts loose like that?" Nate asked.

Guy shook his head. "Hard to say. Depends on how much you drive, or how fast or how rough the road might be. I've heard people can drive for miles like that before they feel something happening. Depends." Guy shrugged his shoulders.

"So somebody could've fooled around with these several days ago, right?"

"Sure, but it's almost impossible to determine with any certainty. Could've been done a few days ago. She landed in a bunch of bushes at the side of the road. If she had hit that tree or if there had been a ditch, she might not have come out of it so well. Fortunately she had her seat belt on."

"I think I might try to get some prints off of those lug nuts and the hubcap. It's a real longshot. A lot of people have already handled them, but you never know."

"Sure, I'll put 'em in bags for you. Hang on; maybe I've got a big plastic garbage bag I can put the hubcap in. I'll be right back."

Guy hurried to the office, returning a moment later with the promised containers. He dropped the hubcap into the plastic sack and the lug nuts into a small paper bag and handed them to Nate. "Good luck with that, Nate."

Nate shook his head. "I'll need it. I don't hold out much hope, though."

"Lemme know if you find anything on 'em, okay?"

Both men turned as a shadow fell across the floor of the shop.

Sage DuBois stood in the entrance to the bay. "Hey, Nate. Guy."

Guy raised a hand in greeting. "I was just tellin' Nate what I found. I'm glad you stopped by."

Sage walked slowly toward the damaged car.

"Sorry about this, Sage," Nate offered.

"I'm not worried about the car. I've got insurance. It's what could have happened to Lucky or Sophie." He turned back to the men. "What did you find, Guy?"

"Somebody loosened those lug nuts on the right front wheel—passenger side."

"I was the last one to change these tires." Sage turned to Nate. "I was real careful about it. I was."

"Hang on, now," Nate reassured him. "We know. Nobody's accusing you. We know somebody tampered with that wheel. The lug nuts from that wheel are all scratched and damaged. They didn't use a lug wrench—that's for sure—'cause the wheel on the other side is fine."

Sage's eyes widened. "So you're thinking this was a last-minute thing, impulsive?"

"Seems that way," Nate agreed. "If you're planning to

hurt somebody, you'd come prepared. This musta been somebody's brilliant last-minute idea," he added sarcastically.

"I'll kill him. I'll kill whoever did this." Sage's lips had
turned white in anger. "Sophie could've been killed if she
had been driving. Thank God Lucky's okay."

"Okay, take it easy, Sage. I know you're real upset and I
don't blame you a bit, but maybe we'll get lucky and find a
print or a partial on something. Don't go making threats and
don't do anything on your own—you hear me?"

Sage took a deep breath to calm himself. "Sophie thinks
it might be that security guy at the Resort. What's his
name . . . Pete Manko, I think."

"Oh?" Nate's eyebrows rose. "Why?"

"Well, she's been off work for a while, waiting for the
summer season, but the other night she got a call from a friend
of hers at work. There's been a labor dispute at the lodge with
the hotel workers and, according to what this woman told
Sophie, they're all afraid and suspicious of this guy. They
think he's a company spy or worse."

"And he might've gone after Sophie because . . . ?" Nate
let the question hang.

"Sophie and Lucky went up to see her. They think this
Pete guy was watching the house. Lucky was able to get a
couple of numbers off his license plate but that's all. Then
he took off."

"I did talk to a woman who works at the Resort. Have
Sophie give me a call and fill me in if there's anything else
she knows, okay? We don't have any proof but I don't like
the idea of somebody maybe stalking this woman or worse."

"I will. I'll tell Sophie."

"You get back to work now, Sage. I've got this covered.
And no more threats, all right? I'll handle this."

Sage nodded. "I'll try. I'm just a nervous wreck these
days."

"Wedding jitters, that's all." Nate smiled.

Chapter 38

"How am I going to keep you safe?" Elias lifted Lucky's chin as he held her close. He kissed her and sighed heavily. "Did you rest today?"

"Had no choice. Sophie wouldn't let me do a thing yesterday. And today, she brought me lunch from the Spoonful. I've been a model patient."

"Good to hear. Come on in. Dinner's almost ready."

Lucky hung her purse on the coatrack in the hallway and followed Elias. She sat at the table as Elias poured two glasses of chilled white wine. She smiled, thrilled that Elias enjoyed cooking so much. This was better than any restaurant she could have named.

Elias checked a simmering pan on the stove. "Tonight we're having chicken piccata with lemon and capers, tender steamed broccoli and pasta." He pulled a glass dish of pasta out of the oven and added the steamed broccoli and olive oil, mixing the ingredients together. Then he scooped servings of the mixed capellini onto two plates and topped each serving with a tender chicken breast. As a last touch, he placed a slice of lemon and a sprinkling of capers over all and poured some of the sauce from the pan onto the pasta.

"I cooked this very quickly, so I can't guarantee how it's turned out. You'll have to bear with me."

"It smells divine." Her stomach growled in response. She hadn't had much of an appetite since the accident the day before but had managed to down some soup that night and a soft-boiled egg on toast that morning. The muscles in her back and arms had been wrenched in the accident and were still very sore. Her neck felt tender but at least the headache had disappeared.

"Fantastic," she said as she took her first bite. "I love the combination of capers and lemons. How did you make this sauce?"

"I sauté the chicken and then add chicken broth with the lemon slices for flavor and reduce it. Oh, and I added a pinch of nutmeg too. I don't know if that's how a real cook would do it, but it seems to work. I'll have to write down how I put it together so I don't forget." He wiped his mouth with a linen napkin.

"Elias, have you heard anything further from the toxicologist?"

He swirled pasta on his fork. "If you mean do I have a report yet, no. I don't. But I do happen to know they've decided to test for the toxin found in water hemlock."

"What? Why?"

"From what Nate's told me, the botanist from the University found it growing next to where Jack picked the leaves from the clump of woodruff."

Lucky groaned. "I know what they're thinking, but Jack could never have made a mistake like that. He used to show me different plants when I was little so I'd be knowledgeable enough not to eat anything strange. He's actually well versed in that stuff."

"I certainly hope you're right."

"What is the toxin in water hemlock, anyway?"

"I was curious too. I just looked it up." He rose from the chair. "I'll show you." Elias left the room and returned a moment later with a printout. "The active ingredient in water hemlock, and the everyday garden-variety hemlock, is a compound called cicutoxin."

"Hemlock. Isn't that the poison that Socrates drank?"

"That's right." He nodded. "The first signs can start an hour or so after ingestion, sometimes even a minute or two. The symptoms are vomiting, widened pupils, convulsions, cardiovascular changes, just to name a few. Central nervous system difficulties can cause respiratory failure, and that accounts for many of the deaths it causes. There's no antidote, but there's been some success with patients who are able to get to treatment fast. Here's a picture of this nasty little compound." He passed the printout across the table.

Lucky looked at a long, black-and-white molecule that zigzagged horizontally. "Ugh. It looks like a centipede."

"Sort of, yes. It consists of seventeen carbon molecules and two hydroxyl groups with three double bonds and two triple bonds."

Lucky raised her eyebrows. "Could you repeat that in English, please?"

"It means that in the human body it is very reactive and not easy to excrete. It's such a dangerous plant because the stem looks like celery and the roots look and smell like parsnips. The root is the most toxic part of the plant, and that even has a slightly sweet taste. When the roots are cut they ooze a thick yellowish substance that's highly toxic. Cattle have been found dead because they've grazed on the roots after fields are plowed and the roots are on the surface to be eaten. Can you imagine what it takes to kill a one- or two-ton animal?"

"Oh, I think I'm losing my appetite."

"Can't say I blame you." He poured a little more wine into her glass.

"Elias, if they do find that water hemlock was in that wine, then it couldn't have come from Jack. He'd never make a mistake like that. Will you let me know if you hear anything more?" Lucky pushed the strands of pasta around on her plate.

"I will. Oh, by the way, I took a walk over to talk to Guy Bessette today. I wanted to have a look at Sophie's car."

Lucky shivered, recalling the tree trunk looming in front of her windshield. "I know Sage went to see him. I feel so bad about Sophie's car. I don't know what she's going to do about getting a new one. I should have gone over to have a look myself."

"Well, Guy said your car is ready. The work is all done. He'll drive it over to the Spoonful tomorrow."

"I've got to talk to Sophie. I feel so responsible. Maybe I can help her with some money or help her find a new car. I don't know if she was covered for collision, her car's so old."

"Can't she use Sage's car for a while?"

"I'm sure she can." Lucky took a bite of chicken. "If she doesn't have insurance . . . Well, even if she does, and she can prove someone messed with those lug nuts, would her car be covered?"

"That I don't know. But . . ." Elias hesitated. "Guy's positive someone did tamper with that front wheel."

Lucky paused with her fork halfway to her mouth. "Definitely?"

Elias nodded. "Guy pointed out some scratches on the hubcap. He was able to find a couple of the lug nuts on the road. And there are no similar scratches on the other wheel. He thinks that right front one was the only wheel that was tampered with. And I don't know about you, but I'm sure Sage was correct that he properly tightened them. I doubt he'd want Sophie driving around in an unsafe car."

Lucky nodded. "I know he wouldn't. Sage is very safety conscious. He'd never do anything so careless. The question is . . . who would want to harm Sophie?"

Elias stared at her. "I'm not so sure Sophie was the target. You've been driving around town in that car for the last few days. And you've been asking a lot of questions. I'm more inclined to think you were the intended target."

Lucky stared across the table at him but didn't speak.

"Who have you been talking to?"

She shrugged. "Just Emily and Cordelia. I was asking about who might have handled the herbs that Jack picked for them. Oh, and Cecily."

"That's all?"

"Well, no. Yesterday, just before all this happened, I went up to Lincoln Heights to talk to a woman who was part of that group. Her name is Willa Persley."

"Just before the wheel came off?" he asked.

"Yes." Lucky nodded.

"I rest my case. Even if none of them wished you any harm, they'd all likely talk to other people."

"You're saying I could have been a target because I'm asking questions about Agnes and the other women."

"I'm worried sick about you." Elias leaned across the table as if to emphasize his point. "Look, any one of those people could have talked to several others. But completely apart from Rick and any conspiracy theories he has, if you're correct, that Jack's herbs were harmless and Agnes was somehow an intended victim, that person would definitely view you as a threat. I'm asking you to stop, Lucky. Stop asking questions. Let Nate do his job."

Lucky shivered, realizing the truth in Elias's statement. "I can't stop, Elias. My only concern is to clear Jack. Surely you can understand."

He reached across the table and placed his hand over hers. "I do. I do understand, but in trying to do that, you might have woken up something very evil."

Chapter 39

"Is that the guy?" Nate turned to Sophie, who sat in the passenger seat of Nate's car.

Sophie nodded. "That's him. Brenda told me he always takes off for lunch the same time every day."

"Okay, don't stare at him." Nate had driven his own car and parked in a public lot near the curving exit of the Snow-flake Lodge. "Just turn toward me and act like we're two friends sitting here shootin' the breeze." Nate had put on sunglasses and wore a casual shirt and a jacket.

Sophie shifted in her seat to look directly at Nate. Nate kept his eyes on the exit as the black SUV coasted down the incline. He focused on getting a good look at the license plate of the vehicle. Once it had passed, he quickly jotted the number down on a small notepad that sat near the gearshift. Then he turned the key in the ignition and the engine came to life. "Put your seat belt on."

The SUV turned right at the bottom of the road. Nate backed out of the parking space and drove very slowly fol-lowing the same path. Nate came to a full stop at the exit and counted to ten, allowing the SUV to gain some distance.

Then he turned right to follow. Sophie remained quiet as they followed the road to the top of the hill where Crestline intersected. Nate stopped again and waited, waving to a crossing car to go through the intersection. "This is a narrow two-lane road; let's keep back a little," Nate said.

"Good idea."

"Have a look at this license." Nate passed the small notebook over to Sophie. "These match those three numbers Lucky was able to catch?"

Sophie studied the scrap of paper and shook her head. "No. They don't match at all. Besides, that was a flatbed truck we saw that night."

"Hmm." He thought a moment. "I know the Resort owns their own vehicles. Do you happen to know offhand how many?" he asked.

"They do. And no, I don't know. I'd just be guessing, but maybe they have four or five on-site. I think they have two small passenger vans, a flatbed truck and two SUVs. This one Lurch is driving may be one of them, but I don't know for sure."

"So it's possible our guy here would have access to those the Resort owns?"

"I guess. He's the Head of Security. I'd think he would."

"When I get back to the station, I can look into it."

Sophie fidgeted in her seat. "Don't lose him, Nate. If he lives around here somewhere I'd love to know."

"Be patient. And don't you go thinking you're gonna confront this guy. We have no evidence at all. We're just checkin' him out right now. For all we know he's an upstanding citizen."

"And a spy for the corporation, don't forget that."

"I haven't. When it comes to labor disputes, all bets are off—on both sides."

"Look!" Sophie pointed. "He just turned up that road."

"That's the entrance to the park and the pond."

"Can we follow him in there?"

"Don't see why not. It's public property. It's a beautiful day, probably lots of people come up here to get away." Nate pulled to the side of the road. "We'll just give him five or ten minutes, though. No point in letting him know he's being tailed."

Sophie heaved an impatient sigh. The minutes dragged by. Finally, Nate turned back onto the road and drove into the entrance of the small park. The road dipped down and curved to the right where a lot provided approximately twenty parking spaces. Six other cars besides the black SUV were parked there. Sophie pressed the button to lower her window. She heard the shouts of children from the play area. Glancing to her right, she could make out a jungle gym, a slide and a set of swings through the trees. Midday sunshine sparkled on the surface of the pond.

"This is nice," Nate said, gazing longingly at the tiny strip of sand that edged the water. A few brightly colored towels punctuated the view where visitors were stretched out enjoying the warm air. "Susanna and I need to get out and relax more. I always forget about this little place."

Sophie wiggled her foot in impatience. "Where is he?"

"Let's take a walk. Real casual, now, let's just chat about small stuff." He climbed out of the car and came around to open Sophie's door.

"Anybody in town sees us here, they'll think we're up to something illicit."

Nate guffawed. "Let 'em. I only care what Susanna thinks. Can't worry about every nosy body."

They strolled across the grass and stood under a spreading elm tree, gazing at the water.

"You see him?" Nate spoke quietly.

"Not yet. Where did he get off to?"

"Never mind. I got him."

"Where?" Sophie spun her head around.

"Hey! What did I tell you? Look casual, I said."

"Right. Okay." Sophie took a deep breath.

"He's at a picnic table to your right."

"What's he doing?"

"Right now, he's taking a last bite of a sandwich. Now he's wrapping up his lunch." Nate paused a moment. "Now he's being a good citizen. He just walked over to the trash can and threw the paper bag in. Keep looking at me." Nate glanced over her shoulder in the distance. "He's walking down to the water."

"And?"

"He's pulling a small . . . looks like a brown paper bag from his jacket pocket."

"Maybe he's going to throw a gun into the pond," Sophie hissed.

Nate remained silent, but focused as he watched. "Well, what do you know?" Nate remarked.

"Whaaat?"

"And now he's coming our way. Must be heading back to work. Come on, Sophie, let's get back to the car." Nate turned and walked away quickly. Sophie hurried to catch up with him. As they reached the car, she grabbed Nate's arm.

"Nate!"

"This guy's a regular menace to society."

"What was he doing?"

"Feeding the ducks." Nate smiled. "Let's get back to town."

Chapter 40

LUCKY PULLED TO a stop in front of a modest cottage on Cranberry Lane in Lincoln Falls. The front yard was full of rosebushes of every color and shape, all surrounded by a white picket fence. She had asked Sophie to take over for a few hours at the restaurant to cover for her while she did some errands. Sophie was curious as to where she was going but Lucky had been deliberately vague about her destination. By a happy coincidence, she had noticed an article about a local potter in the *Lincoln Falls Sentinel*, part of an ongoing series about local craftspeople and artists. A lightbulb went off in her brain. She was sure this was the very same potter from whom her mother had purchased the blue dishes and mugs years before. This woman's work could be a surprise wedding gift for Sophie and Sage. Although she knew it was highly unlikely the very same pottery would be available, and unlikely that Sophie would want the same design that her mother had purchased, she hoped to find something similar.

Lucky opened the gate. It creaked slightly. She climbed the wooden steps to the front door and rang the doorbell. It chimed somewhere inside and then she heard the bark of a large dog. She waited, but no one came to the door. She hadn't had a phone number for the woman; nor had she been able to find one in the phone directory. Coming here had been an impulse move but something had told her to take a chance. She rang the bell again and waited. Again she heard a dog bark. Maybe the sound of the dog was part of the doorbell?

She returned to the front yard and decided to walk down the driveway. In the rear of the property she spotted a large shed. She followed stepping-stones for several yards, and suddenly a huge black dog appeared in front of her. He crouched and growled deep in his throat. She could hear a rhythmic sound from the shed. Someone was home.

"Hello," she called.

"Back here," a voice answered. The dog growled again. "Cerberus! Enough! Let the lady in." The dog immediately whimpered and sat on the grass, still alert.

Lucky whispered, "Good boy."

She stepped forward carefully, not quite sure whether the dog wouldn't change his mind.

"Come on in," the voice said.

Lucky stood on the threshold of a spacious shed, unfinished except for shelves that lined the interior. An aroma that reminded her of gardening in soft, warm earth filled the room. The shelves were laden with finished and unfinished pottery. In the center of the room, a rail-thin, white-haired woman sat at a turning potter's wheel, a tiny human powering a great hulking machine.

"Can't stop now. I can talk to you in a minute."

Lucky watched, fascinated as the woman's arthritic hands shaped a great glob of clay, forming it into a fat vase. She had once seen glassblowers work and it struck her that this process was similar. Amorphous shapes of earth and silica crafted into beautiful objects. Finally the rhythmic noise ended as the wheel slowed and finally stopped. The tiny woman stood and walked to a corner sink to rinse her hands. Wiping them on a towel, she approached Lucky and peered up into her face.

"I knew you were okay. I could hear it in your voice. I'm Persephone, but you can call me Penny; everybody does." She held out a damp hand.

Lucky shook her hand. "I'm Lucky. Lucky Jamieson. I'm sorry to disturb you at work. I just didn't have a phone number to call, so I drove over from Snowflake." Lucky heard the dog snuffling behind her and then a wet nose pressed against her leg. She sidestepped the canine curiosity.

"Stop that, Cerberus. That's not polite," the tiny woman chastised her dog.

"Cerberus?" Lucky asked.

"Yes." Penny smiled. "The dog that guards the gates of Hades. You remember your eighth-grade mythology? He was supposed to keep the ghosts of the dead from escaping the underworld. He was a three-headed dog with a serpent's tail, a mane of snakes and lion's claws. My mother was a student of mythology." She laughed. "That's how I got my name." Penny reached down to pat the dog's head and spoke to him. "I know you don't have all those things, boy, but you're still a good guard dog." She looked up at Lucky. "I thought that was a good name for him, since he's guarding me and I'm so old I'm almost there."

Lucky smiled. "You hardly seem it. Looks like you work very hard."

"That I do. Now, what can I do for you?"

Lucky reached into her carryall and pulled out a paper-wrapped object. She dropped the bag on the floor and unwrapped the blue pottery mug she had brought with her. Cerberus immediately began an olfactory investigation of the cloth bag.

"My mother bought a set of dishes and mugs from you several years ago, I believe."

Penny nodded and reached out for the mug. "That's mine, all right." She turned it over. "Here's my mark right here. See it?"

Lucky peered at the glazed bottom where she could make out the small letter P, the curving part of the letter fashioned in a triangular shape. "Ah. I see it now."

"Are you looking to buy some more? 'Cause I don't have any of those left right now."

"No, actually, I have the full set of my mother's, but my best friend is getting married in a week and I'm helping her with her wedding. I really wanted to get her a sentimental gift. She loves my mother's set. I saw an article about you in the local newspaper and that's what triggered my memory. I felt sure you had to be the person who made this."

"Well, you've come to the right place." Penny turned away and led Lucky to a worktable against the far wall. Her long white hair was plaited in a shining braid. Her back was bent in a dowager's hump and the top of her head barely reached Lucky's shoulder. "I've been working a lot in rust and orange colors these days. This is what I have right now." She indicated a stack of plates in deep muted colors covered with small designs reminiscent of folk art.

Lucky picked up one of the plates. "Oh, these are beautiful!" she exclaimed. "I love these colors." She looked hopefully at Penny. "Are these for sale?"

Penelope nodded. "They sure are. Only thing is, I've only made six of the plates and six mugs."

"That's a good-sized set."

Penelope nodded. "Six is a good number. I always like to stop at six. It's the number of home and hearth; did you know that?"

Lucky shook her head. "No, I didn't. Never gave it a thought, to be honest."

"My house number is sixty-nine. Six and nine are fifteen; one and five are six. See? You should think about that some more. Everything's connected, numbers and colors, humans and animals. Animals always know which humans they can trust. They're more connected than we are. Maybe I'm superstitious but I always pay attention to numbers. Never could figure out why dishes and glasses and such are sold in sets of eight." She shuddered. "Eight's not the right number for stuff for your home. You want to take these?"

"Oh, yes, definitely." Lucky watched as Penelope deftly wrapped each piece in heavy paper and gently laid them in a cardboard box. When she had finished, she put a fitted lid on the box.

Lucky pulled bills out of her wallet in payment. "I'm so thrilled I found you. Thank you again."

"You come back anytime you like. You're from Snowflake?"

Lucky nodded. "I own the By the Spoonful Soup Shop on Broadway. Maybe you can stop by sometime. Soup's on the house for you."

"Well, thanks, dear. That's real nice. I don't drive anymore, but if I'm ever over that way, I will stop in. What's the address?"

"It's One-thirty-two Broadway."

"See? One, three, two—adds up to six. Told 'ya. A good number."

"Very interesting. You're right. I'll have to pay attention." Lucky slung her bag over her shoulder and reached down to pat Cerberus's head. He licked her hand in acknowledgment.

She waved good-bye and lugged her carton of pottery dishes and mugs to the car. She thought a moment and then decided to put the box on the floor of the backseat just to be safe. She didn't like the thought of this box and its precious cargo shifting around in the trunk. As she drove away she recalled that Jack's address was 42 Birch Street. She heard Penny's voice in her head telling her that was a good number.

Chapter 41

LUCKY PULLED TO a stop in the parking lot of the Snowflake Resort. Too late for winter tourists and too early for summer visitors, the lot was virtually empty. Only a few cars were parked in the spacious area. She had decided to take a detour on her way back to the Spoonful. If she couldn't do anything for Jack, she could at least try to help Sophie by attempting to talk to Rick once more. She was also hoping that if she applied some pressure, Rick might break down and tell her the real reason he was in Snowflake. She suspected he knew much more than he was saying about his partner's murder, probably much more than he had told Nate at the police station.

She pushed through the revolving door, a space large enough to accommodate more than one traveler and several suitcases. A woman in her thirties in a black suit jacket and a white business shirt manned the reception counter. Lucky had planned to go directly to Rick's room, but then it occurred to her that his room might have been changed after the discovery of the man in the creek. The clerk looked directly at her and smiled a professional, welcoming smile. Lucky didn't recognize her.

She wasn't a resident of Snowflake—of that she was sure—but then, the Resort hired people from all over the country, people experienced in hotel work and management. The Resort had become a city unto itself. Today, there were no crowds among which she could hide herself. There was no option but to approach the front desk.

"I'm here to see Rick Colgan." Lucky smiled. "I believe he's in Room two-six-nine."

The woman's eyebrows raised. "Well, actually, you're in luck. He's having lunch in the Mont Blanc Room right now." She smiled again. "You can catch him there." The woman at the desk had managed not to deny or confirm Rick's actual room number.

Lucky thanked her and turned away. The Mont Blanc was a high-end restaurant, with prices she could hardly afford herself. It would have rivaled the most expensive restaurant in any big city. She followed the sign to the restaurant down a short corridor and pulled the heavy carved door open. A maître d's desk was directly in front of her. Another woman wearing a similar outfit of a black business suit looked up and smiled. Before Lucky could approach the desk, she spotted Rick at a table by a large window that overlooked a view of the mountain.

But Rick wasn't alone. Tom Reed sat across from him and one of the attorneys who had attended the meeting with Sophie. She smiled at the hostess and apologized.

"Sorry. I was looking for someone but he seems to be busy. I'll wait in the lobby."

The woman nodded in acknowledgment.

Lucky retraced her steps and headed for a comfortable armchair that gave her a view of the restaurant's entrance. As she passed a display of brochures, she picked up one that described services offered at the Snowflake Resort. She sat and opened up the brochure. In an effort to appear casual, she pretended to read it avidly. She could feel the desk clerk's eyes on her, but studiously avoided looking up and catching the woman's eye. After ten minutes or so, she heard voices at the end of the corridor as the door to the restaurant opened. Rick Colgan and Tom Reed stepped out and stood by the doorway for a moment or two. They were followed by the third man. All three lingered in the hallway for a few minutes more, then shook hands all around. Rick headed for the lobby while Reed and the attorney walked away in the opposite direction. Rick seemed distracted and took no notice of her sitting in the armchair.

He was heading straight for the exit. She hopped up and followed him. She immediately felt a twinge in her back. Her muscles were still hurting from the accident. She stopped and took a deep breath, willing her muscles to relax. Walking more slowly, she pushed through the revolving door and was just able to catch up with him as he stood under the awning of the entrance.

"Rick!" she called out as she exited from the heavy glass revolving door.

He turned, surprised. "Lucky. What are you doing here?"

"Well, actually, I was hoping to see you."

"Ah," he said. "Let me guess. My sister sent you."

Lucky shook her head. "She didn't. She doesn't even know I'm here." She took a deep breath. "But you must know why I wanted to see you."

"I figured. Here, let's grab a seat. I can't stay long."

"Are you working?"

"Sort of," he replied vaguely.

"The woman you were hired to locate. What was her name? Washburn? Is she here in Snowflake?"

Rick's jaw clenched. He avoided her question. "What did you want to talk about?"

"Well, first questions first. If you're not interested in selling, how come you're having lunch with Tom Reed and one of his crew?"

He smiled slowly. "'Cause they're paying for my lunch at a very expensive restaurant. Why not string them along?"

"Look, I don't think you're being stubborn just to hurt Sophie. But why won't you give her an answer about the house?"

"I wanted to see what they're offering first."

"And?"

"And they were decidedly lukewarm about it. In fact, they really don't have an interest in the parcel the house is on. They want the other acreage. I was just curious to see how far they were willing to go. It doesn't matter, though. I'm not selling. She won't sell the house and I won't sell the other land."

"But why, Rick? Why do you want to keep it? I don't understand."

His face hardened. "You wouldn't."

"Can you see yourself returning to Snowflake someday?"

"Never. Too many ghosts. Too many memories—all bad."

Lucky sighed. "I'm not trying to bug you. I'm just trying to think of a solution that would keep both of you happy. This means everything to your sister. You can't imagine how much it means to her. She wants to—"

"What? Re-create the family we never had?" he replied bitterly.

Lucky was taken aback by his vehemence. "Maybe. Maybe that's exactly what she wants. Why shouldn't she have that?" Lucky waited, but Rick did not respond. "I just don't get it, Rick. What's the issue? You don't want to stay here. You don't want to come back. Why are you so insistent on not selling?

"This really isn't any of your business, Lucky."

"Sophie is my friend. That makes it my business. I don't want to pry; I just don't understand why you won't give her a straight answer about the house, at least. That's all she really cares about."

"Look, there's no happy here. I had to identify my partner's body a few days ago. He was murdered, Lucky. And he was murdered up there on that land. He didn't wash down from somewhere else. That damage to his face was deliberate. Somebody didn't want him identified. And I think I know who. He was on my mother's property to do me a favor and somebody killed him."

"If you're convinced the Resort had something to do with that, why are you still staying here?"

Rick laughed mirthlessly. "Safest place in the world for me. They're not gonna want any dead bodies found in the hotel. But that's not why I'm still here. I've got a lot of questions I need answers to."

"Like what?"

Rick's face shifted. "I learned a few things yesterday. There's a local woman who died. You know anything about that?"

"A little." Their conversation had taken an abrupt turn. "Why?"

"How did she die?"

Lucky hesitated to give Rick information unless she got something in return, but some instinct urged her to be open with him. "She had a heart attack."

"Oh." Rick seemed to breathe a sigh of relief.

"But they're also suspecting she might have been poisoned."

Rick's face paled. He leaned against the bench.

"Why are you asking?"

Rick hesitated, then finally began to speak. "Eddie kept a notebook. I got to see it yesterday at the station. I read his notes and, reading between the lines, figured out we were lied to about why our client was searching for Alice Washburn. Thing is, Eddie never told me. It was obvious to me that Eddie was worried when he figured out there was more to the story about locating Alice Washburn."

"So Eddie was here to investigate?"

Rick nodded. "He volunteered to come up to give me his opinion about the land, but he never told me he had another reason for coming here. I think he was scared that he hadn't checked our client out more thoroughly before he gave out the location of Alice Washburn, the woman he was looking for."

"Does Nate know all this?"

Rick shook his head. "Eddie's notes wouldn't mean anything to Nate and I didn't want to tell him what we'd done. It's too late now anyway."

"Are you saying Agnes Warner and Alice Washburn are one and the same? Who was your client?"

"I can't tell you that."

"Rick!"

He shook his head. "It's better for you if you don't know. I've said too much."

"There's something *you* should know. Somebody loosened the lug nuts on one of Sophie's wheels."

Rick's eyes hardened. "What? Is she okay?"

"She's fine. I was driving it. My car was in the shop."

"I gotta talk to her. She's not safe here anymore."

He stood suddenly and strode away, heading for the parking lot. Lucky was tempted to follow him but decided against it. She was terrified Rick might be right and that Sophie was in danger.

Chapter 42

LUCKY WALKED UP the wooden front steps to the porch of the library. She glanced at her watch. She had a half hour left before she was due back at the Spoonful. She'd have to hurry.

She peeked through the front window before entering. Emily sat at the large desk in what was once the living room of the cottage, her head in her hands. Lucky immediately felt a wave of compassion. The events of the past week must have been a terrible shock, not just to Emily, but to all the women present. Her questions must have upset everyone she had talked to even more.

She knocked once and pushed open the door. Emily lifted her head instantly. "Lucky!"

"I'm sorry to bother you again," Lucky said.

"You're no bother. Come on in. I'm still so upset about Agnes. I know it's been days but it doesn't seem to get any better. I feel responsible. I keep thinking maybe I should have put a stop to Cordelia and her plans. Maybe if I had, Agnes would still be alive. I can't quite process everything."

Emily sat up straighter and pulled down the sleeves of

her blouse, a brightly colored peasant shirt. Then she smoothed out her long denim skirt. Her gray hair was pinned up in a bun instead of the usual braid she wore. Several strands had escaped. "I'm sorry to rattle on. What was it you needed, dear?"

"I just wanted to talk to you again. I was wondering . . . how did this whole thing get started?"

Emily rubbed her temples. "I don't really . . . It's hard to explain."

"Try me." Lucky sat in a chair near the desk.

"Well, it all started as sort of a women's group, meeting here at the library. One night we got talking about the Stones and the travelers who were in town last autumn."

Lucky nodded. She knew Emily was referring to the Neolithic stones on the hill above the town, one of many well-known structures that dotted the New England landscape and defied solid explanation.

"I guess that was our inspiration. And then . . . somebody brought up the subject of religion and how all the institutions are so dominated by men, how there are no matriarchal-based religious beliefs anymore and there should be. And then someone else referred to the end of April ceremonies in northern climates and how it's a holdover from a pagan ritual."

Lucky listened silently, willing Emily to continue.

"Cordelia Rank . . ." Emily hesitated. "Well, we all know how forceful Cordelia can be." She smiled slightly. "Cordelia decided that we should all take part in a May Day celebration, honoring the earth. It all seemed so harmless." Her voice choked.

Lucky reached out and held Emily's hand. "I'm sorry to make you go through this again."

Emily sniffed. "It's all right. I'll probably be playing this over in my mind for a long time to come." She continued. "Well . . . someone else decided to do a little research and find out what people did on May Day, or the eve of the day. And we learned about Walpurgis Night and the celebrations in many countries. So, that's how it all came to be. It just seemed like it would be so much fun. A bit of an adventure, you know?" She took a shaky breath. "But it wasn't. It was horrible. And we still don't even know what happened for sure."

A door closed in the back of the cottage. Emily looked up as Greta came into the room. She arranged her expression in an attempt to seem calm. "Oh, Greta. I didn't know you were still here."

"I just wanted to finish repairing that last stack of books in the workroom," Greta said.

"You remember Lucky, don't you?" She nodded her head in Lucky's direction.

"Yes, of course. I picked up her books the other day."

Lucky turned to Emily. "Greta and I actually live in the same building. And Greta came to my apartment the other day." Lucky shot a meaningful glance in Greta's direction. "Didn't you, Greta?" There was no doubt in Lucky's mind that Greta had snatched one of the photos from her coffee table.

"Oh, I didn't realize." Emily smiled politely.

Greta's eyes widened. "Uh, yes," she stammered. Lucky was sure the meaning behind her words was not lost on Greta. "See you tomorrow, Emily," Greta replied as she hurried to the front door.

Emily turned back to Lucky and whispered, "I know Greta's such an odd duck and she's not the easiest person to deal with at times, but I'd be lost without her, especially this past week. It's been very difficult to come in, but I'm better off coming to work, I suppose. Otherwise, I'd probably just sit at home and think about what happened."

"How was this ritual arranged?"

"Well, as I think I told you, Cordelia wanted twelve women, thirteen in all, including herself. But we only had seven as it turned out—actually, six. That's why Greta was commandeered to join us. Cordelia had given everyone very clear instructions as to what to wear and how to form the semicircle around the altar. Agnes prepared the altar and we changed into our robes and then . . ."

"Agnes prepared the altar?"

"Uh, why, yes."

"What did that involve?"

"Well, she got the fire started and laid everything out on that big slab of stone, the ladle and the cauldron and the bowl and all. Then we all formed a sort of semicircle around Cordelia, and Cordelia was doing her invocation to Mother Earth, I think, and then . . ." Emily trailed off, a faraway look in her eye. "I just thought of something I hadn't thought of before. I think Greta was first in the circle. I thought it was Agnes who was supposed to go first, but it wasn't. It was Greta."

A chill ran up Lucky's spine. "*Greta* was supposed to go first? Not Agnes?"

"I'm trying to remember. I hadn't thought about it before now. I guess I was just too upset. But yes, I think that's right. I think it was supposed to be the first woman on Cordelia's left. But then Agnes stepped forward and took the bowl from Cordelia. Maybe I'm wrong. Maybe it was the person who prepared the altar who was supposed to go first and Greta was just standing in the wrong place." Emily rubbed her forehead. "Oh, I can't remember it all now. Everything happened so fast. I'm sure Greta would remember." She looked up. "Have you heard anything about the autopsy results, Lucky? Do they know what Agnes died of?"

Lucky was forced to deliberately lie. "No, I haven't." She had no intention of letting Elias's information spread through town. In spite of wanting to take the pressure off Jack, she wasn't willing to volunteer any information about Agnes's cardiovascular problems.

She checked her watch. "Oh, Emily, I better get back. Sorry to cut this short."

"That's quite all right, Lucky. In a way it feels better to talk about it. That night is on my mind all the time anyway."

Lucky said good-bye and walked slowly down Elm Street on her way back to the Spoonful. She had every intention of confronting Greta about the photograph as soon as she caught up with her alone. Was it possible Greta Dorn was Rick and Eddie's client? That she had hired them to locate Alice

Washburn? And was Agnes Warner not who she claimed to be? Was Alice Washburn in fact Agnes's true identity? It had been worth the trip to the library even if she had learned only one fact. If it was indeed true, that Greta was intended to be the first in the circle to drink the wine, what would have happened to her if that had been the case? Assuming Greta was healthy, would she have had a reaction to the wine? Would she have displayed symptoms so quickly? If Agnes had prepared the altar, had she added a toxic substance to the wine? But how would she have managed to do that under Cordelia's eagle eye? And if she had, she certainly wouldn't have chosen to be the first to drink. Had Greta been the intended target? Lucky's head was spinning. She couldn't work it out and wondered if everyone's memories of the incident were foggy or just plain wrong.

THE LUNCH RUSH had ended by the time she reached the Spoonful. She quickly dropped her purse under the desk in the office and tied on an apron as she headed down the hall to the front room. She stifled a quick feeling of guilt over leaving Jack and everyone to deal with the crush.

"Oh, there you are!" Meg said as she came behind the counter.

"Sorry. Didn't mean to leave you shorthanded. Just had to take care of a few things." She glanced over at the cash register. "How's Jack doing?"

"Okay, I think. He's been pretty quiet, but we were fine," Meg said. "Where did you get off to?"

"Oh, some errands for Sophie's wedding and such. And then I stopped at the library to talk to Emily." Lucky deliberately didn't mention her conversation with Rick Colgan.

"Oh," Meg said. Lucky was sure Meg knew why she had been talking to Emily.

Lucky turned around and peeked through the hatch to the kitchen. Sage looked up and waved to her.

"Sophie's not here?" she asked him.

"Any minute. She had some errands to run too." The

words were no sooner out of his mouth than Lucky heard the back door slam. Sophie popped into the kitchen a moment later, tying an apron around her waist.

Lucky pushed through the swinging door into the kitchen. "Have you contacted your insurance company?"

"Yes." Sophie wiped imaginary perspiration from her brow. "We're covered. Still have to find a car, but thanks to Sage, he made sure both our cars were covered for theft and collision."

"Well, I don't want you to worry. I have some money saved up, so whatever the difference is, I'm chipping in. No arguments."

Sage shook his head. "No way. We're fine, Lucky. Really we are."

Lucky started to protest, but Sophie cut her off. "Uh-uh. No, you're not. I'm just glad you're alive. If anything had ever happened to you, I couldn't handle it. It's just a hunk of metal. The important thing is that you're all right."

"Well, the offer's still good. So I don't want you two to have more of a burden, what with the wedding and all."

Sophie came around the worktable and hugged her. "Thanks, we appreciate that, we really do, but no need. Besides, you're covering the cost of rentals and decorations and music for the wedding, which is already far too generous of you. So stop worrying about it."

"It's not a lot, believe me. Besides, that's a joint present from me and Jack, and Elias is chipping in too, so it's no burden." Lucky chose not to argue about the car, but she didn't intend this to be the last discussion. If someone had deliberately tampered with Sophie's car, there was no way to know which of them was really the target. She didn't want to tell Sophie she had gone to the Resort to reason with Rick, and she sincerely hoped Rick was wrong in his fear for Sophie's safety. She hoped Rick would talk to Sophie soon and warn her to be careful.

She returned to the counter and cleared away dishes and replaced the settings with napkins and silverware. Jack was at the cash register. His face looked drawn, and he hadn't said a word since she'd arrived. She walked over and put a hand on his shoulder. "How are you doing today?"

"Hangin' in, my girl," he said without looking up. As she turned to go back to the counter, a figure on the sidewalk outside caught her eye. It was Leonard Warner. She stiffened. Jack followed her look and stared back.

"What's he doing?" Lucky asked.

Jack shook his head and turned back to the cash register. "He was out there earlier. Just stood on the sidewalk and stared in, like he's doin' now."

"Intimidation. That's what it is," she said. "I'm putting a stop to this." She opened the front door and looked at Leonard. "What is it, Leonard? What do you want?"

Leonard continued to stare through the glass at Jack. "I want him to admit what he's done."

"Okay. That's enough. Don't think these tactics will work with us. You'll have to leave . . . right now. I won't have you standing outside trying to freak Jack out and scaring our customers away."

"It's a free sidewalk. I'll stand here as long as I like." He turned to her slowly, a fierce light in his eyes. Lucky wondered if this tragedy had affected his mental balance. "If your grandfather has a guilty conscience, he has no one to blame but himself."

"Well, I hate to disillusion you, but he doesn't, and neither do I, and emotional blackmail won't work. You be gone now or I'm calling Nate Edgerton." As the words left her mouth she spotted Nate coming down Broadway in their direction.

Nate took in the confrontation and nodded to Lucky. He approached Leonard slowly. "Enough is enough, Leonard. This isn't doing anybody any good, especially you. I want you to move on. Go home to your grandson and think about him."

Leonard almost snarled as he turned on Nate. "I'm not going anywhere, Nate Edgerton. I demand you do something. Arrest that man right now."

"Now, Leonard, calm down." Nate's voice became firmer. "I'm asking you again, nicely. I know you've been through a lot, but I'm warning you. I'm not about to arrest anybody until I have all the facts . . ."

"You can't protect that old man forever. He should be in jail before he hurts anybody else."

Nate shook his head. "I repeat. No one is going to be arrested. No one will be accused of anything until all the facts are in. And I'm not going to allow you to harass Jack Jamieson or anyone else. Do you understand?" Nate's voice had changed timbre.

Leonard nodded. "I get it. I get it. You take care of your friends and look the other way when an innocent person like my wife dies. Don't worry. I'm on my way, Mr. Chief of Police, but I'm not finished with him." He nodded in the general direction of the restaurant where Jack sat, then stormed away.

Nate didn't reply but watched Leonard carefully.

Lucky breathed a sigh of relief. "Thanks, Nate. I'm really glad you came along when you did. Jack can't take much more. He's doing a good job on himself as it is. He doesn't need this. It's not fair."

"No, it's not." Nate shook his head. "I feel bad for Leonard but I'm not gonna be bulldozed, no matter how angry the guy is. He's been down at the station every day lobbying for Jack to be placed under arrest."

"He's what?" Lucky was struck dumb.

"You heard me. But don't say anything to Jack. Frankly, I think old Leonard might be going a little off the beam right now. Understandable. He wants to blame somebody and Jack's an easy target, but until those results are confirmed, I'm not doing anything about it—for now."

"Come on in, Nate." Lucky looked behind her. Several customers had noticed the altercation and were staring out the window as she spoke to Nate.

"Don't need to ask me twice. I'm starving." Nate put a hand on her shoulder. "And you give me a call if anything else happens. If Leonard comes back and tries to threaten you or Jack, you call me right away."

"Don't worry, I will. He's really starting to scare me." She turned and entered the restaurant with Nate following in her wake.

Chapter 43

"WHAT'S THIS COSTING you, my girl?" Jack asked.

Lucky shrugged. "It's not bad, really. The material for Sophie's dress and veil and the tulle for the gazebo was super reasonable. The harpist is charging a flat fee, and I think she'll be worth it. She's wonderful and the music will be so romantic. She'll wheel her harp in and I think we should put her on the deck 'cause it's a good solid surface. She's agreed to play for an hour before the ceremony and as Sophie walks to the gazebo. Then she'll play for about half an hour after the ceremony while everyone's milling around."

Jack's eyebrows shot up. "Everyone?"

"Well, that's kind of what I wanted to talk to you about." Lucky watched her grandfather carefully. She took a deep breath. "You see, for the past week or so, I've discovered that lots of people are convinced they're invited."

"Like who? I thought Sophie wanted just a private ceremony?"

"She did, but now I think she's accepted the fact that maybe the guest list needs to be extended."

"Who are we talking about?"

"Marjorie and Cecily are looking forward to it. So are Hank and Barry. They've all asked what they should wear and what presents Sophie and Sage might like. Then Horace asked my opinion about his suit. They haven't even asked if they're invited. They've all just assumed they are. And Bradley asked if he could bring a guest. And if Bradley is coming, we really should invite Nate and Susanna. It's so hard to draw the line."

"I can understand that. Everybody loves Sage's cooking at the restaurant and Sophie too."

"Then Pastor Wilson is under the impression he's supposed to officiate. Plus a few friends of Sophie's from work. And then . . ." Lucky hesitated. Jack looked at her sharply. "Flo Sullivan told me she was waiting for her invitation." Lucky cringed inwardly.

Jack groaned. "Oh no. Not Flo."

"I just didn't know what to tell people. And I'm convinced other people will stop in after the ceremony just to wish the newlyweds well. Everybody knows it's happening at your house. Who knows?" Lucky continued. "What I'm thinking about, if it's okay with you, is we should maybe rent one of those dance floors and hire musicians."

"That's gonna be expensive, isn't it?"

"Not cheap, but it'll give people something to do and it could really be fun. I found a trio of musicians that hire out for small events. Their fee isn't bad at all and I've called a rental company for the dance floor. I can pay for that, no worries. Besides, however Elias and you and I split the rest of the costs, it's our joint wedding present to them."

"But how are we gonna feed all these people?"

"Sage said not to worry. He's taking care of all the food and drinks and champagne. We can set up a huge buffet in your dining room. I'm sure Sage knows what he's doing. He has warming trays and all the accessories, so he can get everything set up earlier and then just enjoy the party. I just hope this is okay with you."

"Well, I think it's nice that all these people want to be part of it. I have no objection. Just one condition."

"What's that?"

"You make sure you stay until Flo's gone home. You can't leave until I'm safe."

Lucky laughed. "Okay. It's a deal."

Chapter 44

FOR NO REASON she could quite put her finger on, Lucky woke the following morning with a heavy feeling in her chest. Was she worried? Yes, definitely. Two people were dead. Her neighbor was more than likely connected in some fashion to the dead woman. And her best friend's life might be in danger. Her muscles still ached from the accident. Her neck was stiff, and she could feel the groaning of her wrenched muscles. Jack was a nervous wreck, and the confrontation with Leonard Warner the day before at the restaurant certainly hadn't helped. Talking about the wedding plans last night seemed to cheer him up a bit but it felt as if every way she turned, her path was blocked. No firm results were in from the toxicology examination. Or if they were, no one was sharing the information with her. Jack still blamed himself and there wasn't anything she could do about it. The only thing she had learned was that Emily thought Greta was supposed to be the first to drink the wine. Lucky definitely needed to talk to Cordelia to confirm that Emily's memory of the night in the woods was accurate.

Cordelia would know, but the thought of going back to talk to Cordelia Rank seemed overwhelming right now.

To add to her frustration, Rick wasn't willing to share the name of his client. Sophie still couldn't get a straight answer from her brother as to why he refused to sell the land. No matter what she had attempted to accomplish, she didn't feel she was any further along the path. And perhaps just as important, she still had no solid idea why her mother had taken so many photos of the Warners years before.

Lucky dragged herself out of bed and headed for the kitchen to make a cup of coffee before starting her day. Once the coffee was ready, she flicked on the computer in the living room. Rick and Eddie had been hired to find Alice Washburn. Was Alice Washburn the real reason Eddie Fowler had come to Snowflake? And if so, why? His client had lied to him. He had discovered there was more to the story. If Agnes Warner really was Alice Washburn, had Eddie tried to warn her? Most important, who was his client?

When the screen came to life, she typed "Alice Washburn" into the search engine. She heard the kettle screaming in the kitchen and ran down the hall to turn off the stove. She poured the boiling water through a filter and swirled it around to make it go through faster. She added a little cream to the mug and carried it back to the living room.

She hit the enter key and waited. When the screen came to life, she scrolled down. A news article appeared highlighting the name "Washburn." She clicked on it. A *Boston Globe* story from five years earlier popped up. A woman named Margaret Washburn was being investigated after the death of her husband from a drug overdose. Farther down, the same name appeared in a Cleveland newspaper article. Margaret Washburn had been indicted for the possession and sale of illegal substances. Lucky read both articles, but no photos appeared. This still wasn't anyone named Alice Washburn. She searched again and a longer article appeared in an Albany, New York, paper, again dated five years earlier. Margaret Washburn was the daughter-in-law of Alice and Lionel Washburn. She had been married to their son, Matthew Washburn.

Lucky shook her head. Alice Washburn. Agnes Warner? And Lionel and Leonard? Could it possibly be? Or just a coincidence? Was this the same Alice Washburn that Rick had been hired to locate? She was sure lots of people were called Washburn. She herself didn't know any, but it seemed a fairly common name. For all she knew, there could be millions of Washburns across the country and maybe hundreds even in Vermont. She continued to search but the name "Alice Washburn" didn't turn up again.

She leaned back in the chair and rubbed her eyes. She pushed an envelope aside that had come in the mail the day before. She glanced at her address. Thirty-two Maple Street. Three and two were five. What would Penny the potter say about that number? She took another sip of coffee and let her mind wander. She pictured the white-haired woman in the potter's shed. *"Everything's connected,"* she had said. Colors and numbers, animals and humans. Two murders. Were they connected? One woman who was perhaps poisoned in the woods, a woman who appeared to lead a blameless life with no known enemies. A man, a private investigator of sorts, murdered with attempts to make the body hard to identify. Could these two deaths be connected? The man in the creek was Eddie Fowler, a partner of Rick Colgan. Was Eddie in Snowflake to warn Alice Washburn or to find his mystery client? Checking out Sophie's mother's land couldn't be the only reason Eddie had volunteered to come. Was Peter Manko, the security guard, involved, as Rick was certain? Could he have been their mystery client? And why had Greta stolen one of the photos? Greta—wasn't Greta a nickname for Margaret? Could that possibly be? Was Greta their mystery client?

Rick had learned that Eddie had investigated their client, worried about the repercussions of revealing the whereabouts of Alice Washburn. If Agnes Warner was really Alice Washburn, then both she and Eddie were now dead. That must be the connection, she thought. Who would have had a motive to kill both of them?

Chapter 45

SOPHIE SAT IN the passenger seat while Lucky drove. "Thank you."

"For what?"

"For coming with me. This isn't easy for me." Sophie had decided to make one last effort to pin her brother down before he left town. Her hands were shaking slightly. She looked frightened.

Lucky reached over and grasped her hand. "It's going to be all right, Sophie. Whatever happens, you and Sage will find the home you're meant to have."

"I know that. Logically, I know that." She giggled suddenly, a hysterical giggle. "Maybe I can have the chimney moved if things don't work out."

Lucky smiled in response. "What's so funny?"

"Oh, I don't know." Sophie wiped tears from her eyes. "Just the thought of me and Sage with a sledgehammer, knocking down that beautiful fireplace and carting it somewhere else."

"Come on. Let's get this over with." Lucky climbed out of the car. She didn't relish the prospect of confronting Rick

Colgan once more, but she had no choice in the matter. She planned to stay back while Sophie talked to her brother, a benevolent observer, a friend.

They entered through the front entrance. A different woman was at the reception desk today. She smiled in anticipation, but Sophie ignored her and headed for the elevator, with Lucky following in her wake. She pressed the button and the elevator door opened instantly.

"Do you know which room he's in?"

Sophie nodded. "I called Mary to check. They moved him after Nate came up here, after we discovered Eddie's body."

The elevator opened on the third floor. The corridor stretched in each direction and Sophie turned to the left, glancing quickly at each door as she passed. Finally, she reached number 315 and knocked on the door. A stiff paper sign requesting privacy hung on the door handle. They heard shuffling and then the door was flung open.

"I said I didn't want . . ." Rick's words died on his lips. "Sophie!"

"Can we talk?"

Rick glanced at Lucky and walked back into the room. "Everybody wants to talk to me. How interesting." They followed in his wake. "What is it now?" He sat heavily in the chair by the desk. A full duffel bag rested on the unused bed. Rick was ready to leave. "Is this about the house again?"

"Rick, I just want a firm answer from you about it. And . . . you said you can locate people." Sophie took a deep breath. "I really want you to find Dad."

Rick's eyebrows rose, and a flush crept up his neck. "Uh-uh. I don't want to do that."

"But why?" Sophie pleaded. "I'm getting married in a week. He's your father too. Why won't you do this for me?"

"If you're gonna be stubborn about this, I can't stop you. You're free to hire somebody, just not me. I don't have any interest in finding the old bastard."

"How can you call him that? He was wonderful."

Rick rolled his eyes. "You know nothing. You were a baby when he . . . left."

"Rick, why are you taking off? I thought you wanted to get to the bottom of your partner's murder?" Lucky asked.

"I'm pretty sure I know who did it and why. I've turned over everything I know to Nate. It's up to him now." He watched Sophie carefully. "If that's it, Sis, I'm taking off. I'll be in touch." He rose and grabbed the duffel and walked out the door, dropping his key card on the table.

Sophie collapsed on the edge of the bed, her head in her hands. Lucky was at a loss for words. "Can you believe him? He won't look for our father, he won't give me a firm yes or no about the house and he won't sell the other parcels." She shook her head.

"I don't think there's much you can do, Sophie."

"Oh no." Her eyes narrowed. "I'm not leaving it. He's not gonna leave me like this with no answers." She jumped up and headed out the door. Her move took Lucky by surprise and she ran after Sophie, who had jumped in the elevator. She barely managed to slide in before the doors closed. She wasn't sure if she should counsel Sophie to calm down or just keep her mouth shut and stay out of the way.

When the elevator doors opened at the lobby level, they spotted Rick standing under the awning of the front entrance. They hurried to catch up with him. By the time they reached him, he was halfway across the almost empty parking lot.

Sophie ran and grabbed his arm. "You are *not* leaving like this."

Rick pulled his arm away and turned to face her, a look of fury on his face. "What the hell . . ."

"I want answers, Rick. You are not gonna drive away and leave like this, not anymore." Sophie's voice had risen.

Lucky took in a sharp breath. She could have sworn Rick's first instinct was to strike out at Sophie.

He pulled himself under control. "I am leaving, Sis."

"No!" Sophie screamed and began to pound on his chest. "I want you to come clean with me. Why won't you sell that land? Why won't you look for Dad? Why?" Tears were streaming down her face.

A frightened look passed across Rick's face. He backed away and stumbled. He seemed to collapse in upon himself, growing smaller. Lucky saw a flash of the young man he had once been as he realized the extent of Sophie's pain. His shoulders slumped; his arms hung limply at his sides. He was silent for several moments, then spoke quietly. "'Cause there's no point, Sis." His eyes held a pitying look.

Sophie grew still. "What do you mean?" she whispered.

"He's dead." A gust of wind seemed to pull the words from him.

Sophie stared at her brother for a long time. "Dead."

Rick stood stock still. Lucky felt she didn't dare to breathe.

Sophie's face blanched. "How do you know that?"

"Because I buried him. I buried him on the other side of the hill."

Sophie opened her mouth to speak, but no words came. Rick waited.

Finally, she spoke. "How? How did he die?" She could barely choke out the words. Lucky had to strain to hear.

"It was Mom."

Sophie's face blanched.

"Mom did it. She finally fought back. After all those beatings, she finally had enough. She went crazy. He turned his back to her and she picked up a hammer." Rick's voice started to choke. He sobbed. "I couldn't believe my eyes, Sis. She wouldn't stop. Even after he fell to the floor, she got down on her knees and kept hitting him in the face and the head. I had to pull her away."

"No," Sophie wailed, a sound that seemed to come from deep within her. Lucky was stunned. She watched helplessly.

"I didn't see it coming. I don't think she saw it coming. When I got her away, it was too late. I could tell he was dead."

"Don't say this!" Sophie screamed. She held her hands up as if to ward off a blow.

"You know what the worst of it was? I was rooting for her. That's the feeling I had. It was so strange, like I was watching something from a long distance away. It wasn't until I pulled her off that it hit me what had just happened. I've thought about it a lot all these years. She and I, we just stood there and stared at him and the blood all over the kitchen."

Sophie started to shake. "And the others?"

"They didn't know; they weren't there when it happened. But I think they knew. They never asked." Rick's face was haunted. "Don't look at me like that. What the hell was I supposed to do? Turn in the one decent parent I had? I was just a kid. You were a baby. We had to survive." Rick sighed. "He's buried under the old white oak that was struck by lightning. You remember that one? It seemed like a good place to put him, under a dead tree. That's why I didn't want to sell that land." Rick reached out to touch Sophie's cheek gently. "I can't do this anymore." He turned and walked away to his car, climbed in and drove away without a backward look. Lucky and Sophie stood and watched him go. Then Lucky put her arms around Sophie and held her while she sobbed.

Chapter 46

SOPHIE STOOD AS rigid as a stone carving, flanked by Lucky and Sage. Sage reached out to hold Sophie's hand, but she pulled away. They stood with Nate watching the men dig. Nate had called in reinforcements from Lincoln Falls, and technicians waited next to their van as the men dug. A chill wind blew down from the top of the hillside. Lucky shivered in her light jacket. Clouds had gathered, threatening rain, after what had begun as a warm spring day.

One of the men shouted and Nate walked toward the group. He looked down at the cavity they had unearthed and nodded once. The other two men rested on their shovels. One wiped perspiration from his forehead. Nate beckoned to the technicians to approach.

Sophie walked toward them. Her legs moved stiffly. Nate turned toward her and warned her off.

"I don't think you should see this, Sophie."

Sophie, with a sudden burst of energy, avoided Nate's arm and ducked around him. She halted at the edge of the shallow grave the workers had uncovered. Lucky rushed forward with Sage following. The skeleton was curled in a fetal position, its legs drawn up as if sleeping. Remnants of clothing still clung to the bones. Sophie covered her mouth and turned away. She leaned over and gagged. Sage stepped close to her but Sophie stood and pushed him away. She ran down the hillside. Sage called out to her as she ran but she didn't stop. Lucky watched helplessly as Sophie climbed into their car and drove away.

Sage, halfway down the hill, came to a sudden stop, watching as Sophie sped away. Lucky caught up with him. "I don't know what to do." He turned to her. "What should I do, Lucky?"

She shook her head. "I'll drive you back. She's probably heading to your apartment. Or if not yet, she will be. Best to leave her alone for a bit."

Sage turned back and looked up at the hillside where the technicians were gathered around the base of the blackened trunk of the tree. He sighed heavily. "Why did Rick have to tell her?"

"She didn't leave him much choice. I think he was just exhausted from keeping the secret his whole life."

SAGE DIDN'T SAY a word on the ride back to town. Lucky pulled up in front of their apartment on Chestnut. Sage jumped out and ran up the stairs. Three minutes later he returned, shaking his head, and climbed back into the car.

"She's not there. And I don't think she's been back. Where would she go, Lucky?"

"I don't know. Maybe we should check my place. She has an emergency key. She might be hiding out there."

"Okay. I can't put myself in her shoes, but why is she driving away the people closest to her?" he blurted out in frustration.

Lucky thought a moment before she answered. "Shame. I think that might be a big part of it. She's spent her whole life recovering from being the poor kid in town, in her mind, looked down on and made fun of. She's made a success of her life and now this has pulled the rug out from under her.

That's just part of it, though. Maybe the bigger part is the fantasy she had to keep alive all these years. That everything would have been different if her father had returned. Their lives would have changed for the better—hers, her mother's, all of them. Instead . . ."

"Instead, the secret ate away at them."

"If what Rick said is true, that none of them ever asked what happened to their father, then somehow, they must have known. They knew not to ask or say a word. And Rick was forced to keep it to himself. What a terrible burden to bear."

Lucky pulled up to her apartment building. "Wait here. I'll run up and check."

"I'll make some calls," Sage said, pulling out his cell phone. "Maybe one of her friends has heard from her."

Lucky ran up the stairs of her building and rushed into the vestibule. Greta's door opened a crack and she peeked out. Lucky called out to her, but Greta slammed the door before Lucky could reach it. Frustrated, Lucky rushed up the stairs to her front door and unlocked it. Somehow the theft of the photo didn't seem so important. Not now. Not with the worry over Sophie. She called out Sophie's name. The apartment was completely still. She quickly checked each of the rooms, the living room, closets, bath, kitchen and bedroom. No Sophie. She hadn't really expected that Sophie would come here, but she had to check nonetheless.

Sage looked up hopefully as Lucky returned to the car. Lucky shook her head negatively.

"No luck, Sage. Sorry." He was just dropping his cell phone into his pocket. "Were you able to reach anyone?"

"No, but I left messages. I didn't say why. I just asked them to give me a call. Maybe she'll come home before I have to explain. Let's get back to the restaurant. If Sophie's looking for us, she may come there when she calms down."

"I certainly hope so." Lucky turned the key in the ignition. "I'm going to drive around the corner to the Spoonful. I want my car parked someplace where I can keep an eye on it."

It was close to lunchtime when they reached the Spoonful. Janie and Meg stared silently at Lucky as she took over the counter. Lucky was certain they had already heard of all the activity on the mountainside and the body the police were digging for. They knew immediately this wasn't the moment to be asking for any explanations. Lucky shook her head slightly to warn them not to talk about anything just yet.

Jack glanced up briefly and caught Lucky's eye. She gave him a nod and held a finger to her lips. Jack would know they could talk later.

BY THE TIME Lucky had a chance to take a break, it was growing dark. Sophie had not returned. Lucky peeked through the hatch and caught Sage's eye. He had been quiet all day, but Lucky knew he was calling Sophie's cell and their home number every chance he had. And he was growing more anxious by the minute.

"Nothing?" Lucky asked quietly. Sage shook his head and slammed a pan on the work counter. He hung his head.

Lucky pushed through the swinging door into the kitchen. She sat on a stool next to him. "Why don't you take off? She may be at home already but just not answering the phone. This had to be unbelievably tough for her today."

"I know. I'm sure it was. I just need to talk to her. I need to know she's okay."

"Go home. She's either there or will be soon."

Sage nodded. He grabbed his jacket from the hook and left through the back door without another word.

The restaurant had emptied out when she returned to the counter. Janie and Meg had gathered all the dishes and carried them into the kitchen.

"We're getting ready to go, Lucky. Are you okay?"

"Sure, you two go ahead," she replied. "Jack and I can handle everything."

Janie hesitated. "I guess they found him? Was it real bad?"

Lucky nodded. "For Sophie it was. She . . . uh, she took off. We haven't been able to find her."

"She's probably hiding out somewhere," Meg volunteered.

"That's my guess too. She'll come home when she's ready."

"Good night," the girls said in unison and left through the swinging door to the corridor. Lucky heard the back door slam. Jack was sitting by the front window, staring out at the street.

Lucky loaded the dishwasher and turned it on. Then she bagged up the last of the trash to unload in the Dumpster · behind the restaurant. She turned off all the lights except for one small lamp and joined Jack at the table.

"Can I get you a beer?" she asked.

He shook his head. "No, thanks. Just don't feel like it."

She didn't know what she could say to lighten his mood. She reached across the table and squeezed his hand. "I know you're really down, Jack."

He nodded. "The worst of it is being here all day and knowing that people are looking at me and thinking that I'm to blame."

Lucky wasn't sure there wasn't some truth in what Jack was saying. "Don't assume that at all." She contradicted him. "You don't know what they're thinking. Most of them probably didn't even know Agnes, much less have an opinion of you or what happened."

"I appreciate that, my girl. It's not true, but I appreciate that anyway."

"Jack, I'm being honest here. I really don't think you made any mistakes. I think somebody intended to harm Agnes. Somebody, in spite of what Cordelia claims, might have tampered with that cauldron or the wine at the ceremony."

Jack looked up. "You think Cordelia might have done it deliberately?"

Lucky shrugged. "I can't imagine why. What possible reason could she have? And if Emily is to be believed, none of the other women seemed to have any connection to

Agnes. There was something I found out from Emily, if it's true, that is. Emily thinks it was actually supposed to be Greta who drank the wine first."

"Hmm. If that's the case . . . then your theory about Agnes goes right out the window."

"I know. Agnes apparently prepared the altar and Emily thought maybe that's why Agnes thought she was to be the first to drink the wine. Maybe just a mix-up."

"So it could just as well have been one of the other women."

"If it's true, if Emily remembered it correctly. And if that's correct, as soon as the first person had a bad reaction, the rest would have known something was wrong with the wine, so no one would take a chance and drink it. Besides, whatever was mulled, it was done at Cordelia's house, and only she and her husband live there. And Cecily swore to me that she didn't stop anywhere or leave the basket unattended after she picked it up from you."

"That lands it smack on my doorstep again, doesn't it?"

"Jack, they believe there was a toxin of some sort involved. We don't know what it was, not yet. We don't know if it came from the wine. We don't know if Agnes was on medication. But we do know she had a heart attack. That's what killed her. What she drank might not even have had a chance to get into her system."

"Lucky, my girl, some toxins from plants can act right away. Not all, of course. Sometimes the effects take a while. They'll just have to figure out exactly what it was and where it came from."

"Right. If the wine is found to be safe, then it had to come from somewhere else. It didn't come from your herbs." Lucky continued, "Jack, we'll find an explanation, I just know we will, and you'll be vindicated. Just be patient. In the meantime, I don't want to see you suffering about this."

The phone in the kitchen began to ring. She looked at Jack quizzically. "Are you waiting for a phone call?"

"Not me," he replied.

Lucky jumped up and hurried into the kitchen, catching the phone on the third ring. It was Sage.

"She's not here. I can't find her. I've called everyone I can think of and no one's heard from her. Not even Nate." Lucky heard panic in Sage's voice. "I've borrowed my neighbor's car. I'm going out to look for her."

Chapter 47

LUCKY DROVE UP and down the streets of Snowflake, starting at her own apartment on Maple. She couldn't imagine where Sophie would be. She'd like to think Sophie would seek her out, especially under these circumstances. She couldn't begin to imagine the range of feelings Sophie must be going through. To yearn for a father who had disappeared and then to learn he had been dead all along, killed by her own mother. And then to actually see what was left of her father's body in the ground. It must have been horrifying for her. She must have been completely overwhelmed.

Sophie undoubtedly had friends outside of Snowflake, but no one she had ever mentioned as being significant. There were work friends at the Resort but again, no one Sophie had ever mentioned being particularly close to. As far as Lucky knew, everyone truly important in Sophie's life was right here in Snowflake—herself, Sage and Jack.

Would she have gone to the Resort? Taken a room to hide out in? That was a possibility. When she completed her circuit of the town and was sure that Sophie hadn't left her car on a side street, she drove the few miles up the mountain to the Resort. She entered through the stone pillars and made a circuit of the parking lot. She was sure that Sage would be making the same kind of circuit. Employee parking spaces were at the far end. If Sophie had come here, she might have parked in her regular spot. Lucky drove to the very back of the area. Several cars were parked in front of signs that stated "Staff Only," but Sophie's, or rather Sage's, car wasn't one of them. Frustrated and exhausted, she made another circuit of the lot, to no avail. Wherever Sophie was, it wasn't here, and she would have had to drive in order to arrive at the Resort. Lucky leaned her head against the steering wheel. *Sophie, where did you go?*

She turned the car around and headed out of the lot, steering back toward town. When she reached Broadway, a thought came to her. It was the last place she would have thought to look, but upon reflection, it made perfect sense. She turned left, passing the Spoonful. The blue and yellow neon sign shone in the front window and a small lamp illuminated the vases of forsythia blooms. She knew now where Sophie had to be.

Lucky reached the road that led to Sophie's mother's house. She passed by the narrow road that gave access to the property where they had unearthed her father's body earlier in the day and continued on. Sophie might have driven around for a while, but Lucky was sure this was where she would have ended up. She pulled into the drive that led up to the house. Her headlights illuminated Sophie's car, half hidden among the trees. She turned off her engine and reached into the glove compartment for a flashlight. She smelled wood smoke as she made her way quietly up to the front porch. A flickering light shone through the front windows. Inside, Sophie sat cross-legged in front of the hearth. A board creaked beneath her foot and Sophie's head turned quickly toward the window. Lucky walked to the door and called out, "It's me, Sophie."

She heard footsteps and the door was opened. Sophie's face was visible in the firelight. "Don't say it."

"I'm not gonna say anything. Except we were worried about you."

"I know. I'm sorry."

"Call Sage, right now. He's worried sick."

Sophie's shoulders slumped. "Okay." She reached into her pocket to retrieve her cell phone and hit a button. Sage picked up immediately.

"I'll be home in a bit." She paused. "I'm fine. I'm sorry. I didn't want you to worry about me . . . Okay." She clicked off.

"Nice fire."

"I got so cold after a while." Sophie returned to the hearth and sat. Lucky clicked off her flashlight and joined her. "It's not looking good—my big plan for the house and everything. I just thought I'd enjoy my grandfather's fireplace one last time.

"All these years . . ." Sophie shook her head. "Since I was a kid, I always held out the hope he was coming back. It used to make me crazy how no one would talk about him. Every time I asked questions they'd all get weird and change the subject." She turned to look at Lucky. Her eyes were still swollen from recent tears. "We were so poor, Lucky. You remember. Other kids used to make fun of me at school, make fun of my clothes. I'd get so angry. I'd think, *You just wait and see. My father's coming back and everything's gonna change.* I'd have fantasies that he was in Alaska working on a pipeline or harvesting salmon and making tons of money and when he came back, our luck would change. We'd be rich and nobody could ever make fun of us again."

Lucky listened in silence. This was everything she had always suspected about Sophie. She had always been her friend and defended her at school.

"And then Rick left, and then my brother Jerry. And then my mom got sick and died. My sister left as soon as I got the job at the Resort. I knew she was just waiting to make sure I had something. I moved out of here and now even my one sister's gone. The others must have known about my father, but no one would tell me."

"They wanted to protect you, that's all."

Sophie sighed. "Am I crazy? Did I remember a different man? I remember how he used to lift me up and hug me. I remember how he smelled, warm and earthy. Was I just kidding myself? I don't remember any of the stuff that Rick talked about. I don't remember him hitting my mom. I swear I never knew any of that."

"You were a little kid. How old were you then? Four? Five? How could you have known?"

"But kids do know. They know when there's something wrong in a house. They may not be able to put words to it—they may even think it's normal; that's how everybody lives—but they know. What's wrong with me that I didn't know?"

The small fire that Sophie had built was turning to embers. "They all did a very good job of protecting you and you needed your fantasies to survive. And you did survive and you built a life for yourself. Give yourself a pat on the back."

"What a bunch we were. He tainted us all. Maybe that's the reason my mother got sick. My sister died young too. Jerry's gone and Rick . . . Well, look at him. He lives in the shadows, can't connect with anybody, has some crazy tracker business with no license. What kind of a life is that? My father ruined them all somehow."

"The secret ruined them. You escaped."

"Did I? How do I know? Maybe I'll just repeat their history. Maybe . . ." She trailed off.

"Maybe what?"

"Maybe I shouldn't even think about getting married. Maybe I'd just mess up Sage's life and whatever family we might have."

"That's not gonna happen, Sophie. That's crazy thinking. You have real love in your life. You're building a life. And maybe Rick will find his way now too. Think about that. I'm sure he's never told a soul what happened, what part he played. Can you imagine what that's done to him all these years?"

"Lucky, that could've been Rick in the creek that day. What if they killed his partner, thinking it was him?"

"They?"

"*He*, I mean. That thug from the Resort."

"I don't know, but I'm sure Nate will get to the bottom of it." Lucky decided this wasn't the time to tell Sophie her suspicions that Eddie's death might have something to do with Agnes Warner. That was a conversation for another time.

"That would have been some irony, huh? The guy who never wanted to come back gets killed in the very same spot he's been trying to avoid his whole life." Sophie pulled her knees up to her chin. "But I'm glad it wasn't Rick."

"Come on, Sophie, let's go. Sage is waiting for you to come home."

Sophie smiled for the first time. "Home. What a wonderful word." She sighed and reached for the poker, tamping down the embers until the last of them died.

Chapter 48

IT WAS CLOSE to eleven o'clock by the time Lucky climbed the stairs to her apartment. She wanted nothing more than to lock her door, climb into a hot bubble bath and grab a good night's sleep.

She shut the front door behind her and walked down the short hallway to the kitchen. She slipped out of her sweater and hung her purse on a chair. Then she kicked off her shoes and went to the bathroom to turn on the faucets. She hadn't even had a chance to talk to Elias all day. He had been seeing patients in Lincoln Falls today. He would have heard about the search for the body. She glanced at the clock wondering whether it was too late to call him. Eleven thirty now. Too late. She didn't want to wake him if he was already asleep.

When the tub was full, she turned the faucets off. Suddenly, she remembered that she hadn't told Jack that Sophie was home. Knowing that he sometimes didn't go to bed until late and often didn't sleep through the night, she reached for the phone and dialed his number.

"I hope I didn't wake you," she said when she heard her grandfather's voice.

"Oh, no. You know me. I'm a night owl."

"I was just about to soak in the tub but I wanted to let you know I found Sophie. She was hiding out at her mother's house."

"Poor kid. That's a bad shock. You just get in?"

"A few minutes ago. Sorry to call you so late."

"That's no problem. I've been going through some stuff in the garage and found some more books I can donate. When I gave Cecily my books last week—"

"You mean Greta."

"Huh?"

"You said Cecily. You mean Greta. Greta picked up your books."

"Did I? Oh, that's right."

A sudden chill ran up Lucky's spine. "Jack? What day did Greta pick up your books?"

"Well . . . I guess it was . . ."

"Was it the same day Cecily picked up the basket of herbs?"

"I . . . I think so. I had the books in the kitchen. When she came to the door . . ."

"Where was the basket for Cecily?"

"It was . . . Why, it was on the hallway table, I think. That's right. That's where I left it so I'd have it handy."

Lucky was suddenly wide-awake. "Jack, do you remember who arrived first that day?"

"Of course I remember. I'm not brain-dead, my girl. It was Greta. I had a box of books on the kitchen table, all ready to go."

"So . . . Greta knocked on your door and you opened it? And then what?"

"I went to the kitchen and carried the box out to her."

"Jack, I think we should mention this to Nate."

"You're sayin' Greta was standing there by the basket and she could have put something in it?"

"Yes. That's exactly what I'm saying. It would have only taken a second or two. And she would have known about it. She was privy to everything that went on at the library. She would have known Cecily would be picking it up from you. She only had to make sure she got there before Cecily."

Jack was silent.

"I'm going to call Nate first thing tomorrow. We should talk about this some more then. Don't worry about it for now, Jack. I didn't want to bring up the whole thing again."

"I . . . Why would that shy little woman want to hurt anybody?"

"I have some ideas about that, but it's the first thing that points to the fact that the basket *was* available to somebody besides Cecily or Cordelia."

"If you say so."

Lucky could visualize Jack shaking his head. "Get some sleep, Jack."

"I will. Good night, my girl."

"'Night, Jack."

Lucky pulled her address book from her purse and looked up Nate's home number. It was too late to call him tonight, but she'd call early tomorrow before he left for the station. She left the address book open on the coffee table and stood. She took a deep breath. This could explain how someone, Greta, could have added something to Jack's herbs. And if Greta was supposed to be the first to drink, then how did she get Agnes to take her place? She turned off the lamp in the living room. That was when she heard the floorboards creak. Someone else was in the apartment.

Chapter 49

SHE HELD VERY still in the darkened room, not daring to take a breath. A shadow moved in the doorway, backlit by the hallway light. Lucky stared, willing her eyes to adjust to the dark. A flashlight clicked on. Greta held it under her chin, illuminating her face, now ghoulish in the harsh light. She pointed the flashlight in Lucky's eyes. Momentarily blinded, Lucky took a step to move away. She felt a searing pain. She had cracked her shin on the coffee table. She struggled to keep her balance.

Greta moved with lightning speed, grasping her arm. She pushed Lucky down onto the sofa cushions. Lucky struggled to break free.

Greta placed her hand over Lucky's mouth and hissed in her ear. "Stay quiet. He's coming."

Lucky continued to struggle but Greta's grip was like iron. She felt Greta's breath on her cheek.

"Be quiet and stay here. Leonard's coming for you." Greta shoved her back.

The sound of glass breaking came from the kitchen. Lucky was sure it was the pane of glass in her back door.

Greta released her grip and stepped into the hallway, moving quietly toward the kitchen. Lucky struggled to her feet. Heavy footsteps came through the kitchen and stopped at the entrance to the hallway.

"Lucky's not here," Greta said. "It's me you want."

Lucky heard a deep howl as Leonard thundered down the hallway. A thump and then a strangled cry came from Greta. She heard grunting sounds and heavy breathing. Lucky's mind raced. She needed a weapon. There wasn't time to wonder why Greta had been in her apartment. No time to ask what Leonard was doing. She and Greta were both in danger. The table leg. She prayed the glue hadn't held. It never had before. She kicked over the table and, leaning down, wrenched at the stubborn leg. It wouldn't budge. In frustration, she kicked down in an effort to dislodge it. It came loose with a crack. She grasped the wooden leg in her hand and ran down the hallway. Leonard's back was turned. He held Greta by the throat, lifting her against the wall. Greta's feet kicked wildly under her. Her hands clawed at Leonard's wrists helplessly. There was no time to hesitate. Lucky took aim and placed the heaviest blow she could muster against Leonard's temple. He grunted. His hands came loose and Greta slumped to the floor, gasping for air. Leonard, still on his feet, turned toward her. He swayed but didn't fall. Lucky took one last swing at his head. His eyes rolled upward and his knees buckled underneath him. She stepped backward quickly as Leonard crashed forward.

Greta was on her hands and knees, crawling toward the kitchen, desperate to move away from Leonard. Lucky stepped over Leonard's body and helped Greta to her feet, guiding her to a kitchen chair. She had to find a way to restrain Leonard. He was splayed on the hallway floor, but he was a big man. If he regained consciousness, she and Greta together could not hope to overpower him. Panicking, she opened one kitchen drawer after another, desperately searching for the length of clothesline she knew was in one of the drawers. She found it. With the clothesline in her hands, she hurried down the hall and quickly tied Leonard's ankles together, then his wrists behind his back. For good measure, she rolled out the end of the long cord and wrapped it around the claw foot of the bathtub. Leonard hadn't regained consciousness. She felt for the beating pulse in his neck. He was warm and alive.

She rushed into the living room and grabbed her phone book from the floor. She dialed Nate's home number with shaking fingers. When he answered, she said, "It's Lucky. Come to my place right away. It's urgent." She hung up before he could ask any questions. Then she returned to the kitchen and carried a glass of water to Greta. She knelt and held it to Greta's lips, urging her to take a sip. Greta hadn't spoken but looked at her gratefully. Bruises were starting to form around her neck.

"Don't talk. Nate will be here in a few minutes." Next she dialed Elias's number. "You better come over."

"What's wrong?"

"You'll see when you get here." She hung up the phone. Elias arrived two minutes later.

Chapter 50

LUCKY SAT ON the sofa sipping a cup of hot tea that Elias had prepared. He put a protective arm around her shoulders.

Greta was bundled up in a quilt from Lucky's bed, holding her mug of tea. Nate sat across from her in the armchair, asking questions and jotting notes. Leonard had regained consciousness a few moments after Nate arrived. Nate had cuffed him to a radiator in the outside hallway pending the arrival of the state police.

"How did you get into Lucky's apartment, Greta?"

"I discovered I had a master key to every apartment. I didn't realize it at first. The cleaning crew who had gotten my apartment ready just before I moved in had given me the wrong key. I planned to return it but I decided I'd keep it awhile just in case."

"How did you know Leonard was coming after Lucky?"

"That's what Lionel would do. That's his real name, by the way. Lionel Washburn. Agnes, his wife, is . . . was Alice Washburn." She looked over at Lucky. "When I heard about your accident, I knew then you were next. Just like he killed that poor man in the creek. You had been asking too many questions."

"So his murder had nothing to do with the Resort or the land?"

"I don't know anything about the Resort, but when I found out the dead man was Eddie Fowler, I knew Leonard had killed him." She glanced at Nate. "I should probably start at the beginning. "My name is Greta Dorn. At least, that was my maiden name. I was married to Leonard's son, Matthew—Matthew Washburn. Matthew was a gentle man, but terribly damaged by his father. Lionel is a manipulative bully who thinks he should be able to dictate everyone's life. My husband, Matthew, had a drug problem he could never control. He kept falling back into that life. What I didn't know was that Matthew was selling drugs to support his habit. When he died of an overdose, the drugs were found in our home, hidden in the garage. I was arrested and charged. The police refused to believe I didn't know or that I wasn't involved."

All the pieces had clicked into place. Lucky realized that Greta had hired Rick Colgan and Eddie Fowler to locate Alice Washburn. Greta Dorn was the Margaret Washburn she had read about, in the flesh, sitting in her living room.

"Lionel and Alice . . . at first they seemed to be very supportive of me. They convinced me that my son, Michael, was better off being cared for by them rather than in a foster home. There was nothing I could do about my conviction but I was so frightened about what could happen to Michael. He was only six months old, an infant, when my husband died. I didn't know what else to do. I never totally trusted Lionel but I knew Alice would take good care of the baby. I agreed to give them temporary guardianship until I was released. It was the biggest mistake of my life."

Greta took a deep breath and continued. "Lionel's a very powerful man. He's always been determined to get his own way. Eventually I realized he needed to believe his son wasn't to blame for what happened. He needed to believe Matthew could do no wrong and that I must have been the cause of all the trouble. He kept his true feelings under wraps because he was determined to get Michael away from me and keep him. I think he figured it was fair payment for, in his twisted mind, what he believed I had taken from him." Greta paused for breath.

"So I signed the papers. What a mistake that was. Once I was sent away, Lionel refused to bring Michael to see me. And when I got out, Lionel did everything possible to keep Michael from me. I was able to see him, but Lionel refused to relinquish custody. That broke my heart. I wanted to tell my son how much I loved him and how I couldn't wait to be with him. In jail, I had written letters to Michael but I'm sure Lionel destroyed them. It didn't matter to me what Lionel did. I was determined not to let Michael go without a fight— not to let him be raised by that man. My husband was such a kind, gentle man who had been so damaged by his own father. And Alice was completely cowed by him. She had given up whatever autonomy she might have had. She was completely under his thumb."

Greta took a deep breath and continued. "It took me a while after my release, but eventually I was able to hire a lawyer, and I filed a petition in court for custody of Michael. Evidence had come to light in another case that could help vindicate me, and my attorney was sure that under the circumstances I'd be able to regain custody of my son. Lionel knew then he would lose. The day we were all to appear before the judge, none of them arrived. They had taken Michael and disappeared. Lionel had cashed out his home equity line, took every dime of savings and disappeared with Alice and Michael." Greta paused again. "I'm sure he was inconsolable after Matthew's death, but he's a vengeful man. He needed to see me punished. He refused to forgive me for Matthew's death. And punished, I was." Her voice shook. "I lost my husband and my son and five years of my life. I went out of my mind with grief."

"Was this in October of that year?" Lucky asked.

Greta nodded. "That's right. It was October. The date of our court hearing was the tenth of October."

"That explains why my mother was trying to capture

pictures of them. She must have read something or seen
something, had some inkling. The story was all over the
news." Lucky glanced at Nate, sure that he felt a twinge of
guilt for not taking her suspicions seriously.

Greta continued. "I'm sorry I stole that photo from you.
I intended to return it. It's just . . . when I saw that picture
of my son, I thought I would collapse. You see, it took me
several years, but I was able to work and save my money. I
wasted a lot of time and money going to different private
investigators to track them, but they had no more luck than
the police did. Everyone had just vanished. Lionel must have
operated only with cash, so there was no credit card or paper
trail."

"Is that when you hired Rick and his partner?" Lucky
asked.

"Yes." Greta nodded. "I happened to run into a friend I
had made in jail, another woman. She told me about Rick
and Eddie. That they would do things for cash that other
investigators wouldn't touch." She glanced at Nate. "I was
desperate. I know what they did was probably illegal but I
didn't care. I had to find my son. It was the only thing keeping me alive."

"So Eddie was afraid you'd find the Washburns and take
some sort of revenge on them for taking your son away?"

"I suppose. You see, I'm ashamed of this, but I lied to
him. I was afraid they might turn me down because of my
conviction. I suspect some of the other investigators I had
tried to hire were suspicious of me. They didn't say as much,
but that's what I think. Some even refused to look into the
case and told me the police were my best bet. I felt this was
my last, best chance. Years had gone by and I was desperate.
I told him I was searching for my sister who was in an abu-
sive relationship. He gave me the information that Alice and
Lionel were living outside of Snowflake. Something that a
licensed investigator never would have done, not without
notifying them and asking permission. Later, he figured out
my story was false and found out I was Margaret Washburn.
He realized his mistake and must have become concerned

I'd do something drastic. I think he went to the Washburns, to warn them. That was a fatal mistake because Lionel knew then he had been discovered. He had to get rid of the man. He must have thought that would solve the problem."

"Once you had their location, why didn't you go to the police?" Nate asked.

"I was afraid that would give them a chance to run again. They had legal custody. They had a court order. And I'm an ex-convict now. Who would believe me without a court hearing, and that would take time."

"How did Rick and Eddie locate them?"

"I gave them the names of every family member, every friend of theirs that I knew of. Everything I could think of. In the end it was very simple. A year before my husband's death, Alice learned she had inherited the house outside of Snowflake from a distant cousin. A cousin named Leonard Warner. The real Leonard Warner had been in a home for years and no one in town really knew him. It was the perfect way for them to hide out. Rick and Eddie discovered the cousin's death and put two and two together. Something the police had overlooked."

Greta took a deep breath. "I changed my appearance as much as possible when I came here. I thought it might buy me some time to figure out the lay of the land. I returned to my maiden name. I couldn't bear the thought of having the same name as Lionel. Greta Dorn was a fresh start. Greta Dorn had no record of a criminal conviction. I wasn't sure what I was going to do, but I thought appealing to whatever human feeling was left in Alice might work. I wanted to take Michael home and then go back to court. After Lionel took Michael and disappeared the way he did, I thought the courts might be able to press charges against him. That's when Agnes first saw me at the library. She almost fainted. She recognized me right away. I managed to get her aside and I begged her. I begged her to bring Michael to me. I even told her she should come away with us and leave Lionel."

"It didn't work?"

Greta shook her head. "No. Alice was lost. Maybe she was lost a long time ago. She had no will of her own. She told Lionel I was here and looking for Michael. He must have been terrified he would be convicted. He hatched a plan to be rid of me once and for all."

"And that was?" Nate asked.

"I think he convinced Alice that I had to die or they would both be sent to jail and Michael would have no one. I knew Agnes had a bad heart but that night in the woods . . . I was convinced she had ingested something awful and that's what caused her heart attack. It took me completely by surprise. You may not believe this, but it never occurred to me that Lionel would try to kill me. He must have coerced Agnes into adding something poisonous to the wine."

Nate shook his head. "The results are back from the lab. The wine was untainted. But a residue of yellowish sap was found in the bowl that Agnes drank from. Sap from the root of water hemlock. Deadly."

"Oh." Greta seemed to cave in upon herself. "That makes perfect sense. Agnes prepared the altar. She must have added it to the bowl we were to drink from."

"But who was supposed to be the first to drink?"

"Me," Greta answered simply. "I was."

"But . . ." Lucky started.

"Agnes stepped forward suddenly and took the bowl before Cordelia realized we were out of order. I could tell Agnes was on her last nerve. She was torn between obeying Lionel and doing what was right. That drink was meant for me. As Cordelia was filling the bowl, Agnes leaned over and whispered to me. She said"—Greta paused, fighting back tears—"she said, '*Please forgive me.*' Then she took the bowl and drank the poison herself."

"You mean . . ." Nate trailed off.

"Yes." Tears sprang to Greta's eyes. "She drank the poison rather than harm me." Greta covered her face with her hands for a moment. Finally, she gathered her strength and looked up. "I cried for her that night. Maybe you think that's crazy, given how she aided and abetted Lionel, but I still cried. Her life could have been so different if she had been able to escape him. There's no doubt in my mind Alice's death was a suicide. At that critical moment, she couldn't do it. She couldn't cause my death. She must have felt that suicide was the only way out of what she had helped to create."

"Unbelievable," Elias replied.

Greta turned to Lucky. "I am so sorry for any trouble your grandfather has suffered. He never did anything wrong. But I didn't know who I could trust or who would believe me. I couldn't tell anyone what I was doing here. I had to focus on getting Michael back."

"I can understand that but what I don't understand is why Leonard . . . Lionel went to such lengths to torture and accuse Jack," Lucky asked.

Greta sighed. "I think Lionel is slightly mad, maybe even insane. He's a man who has always blamed others for his troubles. I can tell you that he will never be willing to believe Agnes committed suicide. He blamed me for his son's addiction and death. In his mind, if I was at fault, it justified his stealing my child. I'm sure it served him to throw suspicion on your grandfather and perhaps he half believed it because he wanted to. He knew full well he was guilty of attempted murder, but at the same time, he couldn't understand why it had gone so wrong. He's just not rational in a way that you or I could understand."

Elias leaned forward in his chair. "Was it Lionel, then, who tampered with Sophie's car?"

"I'm sure of it," Greta answered. "I didn't know whose car it was, but I heard about Lucky's accident and I knew she was asking questions. That's when I knew Lucky was next." Greta turned a hopeful face to Nate. "When can I see my son?"

"Soon." Nate glanced at his watch. "I've sent my deputy to the house to pick Michael up. He'll be with the state police and a social worker by now. We can help you find legal counsel. I don't know if you'll apply to the Vermont courts or New York or both. But I'm sure you can get an emergency hearing in Bournmouth and I'll appear on your behalf."

"Thank you." Tears sprang to her eyes. "It's been a long journey. I can't wait to hold my son in my arms." She swiped at her eyes. "I just hope he still remembers me."

Chapter 51

"IT'S ALL OVER now, Jack." Lucky watched her grandfather closely, thrilled that she could deliver good news to him.

He nodded slowly and looked at her with a cautious glint in his eye. "You're sure about that, my girl?"

She smiled widely and hugged him. "Absolutely. It never occurred to me that Greta might have been at the center of the whole matter. She had done a good job of fading into the background, making herself almost invisible."

"What a terrible story. What that poor woman has suffered. And to think Leonard Warner lived in our midst and we had no idea who he really was. Your mother did, though. Or at least she must have suspected."

"She did. Greta told me her court hearing was October tenth. When it became a kidnapping matter, it hit the news services big-time. Maybe mom didn't suspect them immediately, but when they were so resistant to being photographed, she started to wonder. That's why she kept those pictures. She had been trying to get a shot of the little boy and compare it to the picture in the news, but wasn't able to. Greta never caused anyone any harm. She was wrongly convicted. She was Lionel's victim as much as her husband, Matthew, was. Lionel is a delusional man. He had to believe his son was blameless and Greta was at fault. And he had to believe you were to blame for Agnes's death. Maybe he couldn't bring himself to accept that Agnes drank the poison willingly. Or maybe he was hoping his accusations would draw suspicion away from him." Lucky thought a moment. "I just wish I could have put the pieces together sooner. I had begun to think that both deaths might be connected, but it wasn't until Rick questioned me about Agnes Warner that I realized she was Alice Washburn, the woman they had been hired to locate. That's when I started to put it together. Then Greta stealing the photo—I realized she must be Margaret, but with all the worry about Sophie, it had to go on the back burner. The one thing I was sure about was that you hadn't made a mistake with those plants."

"Well, you're a loyal following of one. I doubted it myself, to be honest." Jack finally smiled. "I'm an old man and I forget things or get 'em mixed up sometimes, but I couldn't live with myself if I thought I had caused someone's death."

Lucky hadn't had a chance to flip over the sign at the front door to open the Spoonful for the day. She heard a banging on the glass. Sophie was outside, knocking and jumping up and down. Lucky hurried over, unlocked the door and turned the sign around.

"Why didn't you call me last night?" Sophie shrieked.

Lucky groaned. "It was so late by the time Nate left, and then Elias stayed with me. He wouldn't go home after what happened, but I was glad he stayed. I certainly didn't want to wake you and Sage up in the middle of the night. How did you hear so soon?"

"Are you kidding? Nate contacted Elizabeth, since Greta was her tenant, and then Bradley called Rowena at the *Snowflake Gazette* trying to make it look like he had apprehended Leonard, or whatever his name is, with no help from you or Greta, and Rowena called several of her friends and it filtered through to us. Sage got a call from his brother, who heard it from . . . I can't remember right now."

"Never mind." Lucky laughed. "It's good to know the grapevine is working just fine."

Sophie turned to Jack and wrapped her arms around him. "See? Lucky was right. It had nothing to do with you!"

Jack laughed. "She's the best, isn't she?"

"Yup."

"And so are you, Jack. I haven't had a chance to thank you properly for hosting our wedding. We'll make sure everything's straightened out and cleaned up after the party."

"Oh, no, you won't," Lucky said. "Elias and Jack and I are taking care of everything. You're leaving for your honeymoon at the lake. We don't want to hear from either one of you for at least two weeks."

Sophie leaned closer. "Sage is really worried you guys won't be okay while he's gone."

"He's irreplaceable, I agree, but really, we'll be fine. We have plenty in the freezer, and believe it or not, I can cook. You both deserve a great vacation, so just enjoy the time."

Chapter 52

LUCKY AND JACK sat in the two wooden armchairs facing Nate across the desk. He had prepared statements for them but wanted them to read the documents over carefully.

"Make sure you read them all the way through. Lucky will probably have to be a witness at trial, but they might want to call you in too, Jack. I want to have all the T's crossed and the I's dotted."

Lucky's eyes scanned the text, which consisted of a bare statement of the facts of the discovery of Eddie's body in the creek, her conversations with Emily, Cordelia, Cecily and Willa, and finally, the witnessing of Lionel's attempted murder of Greta and her efforts to subdue Lionel.

Nate shook his head. "I never suspected a little woman who ran all over town picking up library books was at the heart of this thing."

"It must have broken her heart to have her son taken away from her. I can't even imagine what she's suffered," Lucky replied. "What happens now, Nate?"

"I've notified all the appropriate federal and state authorities. They'll be pressing charges against Leon . . . Lionel Washburn.

Whether they have enough hard evidence to charge him in the death of Eddie Fowler, I don't know, but we got lucky and found a partial print on the hubcap from your accident, and the attempt on Greta's life needs to stick. That's why your statement's so important." Nate pushed his chair back from the desk.

"I can't believe this kidnapping got dropped and not followed up on. Don't the federal authorities keep a case like that active?"

"Technically, the Washburns had custody of the boy and planned to legally adopt him. But once they failed to show up on the hearing date, they were in contempt of court. So, I can't say if everyone considered it a true kidnapping in that sense. The authorities did their best to locate them at the time, but had no luck. The case grew cold, but these things are always on the books. There's just so many, there isn't the manpower to keep looking." Nate continued, "Greta should have no trouble getting permanent custody of her son. She may have to petition the New York court where the original hearing was supposed to be held, but she's decided to stay here in Snowflake and raise her boy in the village."

"How is Michael coping? Did he remember his mother?" Lucky asked.

Nate smiled. "He sure did. I was with them when they met in Bournmouth. Greta had taken off her glasses and let down her hair so she looked as much like she used to look as possible. Michael hesitated a moment; then his face lit up and he ran into her arms."

"That's the best news of all," Lucky offered.

"I suspect the little kid knew something was very off. Lionel and his wife treated him okay, but he knew something was wrong. He said he kept asking for his mother and they kept trying to tell him his mother was dead, but he said he never believed it."

"How could they do that to a child?"

Nate shook his head. "A real sick man. Poor kid didn't ask for any of this."

"I just have one question," Lucky said. "If Rick was able to locate the Washburns, why couldn't the police?"

"Slipped between the cracks. No communication between states, for one thing. Overworked officers everywhere. Like I said, they never close the books on something like this, but maybe because the Washburns had legal custody, it put a different spin on it. Lionel was using the driver's license of his wife's dead cousin and just kept renewing it every year. Pretty hard to survive without credit cards or other identification, but they managed it for several years. These weren't people who'd have had any kind of access to false identification without taking an even bigger risk. Sooner or later, somebody would've got wise. What were they gonna do when the kid got old enough to get a job and needed a Social Security number? Maybe they planned to wait until he started working, or tell him some story and let him use his own Social Security number if he already had one."

Nate pushed back his chair. "Oh, one last thing. Peter Manko's been picked up and shipped over to Bournmouth. Sophie and everybody else up at the Resort won't have to worry about him anymore."

"Picked up for what?"

"There was a Florida warrant for assault. Seems Manko was hired to do security at a hotel there and he put somebody into a coma. Apparently, the Resort wasn't too fussy about who they hired." Nate continued, "Funny how it happened, though. Somebody e-mailed me a copy of the warrant."

"Who?"

"I have my suspicions."

Lucky was sure Nate referred to Rick Colgan. "Are the people at the Resort claiming they knew nothing about this warrant?"

Nate smiled. "You got it. I wouldn't have expected any less. They're, quote, 'shocked and surprised at this turn of events,' unquote."

"What about the man whose house burned down? The one Brenda told us about?"

"Faulty propane tank. Talked to the inspector myself. By the way, any idea where Rick Colgan might have gone? Can't seem to locate him either."

"No. And I'm sure Sophie doesn't either. He's probably just gone underground. If you find him, do you think he'll be charged with being an accessory to his father's death?"

"Might be. Again, I doubt he'd be prosecuted as long as he didn't do it himself and if what he told Sophie was true. He was a kid then himself under extraordinary circumstances."

Chapter 53

LUCKY CLEARED THE leaves and a few sprouting weeds from the flower bed at her parents' gravestone. Her visits to their grave site were regular, but over the past few months she had been too busy to get there as often. The first year had been the most difficult. That milestone had passed last December. She hadn't let snow or cold deter her. The holidays had been the worst time of all. Not only did last December mark the one-year anniversary of their death, but it was at Christmas that she most missed her mother. Martha Jamieson was one of those women who lived for the holidays and loved to cook and decorate. Without fail, a ten-foot tree filled their living room decorated with boxes and boxes of ornaments, some dating back forty years or more, some of them, the ones her mother most cherished, Lucky herself had made in grade school. She had always groaned with embarrassment when her mother would hang them on the tree and point them out to her. She had begged her mother to throw them away, but there wasn't a chance that would ever happen. Martha Jamieson treasured those more than the most expensive ornament she possessed.

Lucky always looked forward to coming to the cemetery. It was the one spot where she could be completely alone, close her eyes, without ringing phones, rushing off to the restaurant, or friends dropping by her apartment. The purple phlox had blossomed again now that spring had come. She had worried they might not survive the winter but they seemed to have done just fine. When she was done weeding, she sat on the ground under the large maple tree nearby and held imaginary conversations with her parents.

This time she talked about Jack. How he admitted to blaming himself for their deaths. She could imagine both of them shaking their heads, saying, *"Oh, no. Tell Jack that's nonsense. It was our time, dear. That's all. It was our time to go."* She knew they'd be happy that Jack was clear of any suspicions, now that Greta had convinced everyone Agnes had chosen suicide.

Most of all, she thanked her mother for the clues she had left behind. Clues about the Warners. She had been in Madison at the time those photos were taken. If only she had been here, in Snowflake, she was sure her mother would have confided her suspicions about the family. *I'm so sorry, Mom*, she thought. *If I could have a do-over, I'd turn the clock back and be here with you, those years after college. I was such an idiot to stay away. Life continued in Snowflake and I wasn't any part of it. I wish I had been here*, she thought, *to be your confidante when you needed one. I hope you can forgive me.*

She could imagine how delighted her mother would have been to see Sophie's wedding. And how proud she would have been to see the dress that Lucky had sewn for her friend. Her mother loved weddings. "Mom, if you're up there somewhere, I hope you can see us all tomorrow, the big day. You will not be forgotten," she whispered.

Chapter 54

"HOLD STILL," LUCKY ordered.

"I'm trying, I'm trying." Sophie wiggled. "I'm just so nervous."

Lucky fastened the last button on Sophie's sleeve and straightened the skirt of her gown. "Nervous about what? It's just us. And a few friends. And it's a happy day."

"I don't know. I mean, I'm thrilled that Sage and I are getting married. Don't get me wrong. All this just seems so *formal*."

"Well, it's about as casual as we could make it. But it is a ceremony nonetheless. And you're the star of it." Lucky straightened up and kissed Sophie delicately on the cheek. "And I'm very, very happy for you!"

"Back atcha." Sophie grinned.

Lucky was already dressed in her gown and had even consented to Sophie's addition of makeup. Their bouquets were ready. They would carry lilacs and lavender. Lilacs for first love and lavender for devotion. Lucky had arrived at Jack's house early that morning to supervise the delivery of the dance floor, chairs and long tables. She had woven white

tulle and flowers through the openings of the gazebo, draping
the fabric around the front and fastening it all with white
ribbon. Jack's dining room was filled with candles in every
shape and size, ready to be lit in the evening. Every surface
was set with food on trays and warmers. Lanterns were hung
around the back deck, and a large table was set up with all
sorts of drinks, including glasses for wine and champagne.
Sage's brother Remy, in town for the occasion, would serve
as the groom's best man. And with Remy's help, Sage had
arrived earlier with all the food he had prepared. He had
outdone himself. There were trays and trays of hors d'oeuvres,
hot dishes of boeuf bourgignon, roasted potatoes, chicken
piccata, wild rice, and a baked shell filled with a variety of
vegetables and mushrooms in a cream sauce, with cups of
chocolate mousse for dessert. Food would be served buffet-
style with Lucky's mother's and grandmother's special sets
of china, silver and linen napkins. Fancy paper plates were
available when the china ran out. Some of the guests had
brought wedding presents, and these Lucky arranged on the
long hallway table in the foyer of Jack's house.

In the garden, strings of tiny white lights covered every
bush and the railings of the large porch. In addition to the
lanterns, Lucky had found outdoor torches that could be lit
later in the evening. The dance floor was in place. The harpist
was already playing and the other musicians were scheduled
to arrive after the ceremony. Pastor Wilson's services had
been arranged, in lieu of a justice of the peace. He was pre-
paring for the ceremony under the gazebo while Sophie was
confined to Jack's bedroom so Sage wouldn't see his bride
until she walked into the garden. She and Jack had done
everything possible to create a memorable and romantic day.

The guest list had certainly grown from the original plan.
Besides the bride and groom, Lucky and Elias, Jack, Remy
and Pastor Wilson, there were Horace, Meg, Janie and her
mother, Miriam, Elizabeth Dove, Marjorie and Cecily Winters, Nate and Susanna Edgerton, Hank Northcross, Barry
Sanders, and even Flo Sullivan. Bradley had invited Rowena
Nash, as his date, even though Rowena had never been a friend

to Sophie. Guy Bessette was in attendance and Lucky was relieved to see that his obsessive crush on Rowena was at an end. Greta was invited and was allowed to bring her son, Michael, plus three work friends of Sophie's from the Resort, including Brenda—twenty-seven people in all. She knew Sophie was upset that her brother would not be attending, but given the unearthing of her father's body, and the role he had played, Lucky was relieved for Rick's sake.

The current attendees were the official list, but Lucky and Jack both knew that many other people from the village would be dropping in all evening with potluck dishes to join the celebration and wish the newlyweds well. They were certainly welcome at Jack's house.

"Okay, now for the veil," Lucky said.

"All right." Sophie took a nervous breath.

Lucky smiled. "You'll do fine. It's almost time. When you're ready, I'll go out and check and make sure everyone and everything is set. Then I'll come back and get you. The harpist is already playing. Listen." The strains of the stringed instrument floated through the open bedroom window.

Sophie's eyes filled with tears. "I can't thank you enough for all this, for organizing everything—the decorations, the musicians, the gown, everything!"

"It will all go very smoothly. Don't worry about a thing." She placed the circlet of pearls over Sophie's forehead and arranged the veil. "Don't forget to walk slowly to the gazebo, don't rush. Just follow me. I'll lead the way. And Meg's volunteered to do the photography—she's very good at that." Lucky stood back and surveyed her handiwork. She smiled. "You look absolutely beautiful."

"If you say so."

"Now, just sit tight. Don't come out. I'll run around and make sure everyone's in place." Lucky peeked out of the bedroom. The coast was clear. Jack, wearing his best suit, waited by the front door to welcome latecomers. "You look very handsome, Jack." She kissed him on the cheek. "It's time. We have to get everyone seated out in the garden. I'll go make sure Pastor Wilson's ready."

Lucky breezed through each room, reminding everyone that it was time to start. After much shuffling, the guests took their seats in two rows of a semicircle on either side of the brick patio. The sun was setting and Remy had lit the torches around the perimeter of the yard. The harpist had said she would start with Pachelbel's Canon in D Major, one of the loveliest pieces of music Lucky had ever heard. Pastor Wilson stood inside the gazebo fidgeting with his collar. Janie had been serving wine to the guests before the ceremony and now busied herself passing around small glasses with tea light candles already lit for each guest to hold.

Lucky stood on the open porch and surveyed the scene. The white tulle stood out in the early evening, lit by the torches. Meg was getting her camera ready. Sage and Remy had taken their places and everyone waited expectantly. She breathed a sigh of relief. It was perfect. Lucky returned to the bedroom and took Sophie's hand. "Ready?"

Sophie, unable to speak, simply nodded. As they stepped outside, a hush fell over the gathering. Everyone stood, small candles in their hands. Lucky caught Elias's eye. He smiled in return. The harpist's music filled the air. Lucky descended the stairway, walking very slowly through the garden with Sophie following. Sage had eyes only for Sophie. Lucky was sure he was in awe at the sight of his bride. Remy smiled widely and he and Lucky stepped to the side as Sophie and Sage took their places. Pastor Wilson smiled at the couple and opened his prayer book to a shortened version of the traditional wedding ceremony. Lucky watched with heightened awareness, wanting never to forget even one precious moment of this day. Before she knew it, she heard the words, "You may now kiss the bride." Sage lifted Sophie's veil and kissed her tenderly on the lips. Then he took her hand as they turned to their guests. Lucky sniffed back tears, moved by the simple ceremony and the knowledge of the love that Sophie and Sage shared.

As Lucky turned, she thought she caught a slight movement at one of the back windows of Jack's house. Was there another guest inside? Or had she imagined it? Something had appeared in her peripheral vision and she could have sworn there was a face at the window. An unwanted guest? An unexpected guest? Whoever it was had now disappeared.

Sophie turned back to hug Lucky first and then Remy as the guests rushed forward to offer their congratulations and wish the newlyweds well. The harpist began to play again, this time a lighter and quicker piece. Then the bride and groom were enveloped by their friends and well-wishers.

LATER IN THE evening, many of the guests had moved inside, a few lingering in the garden to enjoy the evening and sip wine or champagne. Others took advantage of the dance floor and the musicians. Lucky and Jack had refused any help from Sage or Sophie, ordering them to enjoy the time and their guests. Lucky and Remy took charge of clearing away glasses and dishes and generally keeping things organized as the evening wore on. Lucky had kicked off her heels and put on a pair of sandals. She moved through the house, clearing dishes and napkins wherever she found them. Janie and her mother offered to lend a hand and together they stacked the dishes and glasses in the pantry until the guests had gone. Lucky didn't want to disturb the flow of traffic by loading the dishwasher.

She checked the hallway table, now covered with wrapped presents and cards of all sizes. Something caught her eye. It was a large white envelope. A special card? She picked it up. It was sealed, but it didn't appear to be a card. She heard a step behind her as Sophie came near. She turned and showed the envelope to Sophie.

"What is that?"

"I don't know. I don't remember seeing it earlier." She remembered the face she had been sure she had seen at the window, but didn't want to mention it to Sophie. "Open it."

Sophie turned the envelope over and looked at it curiously. Then she slid her finger under the flap, breaking the seal, and retrieved several sheets of heavy paper. Lucky peered over her shoulder.

"Oh!" Sophie gasped.

"What is it?"

"They're quitclaim deeds—to the properties—all of it. Notarized and everything. Oh, Lucky!"

There was no doubt whose face Lucky had seen at the window. She smiled. "Rick was here, after all."

Recipes

MAY WINE

May wine is a traditional drink in many cultures to celebrate the coming of spring on May Day. The brew is a combination of white wine, dried or fresh leaves of the sweet woodruff plant, strawberries and sparkling wine. Sweet woodruff is a perennial herb with dark green leaves and small star-shaped white flowers growing in shady areas in temperate climates. It blossoms in late April or early May. Its generic name, *Galium odoratum*, derives from the Greek word *gala* or milk. *Odoratum* is Latin for fragrant. Sweet woodruff has had many uses for centuries—medicinally to treat various disorders, as a poultice on cuts and wounds, as a fragrant mattress filling, and as sachets to repel moths and insects. Ingesting a small amount of the woodruff leaves is not harmful. However, large quantities can cause dizziness and vomiting. Today, the U.S. Food and Drug Administration considers sweet woodruff safe only in alcoholic beverages.

1 bottle white wine (a Riesling is an excellent choice)
½ cup dried sweet woodruff leaves, a few fresh leaves for garnish
¾ cup strawberries, chopped
1 bottle sparkling wine
Sugar (optional)

Pour the bottle of white wine into a large glass container. Soak dried woodruff leaves in the wine for approximately one hour. Add chopped strawberries and stir. Add the bottle of sparkling wine, mix and garnish with a pinch of fresh woodruff leaves. Add a small amount of sugar if desired, depending on taste. Yields approximately 8 cups. Serve chilled.

CHICKEN POT PIE SOUP
WITH DUMPLINGS

(Serves 4)

1 large or 2 small skinless boneless chicken breasts
4 cups chicken broth or bouillon
4 carrots, peeled and sliced
4 celery sticks, chopped
1 medium onion, chopped
2 cups frozen peas
¼ cup half-and-half (or milk)
Dumplings (see recipe below)

Chop chicken breasts into small bite-size pieces. Add to large pot with chicken broth, carrots, celery and onion. Cook over medium heat for 15 minutes or until carrots and celery are tender. Add peas and cook 1 minute more. Add half-and-half or milk and stir. Prepare dumplings and reheat soup, dropping dough into the bubbling soup and cover. Cook 10–15 minutes more until dumplings are cooked.

DUMPLINGS

(Serves 4)

⅔ cup all-purpose flour
2 tablespoons chopped parsley
1 teaspoon baking powder
¼ teaspoon dried thyme
⅛ teaspoon salt
¼ cup milk
2 tablespoons cooking oil

In a bowl, mix flour, parsley, baking powder, thyme and salt. In a separate bowl, mix milk and oil separately and pour into flour mixture. Stir with a fork until combined.

SAUSAGE VEGETABLE STEW

(Serves 4)

Vegetable oil cooking spray
4 sausages or ¾ lb. of bulk sausage meat
½ onion, chopped
3 cups vegetable broth
1 14-ounce can diced or crushed Italian style tomatoes
3 carrots, peeled and sliced
1 zucchini, peeled and chopped
1 teaspoon basil
1 teaspoon oregano
1 dash nutmeg
1 cup chopped parsley
1 cup rotini pasta (uncooked)
Salt and pepper to taste
¼ cup grated cheese

Spray large pot with cooking oil. If using sausages, remove meat from casing, and saute in pot with chopped onion and cook until onion is tender. Add vegetable broth, and diced or crushed tomatoes. Add sliced carrots and chopped zucchini. Add basil, oregano, nutmeg and parsley. Cook on medium heat for 10–15 minutes until carrots are tender. Add uncooked pasta, bring to a boil, then reduce heat and simmer for 10 minutes until pasta is cooked. If soup is too thick, add a small amount of water for desired consistency. Add salt and pepper to taste. Serve and sprinkle each bowl with grated cheese.

PEAR AND WATERCRESS SOUP

(Serves 4)

4 pears, peeled and sliced
1 bunch watercress
4 cups chicken broth (or bouillon)
Juice of 1 lime
½ cup chopped walnuts
½ cup Gorgonzola cheese

Reserving a handful of watercress leaves for garnish, cut roots from watercress and place leaves and stems into a large pot with the sliced pears. Add chicken broth and simmer for 15–20 minutes. Blend soup in food processor or blender. Add lime juice and chopped walnuts and reheat. Serve and sprinkle cheese over each bowl.

AVOCADO AND ROASTED
RED PEPPER SANDWICH

2 slices sourdough bread
2 tablespoons pesto (see recipe below, or use store-bought)
8–10 strips of roasted red pepper (see note below, or use
   store-bought)
⅓ avocado

Spread pesto mixture on one slice of bread. Layer strips of roasted red pepper. Spread softened avocado on the other slice of bread and cover sandwich.

Note: If you'd prefer to make your own, brush fresh or frozen red pepper strips with oil and grill under the broiler until browned.

PESTO

1 cup basil leaves, firmly packed
½ cup parsley sprigs firmly packed
½ cup grated Parmesan cheese
2 cloves garlic, peeled and cut into quarters
¼ cup pine nuts or walnuts
¼ cup olive oil

Combine basil leaves, parsley sprigs, cheese, nuts, garlic, 2 tablespoons olive oil and blend in food processor until a paste forms. Gradually add the remaining oil and blend on low speed until smooth.